THE HEARTBREAKING VOW

When Lucy found her sister Meg lying in bed, her dress torn, her body wracked with sobs, she managed to make Meg tell her what had happened only after promising to reveal the truth to no one.

Meg was victim of a shameful attack, and felt forever soiled. A short while ago, she had been competing for Dr. Mike Tryon's affection—now she began to retreat into a world of her own.

Lucy knew that only Mike had the power to restore Meg to the lovely, laughing girl she once was. But to break her vow of silence would be to earn Meg's undying hatred—and risk losing the man Lucy so deeply loved. . . .

TO WED
A DOCTOR

ELIZABETH
SEIFERT

A DELL BOOK

CHAPTER ONE

"GET TO WORK, Meg," said Lucy automatically. "The party is tonight. Remember?"

Meg shook her head slightly and continued to stand at the window, looking out through its small panes. "I'm getting an overall view of the town," she said. "How it will look to Mike, coming home after all this time."

"And how does it look, dear?" asked her mother gently.

Meg turned then and smiled at the pretty little woman in her wheelchair. "Red leaves," she said, "and brown, and gold, and green ones, too. Big trees, all full of jeweled leaves, and the ground lavishly spread with them. The hills, the shine of the river below us—the houses—old ones, and new ones. The old college with its red brick and ivy-thick wall about it. The new hospital and the state medical school . . ."

She turned full about. "We have to have the *new*," she said tensely, "or Mike would not come back!"

"He would—to see us, dear."

"Oh, yes. For an hour, maybe a day. But to stay? Never!"

"Is he going to stay now?" asked her father.

Seated at the table, covered thick with newspapers, he was polishing silver, his wife beside him to tell him what and how. Her fingers were too twisted with arthritis for her to do this sort of work.

"We must all concentrate on his staying," said Meg, still tense.

A neighbor came to the side door, her arms filled with chrysanthemums. Yes, she said, she had stripped her beds. But in another week frost would have taken them.

Meg accepted the offering gratefully and brought the flowers to show to her mother.

"I told you not to buy lemon leaves," said Lucy from the living room.

"They'll keep and be handsome after these flowers are gone."

"Didn't we have mums?" asked Anna Goheen.

"Yes, we have some," Meg agreed. "But tonight if people wander out into our garden, and there are no flowers—"

"It'll be black-dark," Lucy pointed out.

"*Aggh!*" Meg cried. "You do not have the romantic approach."

Lucy stood erect and pulled down the tail of her pink shirt. "I'm as romantic as you are," she insisted. "In fact, today I'm all goose bumps and girlish quivers."

Her mother and father chuckled. "It will be nice to have Mike home again," said Anna comfortably. "Dropping in —noisy—"

"He's older, Mums," Meg warned.

"So are we all. It will still be nice. I'm glad you girls wanted to have a party. It will seem odd to Mike to have the old Tryon place gone."

His grandfather's home, where Mike had grown up, down the slope of the hill below the Goheen house, had been an edifice of dark red brick, high-arched, stone-framed windows, and a turreted roof. Two years ago, it had burned to the ground, the fire lighting up all the hills of town.

Now the work went on, the scrubbing, rubbing, and burnishing. For a time, the girls worked upstairs and then came down again. It was a big house, where the Goheens lived—of frame, painted yellow, with dark green shutters at the square windows, slender white columns at the modest portico. It was a well-known house in the town, the garden as popular as its fireside. Sometimes people spoke of it as the "student union," because Doyle Goheen was Dean of the town's small, old, and excellent women's college, and a popular man. His wife, Anna, was as beloved for her wise counsel as for her sugar cookies.

"Are the medical students going to be a problem for you, Dad?" Meg asked.

"And the interns," Lucy added. Meg smiled at her.

"Oh, no!" said Doyle Goheen quickly. "Girls, you know, have to have possible men. And these will be safely busy."

"You hope," said Meg.

"They will be," her father assured her.

"I suppose the medical school here will be a mixed blessing," his daughter agreed. "And the hospital, too."

"Of course, dear. Take the payroll alone. . . . People will spend the money wisely and foolishly. As they do in any circumstance."

"If it brings Mike home," insisted Lucy, "everything about the project is good."

"Listen to the girl," said Meg.

"Don't you feel that way?" Lucy challenged her sister.

"I am the reserved type."

Her family laughed at her—and watched her fondly as she moved about, putting the flowers into a white urn on the drum table, into a brass bucket for the hearth, and a low brass bowl for the coffee table. Meg was a vivid girl, with feathery dark hair and a slender figure that moved with swift and unconscious grace. Today she wore a black jersey blouse and red stretch pants. Lucy, of course, was the beauty of the family. Small, red-blonde—and clever, too, though it was the cleverness one noted in Meg, the beauty in Lucy.

A carful of students came up the hill, rounded the crest, and started off for the observatory. As usual, the girls called out a salute to the home of their beloved Dean.

"They are going to study astronomy," said that gentleman dryly.

"It's nice for the girls, Dad," said Lucy, vigorously rubbing the mop board, "that you are named Goheen."

"And why?" asked Meg calmly.

"Oh, because they can write jingles about him so easily. His name rhymes with all the words they want to use. Dean, queen, lean, serene . . ." Her voice faded away.

"There must be more," said Meg, stooping to plug in the vacuum cleaner.

"There are," gasped Lucy, blowing her bright hair away from her face. "I was reaching behind the couch—you can't write poetry that way."

The cleaner roared.

This day the girls were flying about, preparing their home for the expected arrival of Mike Tryon, the nearest they would ever come to having a brother, although he was no brother in their minds and feelings.

Older than both girls—a difference in age which had diminished as the three children grew—he had lived close to them during their childhood, had grown up and gone away to college and medical school, returning for holidays, summer vacations—always a welcome visitor in the Goheen home, always ready to tease the girls, and, later, to advise them. It was he who had urged Meg to study bacteriology, to take a master's degree. His letter of last week had said that he was counting on her to work in his laboratory.

"Are you going to do it?" Lucy asked again on this day of Mike's actual arrival.

"I have a teacher-contract with the college," Meg reminded her.

"But—"

"With Mike, all things are possible," said her father.

"But, Dad . . ." said Lucy pleadingly.

He nodded. "I think it's wonderful, too, that he is coming back," he asserted, "to set up the internal medicine service in our new teaching hospital. He's done well in the fifteen years he has been studying and working. But do you know? My greatest pride was in what he said about his first interest being in the Goheen home and the Goheen family. . . ."

The girls agreed. Mike was interested in them. He always had been. His boyhood interest in gingerbread and lemonade, in two little girls to tease, had intensified as the years added up. Last Christmas he had sent both girls *sari* silks from India, where he was doing research work.

"We just have to make him stay!" said Lucy, polishing the stair rail.

"Enough lemon oil should do it," teased her father.

"We're his roots," Meg pointed out. "Now, with his grandfather dead, and even the house burned, what other roots does Mike have?"

"He must have established some contacts," said the Dean, not wanting his girls to be hurt.

"He hasn't married! He hasn't stayed in one place long enough—No! We are his roots!"

"And very nice ones, too," said her mother, smiling indulgently. They all loved Mike. He would do nothing to hurt any of them. "Goodness," she continued. "I remember him when he first came to live with Judge Tryon. He was ten, all yellow hair and enormous blue eyes. He would wander up here and watch me cook or bathe Lucy—"

"Mums!" she cried in mock protest.

Her mother chuckled. "You were a baby, and he worried for fear you would always be bald. He didn't think a bald girl had much future."

"He used to try to teach me to throw a baseball over-handed," Meg remembered. "I never made it, but I did learn to bat every one he threw."

"That sort of skill doesn't do much for a girl either," said her father.

"Oh, but that was when I was ten myself. By fourteen I had learned to be on his team, or not to be too good."

"We must have made a nuisance of ourselves," said Lucy. "Help me with these spindles, Meg. We'll never get through! We used to tag Mike . . ."

"And I'm ready to start right in at it again," Meg declared.

"It's funny," said Lucy, sitting on the step, hugging her knees. "I can look back and recognize the way he changed with us. At first, he would throw rocks at us—me, at any rate—to make me stay at home. Then he would explain to me patiently."

"Or go places downhill instead of up and past here," Meg contributed.

"You used spyglasses and saw him."

"I did. And then, in later years, he seemed to like having us go places with him. Remember the canoe he had? And the car—his grandfather never wanted him to have that, but he couldn't deny Mike a thing."

"Mike deserved his trust."

"The Judge," said Dean Goheen, "and Mrs. Tryon, while she lived, realized the obligation they had in serving as Mike's parents. It isn't easy for a man in his late fifties suddenly to be faced with the raising of a ten-year-old boy."

"They did a good job."

"The Judge used to give your father credit," said Mrs. Goheen gently. "He said he—the Judge—disciplined Mike. And we spoiled him. He thought it took both things to raise an orphaned boy."

"I remember when Mike decided he liked to read," said Meg. "That year, he just lived up here and read every book on our shelves."

"I remember that, too," said the Dean, his face bright. "It seemed the books in his home were law books or collected works of George Meredith and James Fenimore Cooper."

"Until Mike began bringing in his science books. They all burned, I suppose. But I've thought—reading Kipling here—Remember how we did it aloud? *Barrack-Room Ballads, Just So Stories*. And the time we read "They," and I cried, and Mike—"

"Mike kissed you," said Lucy. "I thought you were both mushy."

"Would you now?" Meg challenged her.

Lucy threw her flannel polishing cloth at her sister. Chorley, the family poodle, picked it up and carried it to his retreat behind the couch, where he had stayed all day.

"I was going to wonder," Meg resumed, "if reading Kipling came back to him during these two years he's spent in India."

"I'm sure it did," said Mrs. Goheen.

The telephone rang, and Meg ran to answer it. The Dean finished the silver, Lucy went up to take pretty towels to the bathroom on the second floor. Of course people would go up there! she said. Their friends always swarmed.

When Lucy came down again, she asked Meg to cut some of the snapdragons for the vases upstairs. "There're loads of the creamy ones." She looked at the clock, "Oh, good heavens, how the time does go! And so much still to do!"

The telephone range again. It was some man asking Lucy for a date. "Oh, I can't!" her family heard her say. "Not tonight!"

"Why?" asked the distant voice. "Is there another man?"

Lucy's cheeks were pink. "Yes," she said gaily. "Yes, there is!"

Her father offered to set out some lunch.

But he was not to get in Lucy's way—she was going to bake some things.

She did bake them, and the house smelled deliciously of spices and browning cake, coffee—and the flowers.

Meg brought in the snapdragons and asked her mother's advice about vases.

"The girls try to make me feel useful," Anna told her husband.

"I imagine they find you so," he assured her, bringing her a fresh hot cookie on the flattened palm of his hand. He gave Chorley a biscuit.

"In any case, I'm grateful," said the invalid. She was a pretty woman, and seldom let pain, and never discontent, spoil her prettiness. "It is just wonderful," she told her husband, "to be the mother of such *good* girls!"

"Makes for smugness, too," teased the Dean.

Anna dusted crumbs from the front of her pink housecoat. "I know it," she agreed. "But when I think of poor Doshie . . ."

The Dean well knew the problems of poor Doshie, but patiently he let Anna again tell the story to him. It was one with which the Goheen family had dwelt since its beginning. The Chambers family lived down the sloping street from the Goheens; their two daughters had grown up under their observation. Louis Chambers was an engineer for the state highway system. Doshie, his wife, was a friendly person, perhaps flighty, and certainly with no sense of money management. She seized upon every advanced theory by which to raise her two girls, who were younger than the two Goheen girls— But, no, Karen was not. She and Lucy had gone to school together. Judith, of course, was much younger—in her mid-teens, now. Both girls, as the Dean estimated such things, were the logical products of a home background marked by erratic discipline and supervision.

The Goheens loved Doshie and her girls, and their tragedy had been a personal, searing thing. When Karen, at seventeen, had been discovered pregnant, the Goheens had shared Doshie's grief, her shame, her confusion, her protest.

At seventeen, the big-eyed girl had married, then lost her still-born child, and at eighteen, she had been divorced. Since then she had lived at home, sometimes working, generally not—a moody, unhappy girl.

Now Judith was also seventeen, and Doshie, the mother, said Anna Goheen, was in a panic. The same thing must not happen again! Whereas, with Karen, Doshie had made sex a constant subject of conversation and instruction, even discussing the argument for a girl's experimenting; with Judith, to prevent another tragedy, Doshie didn't want the girl to date at all. Really, she didn't want her to leave the house. . . .

"I feel so sorry for that girl!" cried Mrs. Goheen in anguish.

"If Doshie has worked to make her sensible— But then, she should have done as much for Karen."

"I suppose she thought she was doing that, don't you? All that instruction . . ."

The Dean sighed. "And being sensible isn't always a protection to a girl," he agreed. "Judy seems well-balanced. She must know what happened to her sister; she must know that Karen's life has been tragically altered."

"It has, certainly," said Anna. "I've often thought she should have left home, left this town, got a job, and learned to take care of herself."

"It was more what Doshie thought, wasn't it, dear?" The Dean did not want Anna to be upset.

"Yes. But another girl might have left anyway. I believe I would have."

The Dean smiled a little. To imagine his Anna— But, yes, she would have handled her own troubles.

"Judith hasn't been as spoiled as Karen was," Anna was now deciding. "Doshie used to do everything for Karen— she bought her lots of clothes—she wanted her to have lots and lots of dates— But Judith, if she goes out at all, must be home at a certain time, her mother must know the people she goes with, where she goes, what she does. I am sure her behavior must discourage the boys who might want to take Judith places."

"This can backfire," said her husband. "A too-strict home can seem like a prison, and any means of escape subject to a try."

"Oh, dear . . ." murmured Anna.

"Don't let these things trouble you too much," the Dean advised. "We are more help to Doshie as interested onlookers than as participants."

Anna patted his arm. "You're right," she told him. "They'll be here tonight."

"Louis, too?"

Anna shrugged. "Unless he's off somewhere watching a road."

"Does he blame Doshie . . . ?"

"Doshie thinks he does. But at first I thought he blamed his job—that he was away so much, you know."

"Good for Louis! I hadn't expected that of him."

"He has his problems. Doshie is a darling, but she can do some very silly things. Like doing all her Christmas shopping last year out of the Nieman-Marcus catalogue. When the bills came in, I thought we would have at least suicide down the hill."

12

"But we all got lovely gifts," laughed the Dean.

"Oh, we did. Satin slips for the girls— *Doyle!* Go help Meg! She'll kill herself!"

"I've been on a ladder before," Meg called from the dining room.

"Yes, and you have the scars to prove it," said her father. "What are you doing?"

"Getting down the best china. We keep it on the top shelf."

"Am I going to have to wash . . . ?"

"Not with our Lucy such a perfect housekeeper. Look! Everything is in plastic cases. Of course there will be a great washing-up tonight after the party. Give her a yell, Dad. Ask her if she wants dinner or just tea-size plates."

That problem was settled, and others. Meg did not fall off the ladder. The table leaves finally locked into place, and the long cloth was spread. The punch bowl was brought up from the fruit cellar. Where else did one keep so huge a thing as a punch bowl? Lucy wondered if she had cookies enough, and was told that of course she did. And there would be slices of cake, and her delicious nut toffee —punch, ice cream, coffee— Oh, yes! It was all going to be ample!

"We'll get some students," Lucy predicted. "And all the med school staff will come. . . . The neighbors, of course."

"Were students invited?" asked her father.

"No, neither your students nor those of the medical school, but who are the Goheens to close their door against drop-ins?"

He nodded. "Then it will have to be first come, first served," he said. "Latecomers go hungry."

"Provided Mike is one of the first-comers."

"When did he say he would get here?"

"He gets to the city at five and will drive straight here." This had been discussed a dozen times during the past week.

"Seven, then," said Lucy now. "The cookies should last that long."

"We can put a rope or something around the table until he gets here," laughed Meg. "Oh, Dad, Lucy has *piles* of cookies! She's been baking all week. And three beautiful cakes—I think we have a wonderful sister, don't you?"

"I think you have."

"But not much grammar, huh?"

Her father hugged her. "I like you the way you are," he said comfortably. "Could we get your mother down for a nap?"

Meg shook her head. "Watch TV with her. She always cat-naps."

"Smart girl. I'll try it."

The rays of the afternoon sun lengthened and softened; the shadows of the tall trees darkened against the bronze carpet of fallen leaves. Lucy mixed pitchers of punch, ready for the ginger ale to be added.

"Maybe Mike will be too sophisticated for our punch," she worried.

"He won't expect sophisticated punch in this house," Meg assured her. "Have we plenty of ice?"

"Plenty. I bought two bagfuls yesterday. Gallons of ice cream—an ocean of ginger ale— It's good punch, Meg."

"Of course it is. And Mike will love it. He always has. . . ."

"But he could be changed. Do you think he will be? Will he even look the same?"

"Oh, Lucy, of course he will! In three years his hair wouldn't have turned white or fallen out. And I doubt if he got fat in India."

Lucy giggled. "And he'll still stand every young woman in town on tiptoe," she predicted.

"Especially the Goheen girls," said their mother from the doorway. Her daughters whirled. Behind the wheelchair, Doyle Goheen lifted his hands and shrugged. His and Meg's scheming had accomplished nothing.

"Well, of course we have been interested in Mike," said Meg airily, "and have tried to do things for the poor orphan boy."

"Oh, my," said her father.

Meg grinned at him. "He *was* an orphan," she declared. "He used to blackmail us with the fact. And now—well, he still can try it. And that will be just fine if he turns to us for a family. Mums, do you suppose we could get him to stay here?"

"No," said Mrs. Goheen firmly.

"But with his old home gone . . ."

"Yes, dear," her mother agreed. "And he has rooms waiting for him at the hospital. A suite, I heard."

"Meg knows he does," said Lucy.

"Oh, but to live in a hospital . . ." said Meg. "He'll want to get away."

"I imagine he'll do that."

"He's going to be busy," said the Dean, lighting his pipe. "To organize the internal medicine department for a new teaching hospital—that sounds like a big job to me. Mike's a young man—"

"And we think of him as a boy," said Anna. "Though he must be changed a great deal from our thoughts of him. He has travel and experiences behind him. . . ."

"He'll be sunburned," Meg summed up, and they all laughed.

"He'll still like us," said Lucy confidently. "Mike won't have changed that much!"

"I don't think he will either," said her mother. "Of course our town has changed some, too, as he will find out."

"The hospital, you mean."

"That, and the medical school, the students, and certainly the several young staff doctors— For one thing they will offer Mike Tryon some competition. And he didn't use to have a lot of that. Even the state cancer hospital is new for him, and that's only twenty miles away."

"She's trying to console us if Mike shouldn't be interested in the Goheen girls," Meg told Lucy in a conspiratorial whisper. Her spirits were sky-high.

"I know," Lucy answered. "Other fish in the sea. . . . But it won't work, will it?"

"I don't think so. Though some of the fish . . . Tony Bowlin, now, might give him a run. He's very popular—and good-looking. *Wheee-ooh!*"

"Meg!" her father protested. "What's happened to our dignified biology instructor?"

"Oh, I leave her upstairs, Dad, when I change into stretch pants."

"Do you girls like this Dr. Bowlin?" Anna asked, her eyes bright.

"By popular," Lucy explained, "Meg meant popular with 'all the young women.' That doesn't necessarily include us."

"Heavens, no," Meg agreed. "Besides, I understand he belongs to Bee Keel."

"Now, hush!" said her mother sharply.

Meg went quickly across the room and pressed her soft

15

cheek against her mother's. "It's this younger generation," she explained. "They'll say anything!"

Her mother gave her a spank, and then winced with the pain of doing it. But no one ever appeared to notice Anna's pains. Long ago she had set the subject as dull and monotonous, and thus taboo.

"Have you ever met Tony Bowlin, Mums?" asked Lucy, her smile still riffling in her voice.

"I don't remember. . . ."

"Oh, you would!" Meg assured her. "He's the hat-on-the-side-of-his-head, devil-may-care type. Hangs his cigarette on his lower lip, looks at you through half-closed eyes. . . ."

"Meg, *dear!*" protested Anna.

"It's a caricature," said the Dean, "but recognizable. And, yés, he *is* apt to give Mike some competition."

"Is he a good doctor?" asked Anna.

Her husband shrugged. "I don't know. But he's in charge of the surgery—the surgical service, I think it is called—and Chief of Staff of the new hospital. He and Mike will work together."

"That's how he came to know Bee," said Anna. "In the hospital."

Her daughters looked at each other. Bee, certainly, was a doctor; she was affiliated with the hospital as pediatrician, but saying that did not tell the whole story.

"*Will* Mike stay?" Lucy asked for the twentieth time that day. "Do you think he will, Mums? Dad?"

"Not in our house," Anna said firmly.

Lucy flipped her hand. "I meant, here in town?"

"Well," said the Dean, "I think a lot of factors would enter into that."

"It will be wonderful if he does."

"Oh, yes. For all of us, for the town, the hospital—maybe even for Mike."

"Then," said Anna, "we should do everything we can to make him stay."

Meg struck a pose. "Wiles, do you mean?" she asked sultrily.

They all laughed. "Wiles," agreed her mother. "Don't you have a new dress for tonight?"

"I do, and I should be getting into it—once we get you fixed up."

16

"Lucy can do that in ten minutes. Did you get yourself a new dress, dear?"

Lucy shook her head. "Not me. I'm wearing my yellow silk. The last time Mike was home he admired me in it."

"Foul!" cried Meg loudly. "That is definitely dirty pool."

Lucy began to push her mother's chair toward her room. "You go upstairs and get through in the bathroom," she instructed her sister, "and don't splash the mirror. But speaking of foul play, didn't *you* study bacteriology just so you could share Mike's interests?"

"Yes, I did," said Meg. Then she leaned over the stair rail, her black hair falling around her face. "But *you* learned to cook!"

"So," drawled Anna Goheen, "Mike went to India."

They all laughed, the sounds blending happily and lovingly.

"I'd do anything to get Mike," Meg declared. "I'm frankly in love with the guy."

"So am I," said Lucy. "And *I*'d marry him in a wink!"

"That all sounds like bigamy to me," said her father, his eyes twinkling.

"Oh, it is bigamy, Dad," Lucy assured him. "But in this stage, that is legal. Of course I think Meg should step aside. She is clever and has her career to fall back upon. . . ."

"And Lucy is so beautiful," Meg called from the landing, "she can pick and choose among plenty of other men—including the dashing Tony."

"Oh, go soak something, will you?" cried Lucy, and Meg scampered up the rest of the stairs.

They were all dressed and waiting an hour before Mike could possibly be expected, and longer than that before the time set for the guests to arrive. Lucy checked her kitchen and talked to the woman who had been hired to come in and help. Meg wandered about readjusting a flower, changing the way plates and cups were set out on the table.

"Don't do that!" Lucy told her sharply. "I very carefully arranged things! You're worse than a child to move stuff out of place!"

Meg stared at her. "I was just wishing we could have some wine, Lucy."

"Well, you know we can't. Mums won't allow anything of the sort in the house. Mike knows that and won't expect it. Oh, Meg, if you'll just stick to greeting people . . ."

"I will, when they come," said Meg mildly. "No use to get cranky."

Lucy smiled ruefully. "Temper, temper, huh?" she asked. "I'm sorry."

"We're all excited about Mike's coming," Meg excused her. Lucy did look lovely in her pale yellow silk.

"I still don't think we should fight over the boy next door, do you?"

"Oh, yes, we definitely should," Meg assured her. "I told you—I'm in love with the guy. And this time round—"

"All right, then," said Lucy. "I'm in love, too. So watch me."

"Shall do!"

There were quick steps along the front walk, the screen door opened, and Doshie Chambers came into the house. She looked around the hall, the living room, the dining room. "Oh, it's lovely!" she cried. "And you're all ready! I came to help. Let me look—"

The Goheens watched her; she didn't miss a thing; she nodded with approval. The lamps were right. Yes, the flowers—Anna's blue dress, and the blue knitted robe folded across her knees—the Dean's bow tie— "You'll put on your coat, dear?" she asked him. "Lucy . . . Oh, you are a picture! Blondes should wear yellow more. And Meg —well, well, *well!*"

She stooped to assure herself of the length of Meg's flower-figured tent dress. "Not a mini," she decided, "but perfect! Isn't there some little thing I can do?"

Lucy brought her a cup of coffee. "We've been ready since five-thirty," she laughed.

"You would be. Me, I'd be just getting started as the first guest arrived. Have you seen Mike yet?"

"No. I think he plans to come here as soon as he reaches town."

"I see. Maybe I should be getting home. I left Judy ironing her hair, and—"

"Ironing her—*what?*" cried Anna Goheen.

"Of course," said the Dean. "A lot of girls do that."

His wife sighed. "My husband," she said plaintively, "knows more about girls than a baby doctor."

Doshie sat down on the couch, put her cup on the coffee table, and rested her chin on her hand. "Girls," she said in a tone of pained resignation. Then she brightened. "But speaking of baby doctors, as I was coming up the hill, Bee

Keel passed me, and she was driving a sports car. One of those low-slung things—this was white, with wire wheels, and it looked like a baby's bathtub. Has she . . . ?"

"Oh, that's Tony Bowlin's Jaguar," said Meg.

Doshie rolled her eyes toward her. "Tony . . . ?" she asked. "Who's he?"

"Well, honestly, Doshie!" cried Meg. "Don't you read the newspaper? Or listen to gossip?"

"No, I don't," said Doshie, leaning back and extending her feet. She wore white sneakers and denim pedal pushers with the briefest of white blouses. She looked clean, and—but if she stayed around until the party—

"I read the newspaper," she told, "but gossip—uh-ugh. I'm afraid the stuff will splash on my doorstep."

The girls sighed. That was it. Doshie *was* afraid. And, in her panic, she hid in whatever hole she could find. Not to be hurt again, not to let her family be hurt. . . .

"Tony Bowlin," said Meg, carefully calm, "is the new surgeon at the hospital. Or do I mean the surgeon at the new hospital? Chief surgeon. Anyway, he's a fascinating person. Very handsome—the outdoors type. His eyes squint, and he has weathered skin, with deep creases down his cheeks . . ."

"Mike has creases."

"He does, doesn't he?" asked Meg. "But next to Tony, Mike looks like a baby."

"Oh, *Meg!*" Lucy protested.

"Well, he is blond, and his skin is fair—"

"I thought we decided he would be sunburned."

Meg giggled. "I wish he'd get here! Now, Doshie, this Dr. Bowlin is really something. He has presence. When he's in the room, you know it. His voice is good, and he says outrageous things—and he seems to have fallen very hard for Bee."

"She's a nice person."

"Well, she is, of course, but—"

"I know what you mean. She's married. But I don't like Leonard, and—"

"Nobody likes Leonard," said Meg with a glance toward her mother, who was lightly dozing. The Dean was reading the evening newspaper.

"We have to endure him," said Lucy, "because he's the best lawyer in town. I can't imagine, however, what it

19

would be like to live in the same house with such a man. He's—well—cruel."

Meg nodded. "Sardonic. Egotistic, and, yes, cruel."

"I don't like his big nose," said Doshie, and the three women laughed, though softly, to prolong Anna's rest.

"He's big all over," Lucy pointed out. "And called handsome with his silver hair and very blue eyes."

"I still don't like him," said Doshie, standing up. "Your house just looks lovely," she told the girls again. "I know it will be a fine party."

"Aren't you coming?" Lucy asked, in dismay.

"Oh, dear, I don't think so. I'll see Mike later—but I couldn't afford a new dress. . . ."

"My dress is four years old," said Lucy.

"I use my four-year-old dresses for dust rags, sweetie. And I just don't have a thing—I'm broke again, you know. This month the post office sprang a leak. The bills have simply poured in through our mail slot. I guess I went a little overboard during the summer, what with two trips, bathing suits—Louis says I did." She moved to the front door, and the girls followed her out to the stoop. The evening air was like silk—cool and softly pleasant.

"Please come to the party," Lucy urged their friend. "You can wear that white linen you wear to church—it's a warm night. And bring the girls; there will be a lot of young folk here, we feel sure. Some not invited, of course, but a party at the Dean's—" She threw out her hands and laughed.

Doshie touched her cheek. "You are the *loveliest!*" she said sincerely, "and I'll see. Just now our house is in a turmoil because Judith wants to go to the harvest dance next week. And that would mean a new dress . . . and, well—other things."

"But, goodness, Doshie, the child has to go to parties and have clothes."

"Not yet," said Doshie firmly. "I've decided that she should stay home this year. It's better all around."

"Safer all around," said Meg dryly.

Doshie nodded. "Yes. Safer," she agreed.

Meg glanced at Lucy, then she took Doshie's arm and walked her along the flagstones. "I mean to have a little talk with you, Doshie," she said firmly.

"Oh, Meg," cried the older woman, "you don't understand. You're not a mother—you don't *know*. . . ."

"I'm a teacher," Meg pointed out. She walked slowly along beside Doshie. "For four years I have worked with girls; I often have to counsel with them and with their mothers. And it hasn't been too long, remember, since I was a girl myself, and of Judy's age. I well remember what it was like. So you listen to me."

She stopped under a tall oak tree and faced her friend. "Judith is seventeen," she said sternly. "And I know that is a significant age for you. But don't you suppose she remembers what happened to Karen when *she* was seventeen? Don't you suppose she has realized the things that happened, and the results? She was ten, and you had made her wise about things like sex and human relationships. She was no fool. As she has grown up, perhaps Karen has talked to her."

"Karen talks to no one," said Doshie, her tone weary. "Not from the first, she hasn't. She just pretends that none of this ever happened."

"All right," said Meg briskly. "Then let's all pretend. Judith is a smiling, friendly girl—she loves puppies and kittens—she is well liked at school. So I say, give her a chance to live, and live her own life, not Karen's life colored by Karen's mistakes. Let Judith make her own; they won't be many, or great."

Doshie made some small sound, and Meg swept on. "Look!" she said. "Consider this: An airplane pilot figures that each time he takes a plane up, he starts out with a new set of odds against him. Why not consider Judith that way? Mathematically her chances at success, or failure, are exactly that of any seventeen-year-old girl—not doubled because of what happened to her sister. Judy is herself. Look at her that way."

Doshie shook her head. "Oh, Meg," she cried, "I know you want to help, but you are younger than Judith in your arguments. And more naïve."

Meg leaned forward and kissed Doshie's cheek. "What a lovely thing to say!" she cried.

CHAPTER TWO

EVEN AS Meg still talked to Doshie, the first cars had begun to arrive for the party, and when she went back, there was the pleasant riffle of voices in the house and the bright stab of laughter. Mike had not yet arrived, but Meg must greet a dozen friends—faculty from the college, a doctor and his wife, neighbors. The party's pattern quickly formed itself. Everyone first went to speak to Mrs. Goheen, then stepped aside, moved away, out of the living room, into the study or the dining room—sometimes out of doors.

Meg stayed in the hall as she should, to greet the arriving guests. Lucy hovered between the dining room and kitchen. The Dean and Chorley were liaison and seemed to be everywhere.

"Should we put Chorley out?" Meg asked Lucy.

"He'll get stepped on and go behind the couch. Now he thinks the party is for *him*."

"The clown!" cried Meg with an affectionate glance at the big poodle.

And then Mike came, strolling in through the back door, as they might have expected him to do. Smiling, tall, the light shining on his yellow hair, just as everyone remembered. He hadn't changed at all!

He said he had had to park two miles away—somebody was giving a party! He grabbed up a handful of cookies— he was starved! His plane had been late—no dinner—and oh, wasn't it wonderful to be home!

For ten minutes the party frothed around him. He kissed Lucy, he kissed Meg, he shook hands with the men, was charming to the women and the girls. . . .

He looked wonderful! Blue jacket, gray trousers, a dull green scarf tucked into the throat of his white shirt. Chorley remembered him. . . .

"Oh, I'm sure he does!" cried Meg.

"Well, I remember him," said Mike. "I remember everything!" He walked into the living room, where he turned, and turned again, looking, looking. He touched the arm of the couch, lifted a book from the table, opened a little box on another table.

"It's all *here!*" he cried exultantly. "Just as I have pictured it so often."

People watched him and smiled. The tall young doctor was certainly a charmer, though he seemed sincere, too. He was sincere!

He went into the study and put his fingertips on the old, old map behind the couch. "Things were easier when the world was that flat," he told the Dean. "How are you, sir?"

Mike had always called the Dean "sir." Always that, and only that. He liked the calm, watchful man. The two respected each other. "Do you still have problems?" he asked now.

"I do," said the Dean quietly. "Just now it is a matter of the furnace in the big dormitory. Will it, or won't it?"

Mike whistled. "That *is* a problem," he decided. "We'll handle it later."

He went back to Mrs. Goheen's chair. "Oh, Miss Anna Go-*heen!*" he cried, exactly as he had done since he was ten. "You just wait and see what I brought you from India!"

"Presents, Mike?"

"Well, of course, presents." For a minute his fingers lay softly against her cheek. She smiled up at him.

"It's good to have you home, dear," she said.

"And *very* good to be here."

He met everyone, he talked to everyone. He ate cake, and drank punch, and managed to take Lucy's arm and draw her out into the garden for a few minutes.

"I'm needed inside, Mike," she protested softly. . . ."

"I know," he agreed. "But I've been meaning to ask . . ."

Lucy was flustered and flushed by all her housekeeping chores and duties. She tossed her bright hair back from her face and smiled uncertainly up at Mike; though her eyes were still concerned, she was excited by his presence.

"Are you the cook, miss?" he asked her. "Are you the *good* cook?" He drew her into his arms, and he hugged her tight. "And, oh, Lucy, darlin'," he said exultantly, "are you ever the *pretty* cook!"

It was wonderful to have him there—even though Chorley did come out to investigate. Lucy laughed at his antics and hoped she made sense in what she said to Mike.

Then—not much later—he found a minute and a place to talk to Meg. He had, she was aware, been watching her —and she wondered if her dress was the right one.

It was a flowered dress, patterned all over with yellow flowers, and soft rose ones, and green leaves. The thin stuff fell from her shoulders into pretty folds and swirled about her knees. Meg was a slender girl, and vibrant, not very tall, with a cloud of black hair, a slender throat, and huge, dark eyes. Her voice was quick, her manner free and gay. Mike came up to where she stood in a group of young men and women, and he listened to her, smiling; she was quick with a bright word, and just as ready with a flood of earnest ones.

"Oh, if I had a boat of *any* size," she was saying, "I'd *always* name it the *Lizzie Borden.* That's a boat name. And my dog had to be Henry Fothergill Chorley!"

"Though not with permission of the Oxford Press," drawled Mike. "Imagine a woman who will plagiarize the Church Hymnal."

Meg stretched her hand to him. "Oh, *Mike!*" she cried. "It's so good to have you home!"

"I came back to take you for that buggy ride," he explained.

"I'll bet." She looked around at her guests and presented a few of them to Mike—doctors, faculty—the rest were neighbors who needed no introduction. "Mike has been promising me a buggy ride for a hundred years," she explained. "I'm going to hold him to it this time."

"You just find me a horse," he told her, drawing her with him to the hall, then to the front door and outside.

"If it hadn't been for the Goheen girls," said one of the men in the group which they had left behind, "Tryon would not have come back to the Heights."

"Oh, now, he's a town boy."

"He was raised here, yes."

"Which girl does he have his eye on?"

"I don't know."

"I'll bet on the pretty blonde."

"Maybe you shouldn't. Meg, the dark sister, is a live wire. And pretty enough."

"Yes, she surely is."

Outside, Mike seemed content to stroll along the flag-stone walk holding Meg's hand. He was looking down at her, and she tried to think of something to say. Not that anything was needed. They reached the tall oak where an hour ago she had lectured Doshie. She could tell him about that, but of course she wouldn't. She—

"Are you going to help me, Meg?" he asked, his voice deep and warm.

She glanced up at him. "Help you how?" she asked.

"You know how! In my lab—in the work I want to do."

"What do I know about internal medicine and staffing a hospital?" Her voice was bland.

He gave her arm a shake. Not gently. "You know a lot about labs, don't you?" he asked.

"Oh, sure. Everyone calls me Madame Curie."

"That will do to start. Because I mean to do some lab work, and I'll need you to help me. Just now I am interested in filtering water to catch the viruses as well as the bigger bugs. So, will you? Huh? Will you?"

She laughed, acknowledging his reminder of their younger days. "It sounds as if you planned to stay with us for a time." Again she glanced up at him. "Do you?"

"The answer to that," he said quietly, "will somewhat depend on you."

"That will be fun," she decided. "And I really will think about the lab offer. Of course I'm contracted at the college."

"I can blackmail them, too. Now—tell me about yourself."

She spread out the fullness of her frock. "Just what you see. Me, Meg."

"And very nice, too. Lucy—I thought she would be married by now."

"There's Mums, you know, and the house to keep. Besides, Lucy is particular."

"That's good. About your mother . . . ?"

"She gets a little worse all the time, Mike, so far as the arthritis goes. As to her spirit, she's wonderful."

"You're all wonderful. Do we have to go back?"

"I think so. People want to see you and talk to you."

The party was growing by the minute. All the neighbors

had come in. Tony Bowlin arrived, and various ones watched Bee Keel. Leonard had not come, perhaps would not come. But Bee was helping Lucy, laughing—she was a warm-hearted woman. She kissed Mike with a smack and made him laugh.

It was Meg who brought up Tony Bowlin. "I think this may be what is called your opposite number," she told Mike. "Dr. Bowlin, Chief of Surgical Services at the hospital."

Mike fired immediately, his hand thrust out, his voice hearty. "How are you, doctor?" he cried.

Bee looked at Meg and shrugged. "Let's go wash some punch cups," she drawled. "A girl hasn't a chance with these medical types."

But Meg knew that Tony's eyes followed Bee.

"He's nice, isn't he?" she asked ingenuously—or forthrightly, which was Meg's way.

"Who?" asked Bee.

"Dr. Bowlin."

Bee laughed. "Yes, he is, darling," she said. "One of the nicest men I have ever known. Interesting, considerate— and he appreciates women."

"Oh, lovely." No wonder Bee liked him. She didn't get that from Leonard Keel, Meg felt sure. She had heard the lawyer talk about women in a way—

"He's a good doctor, too," said Bee.

"You'd know . . ."

"I do know. But there's more to that than surgical skill, Meg."

"I suppose there is."

"I hope he and Mike get along well together."

"Shouldn't they?"

"I don't know much about Mike as a doctor. His record, of course. But his—well, his philosophy, his—"

"Growing up, he was a pretty nice boy. Honest, and kind . . ."

"Why don't you marry him, Meg?"

Meg laughed. "I'll tell you, Bee. He'd ask me only at his own risk."

Bee patted her shoulder. "Here come the Chambers. . . ."

"Good!" said Meg, and went to meet them. "Get yourself some of the coconut cake," she advised Dr. Keel, speaking over her shoulder. "It's worth a struggle."

Doshie was wearing the white linen dress, straight and slim. She had combed her yellow hair into pretty waves about her face, she wore pearls and a charm bracelet, and she seemed calm enough. The girls—they looked alike, the two Chambers girls. Their kitten faces peered out of a tent of long, ash-blond hair; one could see only one gray eye at a time. Karen was unsmiling, while Judith smiled all the time. Judy was "cute"; she immediately found friends and went with them to the refreshment table.

Doshie endeavored to watch her. "You'll want to see Mike," Meg reminded her. "He's in the living room."

"He's young," said Karen, evidently surprised.

Meg smiled at the girl. "But he used to seem much older, didn't he?"

Karen didn't answer. She now was staring at Dr. Bowlin. "Who's he?" she asked.

"Karen . . ." Doshie protested, but Meg answered. "I'll introduce you," she promised. "We'll break it up between him and Mike. They can talk tomorrow, can't you, boys?"

Mike laughed. "She's the boss, Bowlin," he told Tony. "And we *will* talk tomorrow. Tonight—it's old home night, you see. How are you, Doshie?"

Karen still watched Dr. Bowlin. Meg introduced him to her and then to her mother.

"Perhaps I'm out of place in old home week," Tony said to Meg. "Though I *think* I was invited."

"You were."

"Do you think I should now leave?"

Meg shrugged. "I haven't seen anyone else leave. Have you had some punch and cake?"

"I'll get some. First, I want to talk to your mother."

And he did talk to her, sitting down on the floor beside her chair, his hands clasping his drawn-up knees, his eyes looking up into her face.

"What are they talking about?" Lucy found a minute to ask Meg.

"Quilt blocks, the last time I was close."

"Oh, Meg."

"I swear. Perhaps he has medical reasons for asking Mums if she can piece a quilt, or appliqué— She's having a ball."

"Maybe Dad should watch him."

Bee came to them and touched Lucy's arm. "I'm going to duck out," she said. "Leonard isn't well. . . ."

She was gone. Lucy went toward the kitchen, Meg greeted a group of seniors from the college. The girls were crashing, but had been expected.

"Where did Bee get to?" Doshie asked Meg. "I wanted to talk to her."

"She said that Leonard was not well."

"He can't stand himself," said the rangy phys. ed. teacher, who overheard. Meg chuckled.

"I understand he breeds dogs," said Emma McGee, "and they can't stand him either."

"Oh, now, really!" Meg protested.

"I'm sorry for Bee," said Doshie. Those in the group about her agreed.

"But there's no real need for pity," decided someone. "Not with Tony Bowlin around."

Doshie said something about looking for her girls. Meg tried to change the subject.

"Haven't you seen Dr. Bee driving his car?" Miss McGee persisted.

"Her own was probably giving her trouble."

"Oh, Meg!" The protest was a chorus.

She put her hands over her ears. "Don't all of you shout at me!" she begged.

"And what about her and Tony being caught kissing up on Observatory Curve?" asked Emma McGee. "You heard about that! Everybody heard about that!"

Meg, too. "Oh, well," she said, "what's one kiss among friends?"

"One kiss is a sign there could be more."

"Do you blame her?" asked Bee's next-door neighbor.

"No," said Miss McGee, "I really don't."

Meg did not blame her either, but she would never say such a thing because—after all—Leonard, though probably all everyone said, still was Bee's husband. And Bee had her own profession to consider, as well as Dr. Bowlin's. And, anyway—

By then, the party was very lively and big. Everyone in town seemed to be there, from the Rector to medical students, the president of the college to the barber who used to cut Mike's hair. Mike was glad to see *him* and told some ridiculous tales about having his hair cut in the more remote places of India.

Some of the young people had brought a transistor radio and were dancing out on the patio. "They won't catch cold," Meg reassured her mother. "Not with those gymnastics."

The doctors from the hospital had all come, and some of the younger ones were talking to Karen and Judith. Tony Bowlin had cornered Lucy in the dining room, and she seemed to like it. People were all over the house. Every chair, every couch, was occupied. The stairs were full—a dozen people sat on the floor.

"We're running out of food," Lucy told Meg. "That Bowlin is a fascinating man. . . ."

"Are you being unfaithful to Mike already?" Meg teased her.

"Isn't he just *grand,* Meg?" Lucy asked.

"Yes, he is. He's older. He's all man now, Lucy. The boy is gone. But—yes. He is grand."

"What will we do about food?"

"Are all those cookies . . . ?"

"There still are cookies. But I've run out of ginger ale for the punch. And ice cream."

"Can't I go get some? I could slip out the back way . . ."

"Well—we could send one of the men. Mike, even . . ."

"Oh, no," said Meg. "He's talking to your Tony Bowlin again."

Lucy made a face at her. "Does Mike like him?"

"How would I know? Men don't show such things. Look, I'll get going. My car's right there— I won't be gone twenty minutes. Ginger ale and ice cream, hmmmn? Will do."

And she was gone, with a flirt of her bright skirt, a twinkle of her yellow pumps. Lucy followed her to the back porch and stood for a moment there in the half-dark, her cheek pressed against the pillar which felt cool and smooth. Overhead the stars blinked and a little wind blew among the drying leaves of the tall trees. The dance music came to her from the patio at the side of the house. Down the hill a truck roared along the highway, someone laughed, a voice lifted.

"Mike is grand," Lucy repeated to herself. "Just grand."

She sighed contentedly and went back into the house, her eyes registering a picture which she was always to hold in her memory. Bright colors—Doshie talking to the courtly old professor emeritus of the English department —the Dean carefully transporting two cups of punch. One would be for Mums. The dishes and silver, the candles and the flowers gaily sparkling in the dining room. Talking people again. Out in the hall Emma McGee's pink sweater, a girl's green hairband, a Madras jacket on a tall man. And in the living room where Mike was up on the quilted couch, sitting on the back of it, head and shoulders above everyone else, laughing, talking, and gesturing. Tony Bowlin stood back, watching him, his eyes half closed, a smile crinkling their corners. Karen was watching him, fascinated, and Doshie was watching her daughter. Would she say something or do something?

Doshie seldom, if ever, crossed Karen. Lucy frowned. How *did* she manage? If she couldn't scold the girl . . .

"I can't even talk to her," Doshie had said one time. "Because with one word she considers cross, off she goes. I don't know where! She stays away for hours. When she's in the house, mopey and sullen, as she often is, at least I know what she is doing."

Poor Doshie *did* have a problem! Lucy frowned about it as she busied herself, taking used dishes to the kitchen, straightening the table. Meg should be back quite soon.

Only she didn't come back. The twenty minutes became a half hour, and still she did not come.

Mike was still up on the couch talking—technically, at first, to the doctors who had gathered about him, then telling, informally and amusingly, about the people of India. "I've loved that country ever since I first read Kipling," he said, "right here in this room."

Lucy thought it a shame that Meg should not be there to hear him say that. Earlier in the day she had talked about the Kipling experience.

And before another ten minutes had passed, the Dean asked where Meg was. "She should hear Mike," he said.

Lucy told him that Meg had gone on an errand. Mike said he'd repeat everything—"in private, to Meg, and—" he chuckled—"and to all of you, I'm afraid, again and again and again. You'll get good and sick of me and India."

The punch ran out—and still no Meg. But there was no great harm done, because people were beginning to leave the party. Slowly, as a congenial group does break up, starting, then stopping for a last word here, another one there—but the crowd was thinning. The dancers had left the patio—Doshie took her girls home—and Mike came to Lucy. "Hasn't Meg come back yet?" he asked.

"No, she hasn't."

"Are you concerned?"

He was, Lucy could see. She put her hand on his sleeve. "She's all right, Mike."

"It's after ten. . . ."

"I know. But this is Laurel Heights, remember? Meg went downtown for more ginger ale; she probably met someone, and she's talking. Meg does that and forgets time. . . ."

Mike sighed and nodded. "I thought maybe she had a Tony Bowlin somewhere."

Lucy frowned. "What do you mean by that?" she asked.

He grinned. "Oh, I've heard a bit of gossip here and there this evening."

"Not about Meg!"

"No, dear. No, dear. Not about Meg. But she *is* a clever girl, and fun to be with. Men must like her."

"They do," Lucy agreed. "So what?"

"There's no one special?"

"For Meg? Oh, yes, there is."

He blinked. "Who is it?"

Lucy smiled up at him, her thick lashes shadowing her blue eyes. "You," she said softly.

Mike stretched his lips back against his teeth. "All right, Smarty!" he cried. "You know what I meant. And I *hope* you know what I mean when I ask if there is someone you especially like."

Lucy nodded and took two steps away from him, then turned back. She was laughing. "Oh, yes, there *is!*" she said earnestly. "I've been in love with Mike Tryon since I was ten."

He reached his hand for her, drew her to him, and kissed her, rather hard, full on her mouth. "That makes me very happy!" he said loudly. "And now I am leaving. If anything *has* happened to Meg, will you send me word?"

"Of course. You're staying at the hospital?"

"I understand I have rooms there. Remember now—"

"I'll remember, but she'll come strolling in, the ice cream melted, the ginger ale warm—"

"You may be right. I—well, I'll see you tomorrow, pretty thing. All the Goheens, I'll see tomorrow. Don't have company."

"We won't. Will you come for supper?"

"Oh, sure. I'd like nothing better."

And he strode away, through the kitchen, and out to the wide drive where he had left his car.

CHAPTER THREE

THE PARTY dissolved, still slowly. The Rector and his wife lingered to talk to Anna and the Dean. While they still were there, Lucy began to straighten things, Bonita Sturgeon helping her.

Bonita, recently, had returned to the Heights, having lived, trained, and worked as a nurse in the city for several years. She was a tall, horse-faced woman, and now she would be Chief of Services at the newly operational teaching hospital. Tonight she wanted to talk about Mike Tryon, whom she had known as a boy and youth, though only as one does know the young people of a small town, not as a doctor.

"I understand he's very good, and I hope he'll stay with us," she told Lucy, emptying ash trays, wiping them out with efficient sweeps of a paper towel in her large and capable hands. "I have the idea that we'll keep Dr. Bowlin more readily if he has a good medical chief."

"Is Dr. Bowlin a good surgeon?" asked Lucy, more to show polite interest than anything else. She was, suddenly, tired.

"He's the best I've ever worked with," said Bonita firmly. "And that covers quite a lot of doctors, you know."

"I'm afraid I don't know, Bonita," Lucy told her, smiling. "Meg would, perhaps."

"Where is Meg?"

Lucy repeated what she had, by then, said to a dozen people. Meg had gone for ginger ale, and she had not returned. . . .

"Her car's in the drive," said Bonita.

"Oh, no . . ."

"It sure is. I had to go out and move mine so somebody could get out. I came back up the drive—"

Lucy ran to the back porch. Sure enough, Meg's car sat,

half in, half out of the garage. Well! She would have sworn . . .

But, then, where was Meg? Lucy hadn't seen her come in. Perhaps someone else had driven her for the ginger ale and ice cream. . . .

She was too busy, really, to wonder constructively. Bonita left, and the Rector. The Dean took off his coat and came to help Lucy and the woman hired for the evening finish up the necessary chores. All the dishes were washed, and the good ones were stacked in the dining room to be put away tomorrow.

"There aren't any leftovers," Lucy told Gloria as she paid her. "Just that little plate of cake. . . ."

"It's all right, Miss Lucy. I'll take the cake, and I know before I come that you wouldn't serve nothin' but coffee and punch."

Lucy laughed. "My reputation goes ahead of me, does it?" She took money from the housekeeping purse.

"It's all right," said Gloria again. "I'm churchly myself."

"Can I drive you home?"

"No, Miss Lucy—you got your mamma to tend to. She looks tuckered."

Lucy locked the kitchen door, turned out the lights, and went to help her mother get ready for bed. Her father was moving chairs, setting the lower floor in order. "I keep finding wadded-up napkins," he complained as Lucy went through the living room.

She smiled. "Very few in the wastebaskets, though."

"It was a good party, honey. I think Mike was happy."

"Oh, yes!" She put her hands on Anna's chair. "How about a nice soft bed?" she asked her mother.

Anna gazed up at her younger daughter. "You're a pretty girl, Lucy Goheen," she said.

Lucy was pretty—the sheen of her golden hair, the way her dark blue eyes were widely set, with long lashes and winging brows, the flare of her nostrils, her soft-lipped mouth . . .

"Compliments from you are unseemly," she told her mother sternly. "I get my looks from you, and you know it."

She pushed the chair into her parents' large, comfortable bedroom, where nothing of the party had intruded. There was no tobacco smoke, no crumpled napkins. . . .

Getting her mother ready for bed was a nightly task,

and even as tired as she was, Lucy cherished it because of the chance it gave her for girl-talk with her mother. Tonight that talk was about Mike, of course, and then about Dr. Bowlin.

"He seemed so very nice," said Mrs. Goheen. "He's going to make me some splints for my hands. And I don't believe the gossip about him and Bee, do you?"

"I don't know, Mums. Bee is nice, too. And Leonard must be difficult to live with. I suppose a woman wants love and happiness—don't you?"

"She should decide that before she marries. I hope you girls will be wiser. Lucy, where is Meg?"

Lucy had been turning down the bed, and she straightened and pushed her hair away from her face. "She went into town an hour ago," she said. (It had been closer to two hours.) "For ice cream and stuff. I don't know where she got held up. Probably met someone interesting. . . . Or, you know—the time one of the college girls got sick at the drugstore? Meg helped her home and dropped out of sight for a couple of hours."

"Something must have happened," agreed Anna. She was very, very tired. "Car trouble, maybe— She wouldn't have stayed away so long, otherwise."

Lucy didn't mention Meg's car standing in the driveway. She helped her mother into bed and prepared to give her the usual massage. This was a tedious, care-taking task, for there were many sore and tender spots. Still, circulation must be maintained. . . .

Lucy's hands moved gently, rhythmically; she hoped her mother would not talk—

But she did, of course. About Mike again. "He's like the son I never had," the invalid assured her daughter. "I think your father feels that way, too."

"I don't believe Dad has any complaints about your daughters, Mrs. G."

"No—he doesn't. But we *are* fond of Mike."

"Of course."

"He's grown up now, isn't he, Lucy?"

"Well—he's old enough for that."

Anna smiled. "Yes, of course he is. But he's still the same, sweet and teasing. This evening he talked to me about his grandfather."

"That's good."

"Sometimes young people don't appreciate or understand old ones."

"Sometimes young people haven't the depth. Can you lift this arm, dear?"

"It hurts."

"I know it does."

"Your cake was lovely, Lucy."

"I sent a few ragged leftovers home with Gloria."

"Did you pay her?"

"Yes. Out of the housekeeping money."

"That's right. Did you meet all the doctors who came tonight?"

"I met several. Some of them seemed too young to have studied so long."

"No younger than you, were they?"

"Maybe not."

"I saw a couple of them talking to Karen."

So did Doshie, thought Lucy, but she did not say so. She didn't need to. Her mother had seen Doshie watching her girls, and, often, intervening.

"Does Karen have dates?" Anna asked.

"I don't really know. At first, she was resentful and wouldn't date—or even speak civilly to boys and young men. That lasted for about a year. Things might have been better if she had continued her schooling. But even so, though very timidly, she did begin to talk to them, and eventually she did date. Not often, I think—and of course you know she has held a job or two. She liked working at the newspaper, and I think she did all right. Obviously Karen likes men and is interested in them. The women, perhaps, have given her a bad time, but the men . . . Some of them could be problems, I suppose, but others are nice to her, and she likes them. It's not entirely sex interest, just —interest. She helps me at the church sometimes, and I think I could persuade her to work in the children's clinic at the hospital. Bee said I might ask her."

"You'll like that work," murmured Anna.

"I believe I shall." Lucy hoped her mother was getting drowsy, so she talked softly, her voice a monotone. Sleep was a rare gift for Anna Goheen.

"The trouble is," she said, "Doshie is suspicious. She'll think Karen will want to work at the clinic to be near the doctors."

"And me too, eh?" laughed Lucy. "All right. That's

36

normal girl-stuff. If Karen had married normally, and had been divorced, Doshie would want her to work where she'd meet other men. But as things are, it's Doshie who thinks of the sex side all the time. She watches Karen and questions her—and very soon Karen gives up going with a boy—any boy—or man. I often wish she would show a little more spunk."

"The one time she did, dear . . ."

"Oh, I know. But one mistake! Is she going to have to pay for that all her life?"

"To Doshie, she is. And we must not forget, Lucy, that Doshie knows more about the girl than we do."

"I still don't think she is handling the situation very well."

"She needs someone expert at these things to talk to her and advise her. Will the new hospital staff have a psychiatrist?"

"Oh, I suppose it will. For a medical school. But I don't believe Doshie would ever— I can't help but be sorry for her, Mums."

"And for Karen."

"Oh, mercy, yes! And Judith, too. Because Doshie—and maybe even Judith—fear that she will do as Karen did."

Her mother sighed. Lucy folded the sheet and the light blanket neatly under Anna's chin. She bent over and kissed her mother's soft cheek. "Go beddy-bye now," she said, as had become ritual. She took her powder and lotions to the bathroom, came back and put her hand on the lamp switch.

"You ask your father," said Anna softly, "to find out what happened to Meg."

"Oh, Mums, Dad is tired. And Meg can take care of herself."

"I know, but—Mike would help you."

"We'll tend to things. She probably is home by now." Lucy turned out the light and left the room.

She decided to say nothing to her father about Meg. He called Chorley in and locked the front door. "Good night, Lucy, dear," he called to the girl. "Is your mother settled?"

"Yes. And tired. Try not to let her talk. . . ."

"I know the routine."

He did, poor dear. For ten years and more—the rheumatoid arthritis had begun earlier—Doyle Goheen had

had an invalid wife. Not many men could take such a thing as he had done, patiently, sympathetic always with Anna, appreciating what the girls did, anxious always not to overburden them. The situation was distressful, but warm love had helped them all carry the load.

Lucy checked things again and started upstairs. She was, she would admit, a little upset. Surely nothing had happened to Meg. But it did seem thoughtless of the girl to have caused any concern.

A few years before, the entrance hall of the old house, and the stairway, had been remodeled, and Lucy, even tonight, could cherish the prettiness of the delicate hand-rail and its supporting spindles, the thick gold carpeting on the stairs. The double front doors were wide, with a fanlight and side windows through which Lucy could see the shadows of the blowing trees and the passage of a car along the street.

Since their mother's illness, the second floor had belonged to the girls; each had her own room, furnished and decorated to her own taste, each showing the girl's interests and character. Lucy's furniture was white, her carpet blue, the walls a pale yellow. It was a pretty room which had supported college pennants, invitations, cheerleader pompons, and now still contained many pictures of her family and friends.

Meg's room was more austere—comfortable, peaceful, and elegant. There was walnut furniture, a green carpet, green walls, and blue and green tapestry hangings. She and Lucy shared a bath which was both light blue and dark green; it contained a cabinet shower in which the girls reveled, and which, tonight, contained Meg.

Having reached the upper hall, Lucy could hear the shower going, and she sniffed at the acrid smell of burning cloth. What on earth . . . ?

Just then, the shower water shut off, and Meg came out, wrapped in a large green towel, her hair plastered against her head, and her eyes— Why, she looked terrible! Lucy followed her into her room.

"Shut the door," Meg croaked. "That smell— We don't want Dad up here."

"But, Meg—"

"Shut the door!" Meg cried shrilly. Roughly, she pushed Lucy aside and closed the door herself. Every window was open, the curtains billowing out into the room. "Don't talk!" she cried. "Don't *talk!*"

She spoke gaspingly, her voice high and thin. Her eyes bulged, and her face . . .

Hysterical, thought Lucy. *Meg is hysterical!* Her black, wet hair clung to her head; she had not bothered with a shower cap. She stood shivering, but when Lucy would have closed a window, she protested excitedly against it. And the room was warm enough because of the fire on the hearth. Why, Meg had been burning her new dress! There was a half-burned remnant of the flowered stuff, and one of her yellow shoes lay scorched, and—

Lucy whirled. "What's happened?" she cried. "What has happened to you?"

Meg could not speak. She just stood there shivering and clutching the green towel around her, now and then bending her head to wipe her cheek against it. She opened her lips and closed them again—her eyes stared and stared. . . .

Frightened, Lucy went to her and put her arm around her sister. "Tell me," she urged gently. "Tell me . . ."

Meg shook her head. "I—" she said, her teeth chattering. "I—I have had a terrifying experience. Oh, *Lucy!*"

Terrifying had to be the word. It was the one which Lucy was ready to believe. The way Meg looked—she kept rubbing her knuckles across her mouth—

"Are you hurt?" Lucy asked sharply. "Should I get Mike?" She had promised to let him know if . . .

She felt, and she saw, Meg freeze—literally. The lines of her face, her lips—the muscles of her slight body—stiffened into ice. Lucy watched in terror.

Slowly Meg's head began to shake from side to side. "Don't—need—Mike," she whispered with an agonizing effort. "Don't—want— Never, never, never—see—him—again." She began to tremble, but when Lucy would have led her to the bed, she resisted strongly. And Meg was strong. She played tennis, golf and swam. . . .

"What's this about Mike?" Lucy asked anxiously. *"He* didn't hurt you?"

Meg shuddered. Her teeth rattled together, and she shook all over.

Lucy decided that patience was needed, first of all. She went to the bathroom, got a dry towel, her glance touching the vase of white flowers which, earlier on this day, Meg

39

had placed on the counter. She came back and wiped her sister's face and her hair.

"You love Mike," she said gently, in the soothing tone which she used to Anna. "Don't you, dear? He—"

"I—" Meg attempted. "I have—loved—him."

"Then—"

"No." She walked toward the fireplace and stood there looking down into the ashes. She seemed completely dazed —in shock, probably would be the term. Now and then a spasm shook her from head to toe. Lucy wondered if she might call Mike anyway. She would need to go downstairs to do it, and his coming would frighten their parents. But—

"Meg," she said firmly, "I am going down to tell Mums that you are at home. She was worried. . . ."

Meg turned and looked at her. "Don't phone Mike," she said.

"All right," Lucy agreed. "All right. I won't." She started for the door. "I'll be right back."

She whispered her news to her father and came upstairs again, Chorley following her. He sniffed at the sill and sneezed when Lucy opened the door of Meg's room.

Meg was in the shower again, the water pounding, rushing.

Lucy stood in complete terror. What had *happened* to Meg? Was this a breakdown? What should she do? There must be something— Something must have happened, and —and—

Meg came out of the bathroom again and went over to the bed. This time she had put on a robe. Lucy helped her get under the covers and again she wiped her hair, not talking. She went into the bathroom and straightened things there, wiping up the puddles, putting the wet towels on the racks.

Her eye on Meg, who lay staring at the ceiling, Lucy went to her own room, took off her dress and put on a loose robe. She came back and knelt beside Meg's bed. She stroked her sister's cheek. "Tell me, Meg?" she asked. *"Please* tell me. Did you go into town . . . ?"

Meg turned her head to stare at Lucy. And she began to weep—slowly at first, then with tears gushing from her eyes and great sobs shaking her. Lucy had an idea that weeping was good for someone with hysterics, that it would relieve tension, or whatever—but the trouble was that after five minutes or so of this, Meg quieted into her former rigidity. She stared at the ceiling, her arms lay stiffly at her side, her feet—

Lucy began to weep herself, gently, putting her head against Meg's shoulder. "Tell me," she whispered. *"Please* tell me. I love you, Meg. I want to help you. . . ."

She could feel Meg relax—not much, but there was a softening, a slumping. "I'll tell you," she said, after a time, "if you will promise me— Just you, Lucy. No one else is to know, ever. Will you promise me?"

Lucy kissed her lips. "I promise," she said softly.

"All right." Meg sat up and hugged her arms about her updrawn knees. "Turn out the light," she said.

Lucy did. The lamp on the dresser, the one beside the bed. She sat down again on the stack of cushions which, by day, were scattered across the bed—a dark green square one, a brownish green square one, two yellow ones, one of them square, one round . . .

She waited.

"In other towns," Meg said finally, speaking as if she were a thousand miles away, "everyone's life, it is said, is like a novel. A novel could be written. But here—in Laurel Heights—everyone's life is a scandal."

She turned, and her hand clutched at Lucy's shoulder. "But not me, Lucy!" she said harshly. "Not *me!*"

"Shhhh," said Lucy. "Shhhh."

"How can I tell you if I hush?" Meg demanded.

"Just—tell me." Lucy was more frightened by the minute. Soon she, too, would be having hysterics. "I promise you," she said, "if that is what you want, I won't say a word."

She nudged and pushed Meg to the middle of the bed, heaped the pillows, and sat beside her, putting her arm around her sister. *I don't want to hear,* she told herself. *I want Meg to fall asleep and not tell me. I want to go back to six o'clock this evening, before the party— We were happy then. Mike was coming . . .*

But Meg was beginning to talk. Lucy could feel the difficulty with which she formed each word and spoke it. "I—" she said, and paused.

Then she tried again. "You needed—things—"

"Yes," said Lucy, "ginger ale and ice cream."

Meg's big eyes questioned her. "All the people . . ." she said.

Lucy waited. Meg began to shake again, and her arm tightened. Chorley moved from the hearth rug, lay down, and sighed. His beady eyes watched his people.

"I took the car," said Meg then. "I drove it—there was a moon. The hunters' moon, it is called Enormous. The trees latticed . . . Black, you know, against its brightness."

Of all things to talk about! thought Lucy.

"Colors look different—by moonlight," said Meg. "Who was it painted a picture—a study in black and gray—?"

"Whistler," said Lucy softly. "Go on, Meg."

"I'm telling you," said Meg, leaning forward to rest her chin on her knees. "I drove downtown. I got the things you wanted." She turned her head. "Oh, Lucy!" she cried. "I didn't put the ice cream into the freezer."

"We'll clean up the mess tomorrow."

"Mess," said Meg, savoring the word. She shook her head from side to side. "That mess won't be hard to— clean up."

"No . . ."

For minutes, Meg did not speak again. Chorley, stretched out on his side, was snoring. Lucy slid down in the bed to be more comfortable.

"I drove back on the Observatory road," Meg said then, speaking more readily—as if she had gone over this part of the story many times. And perhaps she had—to herself —in her mind. "It's a dark road, but there's not much traffic—the trees lean over it up on the curve and form a tunnel—and there, almost to the top, my headlights picked up this dog. It was right where the footpath cuts down the hill, Lucy. I've walked there many times. You have."

"Yes."

"There are low bushes back from the road. But on the shoulder, there's a stretch of grass which the college keeps mowed, and now, of course, there are leaves."

Lucy waited.

"And on the road there was this dog—he had been hurt —he dragged his back legs, and would fall, and—well—of course I pulled up and got out of the car." She straightened. "Don't tell me I shouldn't have!" she cried loudly. "Don't tell me *that!*"

"Shhhh," said Lucy.

Meg sighed. "I had to get out," she said wearily, "to see if I could help that dog. I could at least have moved him to the side of the road. I thought—"

She stopped speaking again, and there was that about her silence which sent shivers up Lucy's spine, which tingled in her arms.

"Then," said Meg, and she stopped again, staring before her, not seeing the green wall of her room, Lucy was sure, not seeing the bowl of yellow and bronze chrysanthemums; Meg's dark eyes widely stared at things beyond.

Lucy, in her turn, had a vivid picture of Meg in her bright, pretty dress, bending over the injured dog.

"Then," Meg began again, her throat dry, the words hurting it. "Behind me, the car lights went off. I looked up to see what was wrong, and a man— A man," she said. "A *man,* Lucy, seized me! His arm went around my shoulders, his hand clamped down over my mouth—a big hand it was, hot—and it smelled— Oh, I don't know! That smell—I can't describe it. I can't forget it. I won't . . . He half lifted me, half dragged me—and he threw me down at the side of the road—on that grass, covered with leaves—down on all those scarlet leaves, Lucy! Oh, all those beautiful scarlet leaves. . . ."

"Don't," Lucy begged. "Oh, Meg, don't. . . ."

Meg nodded and shuddered. "He—he tore at my clothes, Lucy. Do you know? We read in the paper nearly every day? 'Disheveled clothing,' they say. He—he—" She gulped and shivered, and she began to cry again, with great, tearing sobs. Lucy clutched at her, and Meg pushed her away. Now she seemed to be laughing.

"Me!" she cried shrilly. *"Meg* Goheen! Not the pretty Goheen girl! Not Bee Keel. Not Karen Chambers. Oh, no! *Oh, no!* But *me!* Margaret Goheen, instructor in biology at the college. *Biology!* Do you get that? *Biology!* She laughed and said the word again, and laughed again. "Biology," she repeated. "Me, the teacher. Me, the woman of brains." Her voice fell. "Brains," she repeated dully. Then she turned fiercely to look at poor Lucy. "But I was a woman, too!" she cried. "That man—he knew what he wanted. And he—he—"

Lucy could take no more; she turned and buried her face in the pillow. She could feel the whole thing; this was all happening to her! The brutal hurt of it, the protest; she cringed at the violation; she fought against it as Meg must have fought—and after it, she had dragged herself home, like the hurt dog, her clothes torn, her body bruised and hurt—and Lucy, too, even as Meg, wanted to scrub the thing away.

It had happened to *her,* it had happened to Meg—she knew it even as she refused to believe it. This was a nightmare which went on and on—because it could *not* have happened! It could not. Not to one of their family—

She sobbed and sobbed, and finally she sat up, wiping the palms of her hands down her wet face. She looked across at the fireplace. Meg's pretty dress . . .

"Who was the man?" she asked woodenly.

"I don't know," Meg answered in the same tone. "A man. I saw him against the sky—an ape—a man—a—*man.* He didn't speak—he made sounds— When he left, I just lay there—and finally I crawled on my hands and knees to the car—and I got home—somehow. Up here."

Lucy drew her close, and they sat so for a time, comforting one another.

"A horrible thing . . ." Lucy whispered.

"Yes," said Meg. "It was. It is. And it will be, Lucy. It *will* be!"

Lucy, too, knew that it would be. "I am going to call Mike," she said, putting her feet to the floor.

But Meg clutched at her in a frenzy. She must not! She had promised! She— "Oh, Lucy, Lucy, no!"

Lucy tried to calm her and then to persuade her. "You must see a doctor . . ."

Meg laughed harshly. "The newspapers again. The paragraph always ends, 'the woman was treated at the hospital.' "

"But— Oh, Meg, you *have* to! Mike wouldn't tell anyone."

"That's debatable. But even if he wouldn't— Oh, Lucy, not *Mike!* He mustn't know. Not ever!"

"All right then. There's Bee. She's a doctor. She lives down the street—"

But Meg would not consent. Firmly, stubbornly, she refused, and soon it was Lucy who was in a panic and Meg who must comfort her sister, reassure her, and, in doing so, she herself became somewhat calm. Enough that she could talk to Lucy and help her.

"I've told you what happened," she said. "I thought I must tell you, though I would have saved you if I could. . . . But no one else is to know, Lucy. If for no other reason than Mums and Dad. This would perhaps kill

Mums, to know—what—" She gulped. "And then—if the story got out—as it would—there is Dad's position at the college. He could not take the whole thing which this would mean. So no one must *know!* I won't have people looking at me and knowing—"

Lucy sat mournfully shaking her head. "But that—that *creature!* Someone must be punished."

Meg lay back on the bed. Her face again was dead white. "Someone is being punished," she said gravely. "Someone will be."

Finally she agreed to take a sleeping pill, and Lucy moved about quietly, getting herself ready for bed. She turned out the lights and lay quietly. Meg seemed to be sleeping—at least she, too, was quiet.

A little breeze riffled the window curtains, and acorns dropped upon the crisp red leaves that covered the ground. The sound was a small one, only to be heard in the silent hours of a long and wakeful night, a small sound that became too much to bear, and Lucy sobbed aloud, suddenly frightened by the terrors which were all about her.

There was that sound, and the smell of burned cloth—and the *hurt* of Meg across the hall—

Next there was anger.

Protest.

Oh, *anyone* would be terrified!

She was glad when dawn came at last with small flaky clouds which turned from gray to silver and then to rose. Neither Lucy nor Meg had slept. All night Meg had lain in the silence of despair, and Lucy had watched over her with pain and grief. They had been so happy. But now, to rise, to dress, and clean away the litter of last night's joy—to go to church to pray and praise. . . . How *could* they?

CHAPTER FOUR

IN THE DOING of familiar, routine things, there was a physical relief for Lucy to get up at six o'clock, to prepare breakfast, to go in and dress her mother—then to go to church and play the organ for the nine-thirty service and again for the eleven.

To come home, not too closely watching Meg, who was in the driveway cleaning her car. Lucy changed her clothes and came downstairs again to cook and serve their usual Sunday dinner.

It was a full day, and Lucy was glad that it should be one. Meg was white, listless, silent, but she washed the car and pretended to eat. She helped Lucy with the dishes, then asked, piteously, if she could go upstairs.

"Mike is coming for supper. . . ."

"Oh, Lucy! I can't . . ."

Lucy nodded. "I'll tell them that you have a headache. You do, don't you?"

Meg frowned. "No . . ."

"Then I'll lie a bit."

It was to be the first of her many lies. She told that one to her parents, and to Mike, when he came.

"She had too much Baptist punch," she said as pertly as she could manage.

But seeing him brought back the whole story. If *only* she could tell him! She prepared her salad, thinking, thinking. Meg was right. This should not have happened to *her*.

Men liked Meg, but sex was not the prime interest they had in her. She could talk, she could play tennis, or even golf, on a basis which they understood and appreciated.

If this dreadful thing had happened to Karen Chambers, to Bee or even to Lucy . . . But it should not have happened to Meg. All day, at church, and during the afternoon when a few students came in and brought some

"boys" with them, Lucy had looked at the men and wondered . . . Had it been someone they knew? Someone at
the party who had seen Meg leave . . . ?

Oh, it didn't bear thinking about, but Lucy could not
peel an apple without thinking about it.

Mike had accepted her excuse for Meg's absence, asking
only if there was anything he could do.

"No. She worked too hard yesterday, perhaps. Meg
throws herself into things."

Mike nodded.

He talked to the Dean, and to Anna, mostly about the
hospital layout. He drew plans on sheets of yellow paper,
explaining how the center core system would work. Yes,
he liked it, and would.

He ate Lucy's supper and wiped the dishes for her
afterward. He played with Chorley out in the garden, and
with Lucy he watched the sunset turn the western sky to
gold and crimson, turquoise and mauve, sweeping their
banners aloft while dusk enfolded the river valley below
them.

Lucy wanted to talk to Mike! She *wanted* to! It would
have been hard to talk to her father, and certainly to her
mother, who must be protected from emotional crises, but
— Not being able to talk to anyone, she could barely manage to speak and answer as if nothing had happened.
Because something *had* happened! And what was Lucy
going to do? She herself felt violated and ashamed—for
Meg.

To Lucy's surprise, before Mike left, Meg came downstairs. She had put a little rouge on her cheeks, her hair
was drawn back from her face. She said quietly that yes,
her head still ached, but—

Lucy brought her a cup of tea and a sandwich. "You
can eat this," she said firmly.

Meg glanced up at her, then obeyed, even seeming to
listen to the Dean and Mike discuss one of her father's
"problems." At another time, the girls would have made a
great joke of the whole discussion, but tonight—

"She's a really nice girl," said the Dean of a student,
"but she doesn't get along with the other girls. I cannot
understand why. But you never see her in a gossip huddle
group or hear anyone call after her—"

"She should be going to a coed school," said Lucy. "Men
often like her kind, and she would make friends there."

"Huddle group?" asked Mike innocently, and everyone laughed except Meg.

She didn't laugh or smile for the remaining hour, and she spoke only when directly addressed. Everyone noticed her quietness.

As the next days came and went, people continued to notice it. They had to see the great change in the vivid, talkative girl.

She went to the school; she must have taught her classes; she returned home—and stayed upstairs in her room.

It was on Thursday that Lucy first smelled the whiskey. On Saturday she spoke of it.

"Don't you ever take a drink?" asked Meg defensively.

"At parties, yes, I do," said Lucy. "Dad knows that I do. I suspect Mums does. But you—"

"I have to do *something*, Lucy! I *have* to!"

"Does a drink make you forget?"

"No, but it blunts the sharp edges."

"Oh, dear Meg! *Dear* Meg!"

"Don't *look* at me!"

"Now you hush." Lucy went to her sister and put her arm around her. "I'm hurt, too, Meg," she said gently. "You have to believe that I am."

"Yes, I will believe it," said Meg. "Because I'd feel that way if—"

"I wish it had been me."

"You don't know what you are talking about." Meg spoke coldly and drew away from Lucy.

But Lucy stood her ground. "As for the drinking—" she began.

"I have to do something!" Meg said again.

"Perhaps. But don't think you are fooling anybody."

"I don't care. . . ."

"You do care. You know Mums has a thing about drinking."

"Then I can move out."

"She'd have a thing about that, too."

"But what can I do, Lucy? I'm drawn as tight as wire. I can't sleep. . . . It—it— You can't *imagine!*"

"No. Though as I said, I am having my own bad time."

Meg gazed at her. "Do you think that makes me feel better?"

"I know it doesn't, but—"

"Perhaps I should leave."

"You can *not* leave!" Lucy cried. "We decided years ago that Mums should never be Dad's burden alone."

Meg must remember that solemn day when she, twenty, and Lucy, eighteen, had made that promise to each other. They had been picking cherries that day, both girls in jeans and up on ladders. Now the feel and taste and perfume of the laden trees were with them again.

"We're just going to have to see this thing through together, too," Lucy now told Meg.

"I won't promise—"

"I don't want your old promise," Lucy cried. "Just don't forget that the rest of us have to live with you!"

Meg sighed. She looked so tired. "I'll try to work this out, Lucy," she said wearily. "I'll honestly try to do that. But—I cannot forget it! I cannot talk to people as if nothing had happened to me. Because it has. It *has!*"

Yes. It had.

And in the days following, its happening got no easier to bear. Meg settled into a hard shell of nonresponse. She moved automatically through her usual routine of school and home, meals and bed. She talked only as she must and offered nothing in the way of interest or ideas. Lucy was sure that she continued to drink, but probably only at bedtime. She wouldn't do it at school; she would not go to a bar in town.

And Lucy would often determine to let her alone, to stop trying to figure things out. Something must break, something must change—but what those things would be, Lucy was unwilling to consider. She, too, leaned upon and followed her usual routine. She did make an effort to be especially gay and talkative to cover up Meg's silence.

And people noticed *that!*

Mike did.

He came frequently to the Goheen house, and at irregular times and intervals. In his boyhood he had always done this, showing up for a piece of breakfast toast, popping in through the back door or knocking on the study window rather late in the evening, then coming in to sit by the fire with the Dean while Lucy put her mother to bed.

"Could I coax Miss Anna to take me on as her doctor?" he asked the Dean.

"Would you help her?"

Mike shrugged. "There are always new drugs. Today, if we get a rheumatoid in its early stage, we do quite a lot for it. And I'd do anything I could for Miss Anna."

"I know you would, Mike. How's the work going?"

Mike shook his head. "Slowly. You wouldn't have about ten interns in your pocket, would you?"

"I thought the hospital was going to use only residents," said Meg unexpectedly. Seated at the far side of the room, she had been pretending to read.

Mike glanced across at her. Meg must have lost five pounds in the past two weeks. "We are going to do our level best," he said, "to get interns. And I have to hustle to get our name on the list before placement time."

"I'll put it in our college brochure, too," said the Dean. "Such bait should be appealing. Ten interns. My, my."

Meg made no comment. And Mike continued to look at her. She was clean—tidy. She wore the sweater, blouse, and skirt he could have expected her to wear—but there was something about Meg—he was too much her friend, too much the doctor as well, not to—

She knew that he watched her, and soon she stood up, saying brusquely that she was going to bed. Her father nodded, but Mike got to his feet and followed her through the living room and out to the front hall. His hand fell on her shoulder, and he could feel the muscles draw into knots. He frowned.

She would have gone up the stairs, but he stepped quickly in front of her to prevent this.

"Don't touch me," she breathed.

"Then stay put for a minute, will you?" he asked.

So she stood where she was, her shoulders down, her head down. Mike shook his head. His mouth was pressed in tightly, deep creases bracketed its corners.

"What's happened to my girl, Meg?" he asked softly.

She looked up at him, she began to tremble—and her face fell utterly to pieces. "Let me go," she begged. "Let me *go!*"

He stepped aside and back. She ran up the stairs, stumbling.

He made a move to follow her, then, shaking his head, he walked slowly back to the study and to the Dean. By the time he reached the lamplight there, his face was composed; he was a doctor trained not to betray his puzzled wonder and concern. But, within, Mike was about as devastated as Meg had shown herself to be.

Snow for the pretty college town was both a blessing and a curse. Come early as it did this year, or late, the students reveled in the white stuff, and the same hills rang with the laughter of coasters as echoed with the growl and snarl of cars unable to negotiate the steep and slippery grades.

In every other year of her life, Meg had loved the snow. The bobbing tassel of her stocking cap had been a bright badge upon the white slopes. She had hung suet baskets for the birds and scattered sunflower seeds; just last year she had joined the hardy souls who had tried to ski down their short, steep hills.

This year she said nothing about the snow; she put on boots and had chains fastened to her car wheels. She carried in the wood for the fireplaces, but she showed no interest in the snow ice cream which Lucy ritually made.

"I can't understand Meg these days," Anna told her younger daughter.

"She has something on her mind."

"It can't be a happy something."

It was not, and its unhappiness on *her* mind caused Lucy to wonder with increasing fear if Meg might not be threatened with a mental disturbance that could grow and grow . . . These times of panic which Lucy felt, these moments of acute fear—how much worse, and how much more dangerous they must be for Meg!

She seemed, by great effort, to be doing her usual tasks at school and at home, but at choir practice one evening Lucy overheard a couple of Meg's students speak of her as "Naggy Maggie." This was a shock, because Meg had always been one of the most popular teachers at the college.

But now she was cross at home—even with her parents, and in their home such a thing amounted to a phenomenon. The time she snapped at Anna, Meg herself instantly realized what she had done. She rose and walked out of the room, her spine stiff. For the next two days she joined the family only at dinner, and then not speaking except in monosyllables. She did not mention the incident to Lucy, but it was on both of their minds.

Lucy knew that Meg had periods of prolonged weeping, that she dreamed—that she drank.

There came a cold night when she came into Lucy's room, her red robe pulled on any which way, and her dark hair wild about her white face. She clutched at her sister's shoulder and shook it.

Lucy struggled up out of sleep. "What . . . ?" she asked groggily. "What time is it, Meg?"

"Oh," said Meg, "it isn't any *time!* I mean—" She stood looking down at Lucy. "I just thought of something," she gasped.

Lucy stifled a sigh. "Go back to bed, Meg. You were dreaming."

"No. Not this time. I was lying there, I was looking at the window, and the sky—the stars are always brighter when there's snow on the ground—I've noticed that—and I thought—"

"Do you have your slippers on?" asked Lucy practically. All she needed was to have Meg down with a cold.

"Oh, Lucy!" Meg protested. "Let me tell you!"

"All right, but make it quick. I need my sleep, and so do you."

Meg ran her hand up and back through her hair. "I don't sleep very much," she said pitiably.

"I know," said Lucy gently. "But, dear—put my blanket around you or get into bed. . . ."

Meg sat down on the bed and tucked her bare feet up under the red robe. "I just had this thought," she said again. "Lucy, what if he— What if he was a man we know? Or a boy we know?"

Lucy sighed again. She had had this "thought" sometime earlier.

"What if it was one of our neighbors?" cried Meg, tensing unbearably. "Or one of the students at the med school? One of those nice young men who came here to meet Mike?"

Lucy moistened her lips. She had had this thought and had found herself looking speculatively at every man.

"You don't have any clues?" she asked carefully. "You couldn't identify him in any way?"

Meg shook her head. "He was—big," she said between stiff lips. "I couldn't fight him off. It was dark under the trees—he had turned off my car lights—he came up behind me, and his face always was in the dark. He wore a dark jacket— It was rough against my cheek— He—he— he" She gasped for breath. Lucy rubbed her arm. "His shirt was light," Meg said more quietly. "White perhaps. He didn't speak—he made noises—like an animal—in his throat—but he didn't say one word."

"Didn't you scream?" asked Lucy. "You say you tried to fight. Did you try to get away?"

Meg stared at her. "I— Yes. I think I did try to scream. But I don't remember making a sound. I must have fought —my dress was torn. I—" She sighed wearily and sat, head down, gulping for control. Then she looked up. "Oh, Lucy!" she cried thinly. "Suppose it *was* someone I know! Someone who sees me often—and *knows*."

Lucy sat up in bed. "It could be," she said. "It could be someone who would do such a dreadful thing again. So— we have to go to the police, Meg. They have ways of finding such people. People like us should help the police. . . ."

She had thought Meg would fire, but she only sat there shaking her head. "Maybe he's not here any more," she said. "Maybe he was just someone—a tramp, you know. A hitchhiker. Someone watching for a college girl—"

"That could be true," said Lucy. "But what if it *was* someone we know?"

"I can't bear the thought. . . ."

"But it is a possibility," Lucy insisted. "Oh, Meg, we have not done right. You should have seen a doctor. We should have gone to the police at once."

"And what could they have done for me?" asked Meg coldly. "Could they have changed anything?"

"If they had caught the man, you wouldn't have waked up tonight wondering who he was."

"And *you* might consider the personalities of our local police, Lucy. Which one of them do you want to know and handle your most personal affairs? The Chief is a ham-fisted bungler, and you know it. Then take the City Prosecutor . . ."

Lucy didn't need to "take the Prosecutor." He was a man who, the town said, was brilliant; the town said it was a shame he drank more than he should. He got into office and stayed there; he controlled almost any election by his relationship with the poor, the ignorant, and the inmates of nursing homes. The means by which he gained and held this control were suspect, intimidation being the least of them.

"We have reputable lawyers here in town," said Lucy. "Mike would have helped us. All right, all right. I know you didn't want to bring him in on this, but what do we know, what do *you* know about handling this sort of thing, Meg? No more than I do, of course, except that I know we haven't gone about it as we should have done."

Meg made no reply. She sat huddled on the foot of the bed, her head down, a figure of despair.

"You know what I think?" Lucy asked, sitting more erect. "I think we should tell Dad."

"Oh, Lucy . . ."

"Yes, we should. If he ever finds out, our not telling him would hurt him more than— We *should* tell him, Meg! He's a wise man; he would know ways to help you."

Meg sighed deeply, shudderingly. "How can he rub out what happened?" she asked. "How can he help me find my pride and self-esteem? That's what I need now, Lucy. And that's what I don't think I'll ever have again." She got off the bed and went back to her room.

"He'd help *me?*" Lucy thought, sliding down again into the nest of warmth under the blankets. "I don't know that I can bear being the only one who knows."

As for Meg— Poor Meg, dear Meg—

Would she ever again know the carefree joy of hopping into her car and going where she wished, when she wished?

Getting up in the morning now was a drag, going to bed was an invitation to dream horribly and to waken three or four times during the night remembering the feel of that man's hands. . . .

Even Lucy— Whatever she was doing, she would remember. While mixing a cake, she would put her hands over her eyes to shut out the thought of . . .

Why wouldn't Meg go slowly out of her mind—with Lucy not far behind her?

Meg knew that she was gravely troubling her sister, and this added to her own burden a sense of guilt and error. She was sorry that she had told Lucy the story; somehow she could have avoided telling her.

Now she made various attempts to tell Lucy to forget it. "Just put it out of your mind," she said.

"Can you do that?" Lucy asked, her blue eyes wide.

"No," said Meg forthrightly. "I can't, but you might, if you would try."

Lucy did not answer her. And she went on being troubled.

Meg still took at least two baths a day. Each day it took a real effort for her to eat dinner with her parents and Lucy, and to sit with them during the evening.

Then, finally, not quite a month after Mike's homecoming party, Meg resigned her teaching position at the school without saying a word to anyone.

It was Judith Chambers who told the family. The Dean and Mrs. Goheen were out in the kitchen that late afternoon watching Lucy make gingerbread, which they would eat, still warm, for dessert at dinner. Doyle Goheen sat at the table looking through a cookbook to see if he could find a sauce better than the "dishwater sauce" they usually used for gingerbread.

"When gingerbread is hot," said Anna, "I like it best plain. After that . . ."

"Don't worry," Lucy told her mother. "He won't find anything better. Besides, Dad likes dishwater sauce."

"All but the name," said the Dean staunchly. "It isn't in this book, I notice."

"Oh, yes it is," said Lucy. "It's called either clear lemon sauce or vanilla sauce. I make it lemon for gingerbread."

She had a smudge of flour on her cheek and another dusted down the front of her pink apron. She moved with speed and grace, a good cook who liked to cook. "It's the color that makes us call it . . ."

She broke off and turned at the sound of steps on the back porch. "Oh, it's Judith," she said gladly. "Come in, sugar."

Judith did come in, shedding her fleece-lined coat and smiling shyly at the Dean and at Anna.

"Sit down," Lucy told her. "I'm making gingerbread."

"I can smell it," said the girl, brushing her hair away from her face.

"Want a cookie?"

Judith got up and went to the big brown jar on the counter and took out two round sugar cookies.

"There's milk, Coke, orange juice," said Lucy, carefully filling a square pan with her batter.

Judith poured herself a glass of orange juice, and nicely answered Mrs. Goheen's inquiry about her mother. She again pushed her long hair out of her eyes and sat down to eat and drink. She wore a shapeless overblouse of red and blue striped jersey, a very short blue skirt.

"Where's Meg?" she asked.

"I don't know whether she's upstairs or not," said Lucy, closing the oven door.

As she came back to the table, she lifted a strand of Judith's long, straight hair. "I'd love to see you with a really sharp shingle," she said.

Judith shook her head, then again pushed her hair away from her face, a gesture which was automatic. "I came," she said, leaning forward to look at the Dean intently, "to ask you why you let Meg resign."

The Dean looked at her. Then he closed his cookbook, took off his glasses, and looked at her again.

"What do you mean, Judy?" asked Anna. "Meg hasn't—"

Lucy glanced warningly at her mother. There was no telling what Meg might have done.

The Dean caught her gesture and asked, "What do you know about this, Lucy?"

She shook her head. "Nothing, Dad."

"Well, lately you girls . . ."

Of course he had noticed. "I know nothing about this," she said again, and firmly.

"Didn't you know?" asked Judith. "I thought, being Dean—"

"I am Dean of Women, my dear," said Mr. Goheen. "The faculty and other personnel are not my immediate concern. But you, as a student, are, so tell me what happened."

Judith drank the rest of her juice. "I just— Well, when we went to Biology class today, there was this other teacher—Mr. Shead, you know." She made a face.

"Don't you like Mr. Shead?" asked the Dean.

"Oh, he's all right, I guess. Teaching *botany!* But not— Oh, Meg can't resign, Dean! She's the one teacher we really *like!*"

The Dean sat thoughtful. But the announcement had shocked him, Lucy could tell. However, he was being careful of what he said before Judith.

He let Lucy and his wife comment. He let Judith say all she wanted to about petitions and refusal to have another teacher. When challenged, he said he didn't like the situa-

56

tion any better than she seemed to, but he really did not think a petition was in order. "Though I'd be inclined to sign one," he declared.

"Didn't you know, Dean?" Judith asked. "Didn't she ask you . . . ?"

"Judith," said the Dean, waving his dark-rimmed spectacles at her. "A half-dozen years from now, when you are married or are earning your own living, do you plan to ask *your* dad if you can do things?"

Judith grinned at him. "I don't like to do it now," she told Dean Goheen. "Well! I must be going. The gingerbread smells wonderful, Lucy. And you tell Meg I'm mad at her."

"Will do," said Lucy.

Left alone in the kitchen, the three Goheens faced each other blankly.

"I am not a profane man," said the Dean finally, "but I would like to know what the hell goes on with Meg?"

Lucy put her hand on his shoulder. "Why don't you ask her?" she said. "But gently, Dad. Gently."

"Is she sick, Lucy?"

"You could ask her that, too."

"Is she upstairs now?"

"I think so."

"All right."

"And Lucy and I won't let ourselves be upset," said Anna Goheen. "Don't bother to tell us, Doyle."

He smiled faintly and left the room.

It was an unusual thing for Doyle Goheen to go upstairs. Those rooms belonged to the girls. But when he did go, his custom was to slap the wall with the flat of his hand and call, "Coming up!" He did this now, expecting Meg to call out to him or even to meet him. She did neither.

He went up and into her room, to find her standing at the window looking out at the bare tree branches and the snowy garden.

"Will you talk to me a little, Meg?" her father asked, coming across the green carpet.

"Of course," she said. "Sit down." She indicated the low armchair; she sat on the bench at the foot of her bed.

The Dean snapped on the lamp beside him and studied his elder daughter. She was wearing a dark suit and a white blouse. Her hair was neatly trimmed and arranged. Her face was quiet, her eyes—

"Meg," he said deeply, the hurt sounding in his voice. "Are you sick?"

Meg brushed the back of her hand across her hair. "No," she said quietly.

Her father frowned. "Have you robbed a bank?"

She did not smile.

He leaned toward her. "My dear! Has Mike's coming home anything at all to do with the way you have been acting for the past couple of weeks?"

Her eyes widened. "What could he have done?" she asked blankly.

"I don't know," said the Dean. "That's what I am asking *you*."

"Mike—I haven't seen him very often—"

"Did you resign to work with him?"

Meg frowned, honestly not understanding what her father had in mind.

"There was talk about your working with Mike, wasn't there?"

Again she made that weary gesture with her hand. "It was just talk, Dad."

"I see. And all the talk about your marrying him, and Lucy marrying him—you didn't mean any of that?"

"I won't speak for Lucy. As for me, I have no plans."

"Other than to leave our faculty."

Meg sighed. "I didn't even plan that," she said. "Friday, in the lab—the subject was acid and base experiments, and all the girls seemed interested in, all they talked about, was sex. Not sex in frogs or amoeba, you understand. They discussed and *discussed* whether they—those fifteen young girls—had sex as individuals. Sex appeal, I believe would be their term."

The Dean shook his head. "They are young, dear. They pretend they are wise, but they are not. They are just curious young people, anxious young people. Even a-little-frightened young people. And like any group of frightened animals, they huddle together, they talk together for courage against the future."

"Sex," said Meg stonily.

"Well, yes. That's a part of maturity. You know it is—"

"Yes. I know it is. That's why I decided that I could no longer be around or teach young people."

"Oh, *Meg!*"

"I'll work this out, Dad. You are not to worry. I know I must pay my way . . ."

"Now, look here, Meg Goheen!" His tone sharpened. She hunted for a smile to give him.

"I am able and willing to take care of you girls," he said sternly. "Your home is here. It was your own choice to take a job and pay for your clothes and your car—just as it has been Lucy's to play the organ and direct the choir for the church. But—"

Meg got up and came to his side. Her fingers smoothed his short white hair. "Calm down, sir," she said, almost in her natural tone. "I have been in a flap, I am in a flap, and probably the flap will hang around for a time. It is something I shall have to work out for myself. But I am not sick, and you are not to worry."

The Dean stood up. "All right, Meg. I have always been able to trust you. But as for my worrying, I am afraid that is my department, and I'll attend to it as I find necessary."

She stood away from him. "Yes, Dad," she said softly; her face was dead white.

"And there isn't anything more to say?"

"No . . . No."

He went downstairs, knowing that he would continue to worry about Meg. He let Anna decide that something had happened between Mike and Meg. She didn't specify what —and he suggested that they not talk about it just now.

And nothing further was said to Meg or in the family's conversation with each other. But on Thursday, which was Thanksgiving, when Meg announced that she did not believe she would go to church, Lucy spoke sharply and angrily to her sister.

"You will too go!" she cried. "You know how much Mums counts on Thanksgiving service. It is one of her rare excursions out of the house; she prepares for it a week ahead of time, rests, plans her clothes— Oh, Meg, you cannot do this to her!"

"Lucy—"

"All right!" said Lucy. "Last Sunday you told me that you could not take communion, that you were not in love and charity with your neighbors, and I told you to talk to Father Finlinson. But you didn't, did you?"

Meg only sighed.

"Now!" Lucy demanded. "Aren't you in love and charity with Mums and Dad?" Her eyes shot sparks, and her face was pink. Today she meant not to spare her sister.

"Look, Lucy . . ." Meg attempted.

But Lucy was not to be deterred. "I know what happened to you," she cried. "It was a terrible thing, but it was an accident that it happened to you. However, if you don't go to church with us this morning, what you will be doing to us will be deliberate. You will do it knowing that it will hurt us."

Meg stood shaking her head, and tears began to fill her eyes. "You shouldn't be hurt," she agreed. "I— You shouldn't be. Oh, Lucy, don't you think I should leave this house, go away?"

"No," said Lucy, "I don't."

"But—I can't stand hurting you!"

Lucy glanced over her shoulder at her sister. Poor Meg. She was living in torment, and showed it. She had no color, her dark eyes no longer shone. She looked small and pathetic.

Contrite, Lucy went to her and put her arms around her. "Oh, dear Meg," she said. "I am sorry! I *am!* I wish I could help you!"

Meg sighed, the breath seeming to shudder up from her heels. "If you would just tell me what to do!" she begged. "I know this thing will pass. It has, for others—"

"It will," Lucy agreed. "And for now, I will tell you what to do. You are to get out your red suit, your little fur cap, your high-heeled pumps, and you are to come to church with us. You're to take communion because it will please Mums. The Lord will forgive any small sin you may do. And when you say your prayers, you are to pray for yourself, for help. I'll do the same."

"I'll try . . ." Meg agreed.

"All right. You go dress. I'm ready, and I want to put the turkey in the oven before I go."

"Are you going to the Keel party?"

"Tonight? Of course I'm not. We're having our own party right here."

"With *company?*"

"Mike. And some orphans from the college." She was down the stairs before Meg could comment or protest.

Meg dressed in the red suit, and she went to the Thanksgiving service. When the family returned home, she, almost shyly, offered to help Lucy with the dinner preparations.

"Sure you can help," Lucy told her. "You can set the table—get down the good dishes. There will be—" she counted on her fingers— "there will be nine of us. Four Goheens, Mike—the Beyes—"

"They are *orphans?*" Meg demanded. Mr. Beyes was the vocal music instructor at the college; he was a handsome young man, possessed of a fine baritone voice.

"He and his wife live in a small apartment," Lucy explained. "They can't go to their families in California—"

"All right," said Meg. "Who else?"

"Two foreign exchange students. Dad hasn't yet taught me to say their names, but there's a Hindu girl and a Korean."

"I hope they like roast turkey," was all Meg said.

Lucy thought her small lecture might have set Meg on a more stable course.

During the afternoon she worked, setting the table and arranging flowers; she read aloud for an hour to her mother while Mums rested.

Dinner was set for five. By that time cars were beginning to fill the street because of the Keels' big party. Mike was going to look in on that first, he had said. "I may snitch some cocktails and bring you one," he had promised Lucy.

Evidently the party was a very large one; the Dean reported that there were "fur coats and high heels all over the street."

"You girls should have gone," suggested Mums.

"On *Thanksgiving?*" Lucy asked her. "It's my year for the wishbone."

Their own guests arrived and there was considerable hilarity over trying to translate the American feast into understandable terms for the Hindu girl. The Korean one was more knowledgeable. When Mike came in with a bouquet of roses for Mums, which he insisted he had stolen from a patient's room, the small, dark girl from India was delighted to find that the tall, blond doctor knew her country.

Meg went to the kitchen to help Lucy. "They are having a good time," she told her sister timidly. To hear Meg speak so hurt Lucy.

"Did Mike say anything about the Keel bash?"

"I came right out here."

"They are having ten pounds of shrimp for *hors*

d'oeuvres alone," Lucy said, shaking her hair back from her face. "Fill the water glasses, will you, Meg?"

The meal was delicious, the talk was good. Hardly anyone noticed that Meg said very little. The Korean girl ventured to ask Lucy how she got her hair the color it was, and the two young men insisted on answering her, until Lucy took pity on the stranger and explained that it was a matter of having the right mother, who, in her youth, had had this particular shade of golden hair.

"And Dr. Tryon's mother?" the visitor asked softly.

This turned the teasing Mike's way, and he ably handled it. Next he told vividly about the Keel party. He was sure they had had turkey—"It isn't legal not to!"—but the noble bird did seem to have been buried under a wealth of country ham sliced in the serology lab. . . .

Meg's head went up, and his eye glinted to notice that it had. "There was such a salmon in aspic," he continued, "with a stuffed olive eye. When it winked at me, I decided that I'd had enough to drink and came up here to safety and sanity—and Lucy, darling, what did you *do* to this mince pie?" He leaned back in his chair and sighed deeply.

All Goheen parties had a way of ending in the kitchen, and that night nearly everyone helped clear the meal away and wash the dishes. The Hindu visitor sat with Anna Goheen by the living room fire and talked to her shyly. After the work was done, Mr. Beyes played the piano and sang nonsense songs until the telephone rang sharply, insistently.

Mike got up to answer it. "That sounds like a professional call," he said.

He came back, shrugging into his topcoat. "I was right," he told. "Something's happened down at Keels'. They knew I was up here."

"Wasn't Dr. Bowlin a guest there?" asked Anna.

Mike shook his finger reprovingly at her and left, promising to come back. "If they've just called me for a falling-down drunk," he promised, "I'll be right back!"

"It must be something," the Dean decided, coming back from the front door. "Bee would have been at her own party, and she's a doctor."

It must have been "something," for Mike did not return. The guests stayed until after nine, the Hindu girl carrying away with her the wishbone wrapped in a paper napkin.

The Goheens settled down by the fire for a time of

talking about the evening. Mr. Beyes did sing beautifully, they said. Why wasn't he on the concert stage?

"I think he does make some appearances," the Dean told them. "His contract allows him six weeks off during the school year."

The Hindu guest had been charming, they said; the Korean girl seemed a bit on the defensive . . . and was Mrs. Beyes expecting?

Lucy put the now-cooled turkey away and brought her mother a glass of milk and a plate of cookies. The others, she said, could fetch their own snacks. The Dean promptly went off for cheese and crackers, Meg took an apple from the bowl and sliced it into crisp wedges. Lucy nodded approvingly and checked herself, lest Meg notice. These little signs of Meg's return to her normal self must be cherished like delicate seedlings.

Twice Lucy had gently mentioned bed to her mother. The first time Anna said that she was not yet ready; the second time she remarked that the Keel party would have broken up early—which meant that she hoped to stay up until Mike came back or at least sent them word.

At ten-thirty he came in, wearing a heavy sweat shirt and his hospital ducks. Even as he opened the front door, he demanded a turkey sandwich. "And none of your paper-thin slices, either," he admonished Lucy, who went at once to oblige him.

He came into the living room, stretched his length in the green leather chair before the fire, and told Miss Anna Go-*heen* that she was losing her beauty sleep.

"I don't need it," she assured him. "But if you'll tell us pretty soon what happened at Keels'—I'm being afraid something happened to Leonard."

Mike took the plate and glass of milk which Lucy brought to him. "How did you deduce that?" he asked Anna, gravely inspecting his sandwich.

"Oh, he hasn't been well."

"That he hasn't," Mike agreed.

"And the fact that you were called, with Bee right there . . ."

Mike nodded and bit off a corner of his sandwich. "You're a smart cookie, Miss Anna Go-*heen*," he told her.

"Don't talk with your mouth full," she admonished him.

"Now which do you want?" Mike demanded. "My news or manners?"

She chuckled and settled back in her chair.

Mike nodded and finished half of the sandwich, relishing it. "It was Leonard," he said then, touching the corner of his mouth with the napkin. "He had collapsed. At first, I thought it was a matter of too much to drink and too much excitement. The short time I was at the party, he was riding high. He's a big man, you know—"

"He's not been well," Anna said again. Lucy was sitting on the hearth rug with Chorley's head in her lap. The Dean sat across from Mike, with Anna beside him. Meg sat in a deep chair several feet away from the others. She was listening, but had said nothing.

"Leonard seems to have," Mike said then, "a paralysis of the lower limbs."

Anna made a soft sound of protest.

"A stroke?" asked the Dean sharply.

Mike shook his head. "Not in the usual sense, sir. I mean, not a cerebral hemorrhage or clot. Probably." He drank some milk.

"I don't know if that's good or bad," said Doyle Goheen.

"In this case I am afraid it is not good," said Mike. He began to eat the rest of his sandwich. "I made a fairly thorough examination," he told. "And I suspect that his condition may be due to an abdominal aneurysm. Meg, you tell them what that means, while I eat."

For a second or two, Lucy was afraid that Meg would refuse—but she spoke quietly. "I expect Dad and Mother both know what an aneurysm is, Mike. It's a thin place in a blood vessel, and if the blood is sluggish for any reason, it gathers and bulges out the artery wall. Sometimes—" she looked questioningly at Mike—"a tumor forms."

He smiled at her, the lamplight shining on his hair, marking the strong lines at his face. "Good girl!" he said. "My examination was thorough only to a degree, but a tumor may be there. In any case, there seems to be a blockage of the vena cava. This has caused edema and the paralysis."

"Why would there be paralysis?" asked Lucy. "Remember, I'm not the smart Goheen sister."

Mike glanced down at her, his eyes smiling. "No," he agreed. "You're the one who stupidly puts something deliciously caramel on your mince pie. Why, pretty sweet, the blockage—even the swelling—causes pressure—on nerves, on contiguous parts—and the circulation of blood becomes affected. You know how your hand or foot can go to sleep?"

"Oh," said Lucy, "if it's that simple—I always take off my shoe."

"No," Mike told her, "it is not that simple. Of course we'll make tests—do X-rays—but already I can hear a definite bruit. . . ."

Lucy's head went up, and Mike laughed. "It's a noise," he explained, "a pulsation. The blood is trying to get through. We think there is an aneurysm or a clot."

"That sounds serious," she said anxiously. "Is it?"

"Oh, yes."

"Hopeless?"

"Not necessarily. We may be able to handle things without surgery."

"If not, will you do the surgery?"

Meg stirred a little in her chair.

"No," said Mike, "of course I wouldn't."

"Would Tony Bowlin do it?" asked Lucy. Each one in the room thought of Tony and Bee.

"Any surgeon," said Mike quietly. "Any capable surgeon."

"Is he conscious?" asked Mrs. Goheen. "Leonard?"

"He was in great pain when I reached their house—and scared silly by the paralysis. Now he is under sedation—at the hospital, of course."

"Is Bee with him?"

"A nurse is with him. I took Bee home as I came here. There was no need for her to stay."

"We'll go down tomorrow and help her clear the party mess away, won't me, Meg?" Lucy asked her sister.

Meg nodded almost indifferently.

She sat with them, she listened, but she made no comment nor offered any suggestion. Mrs. Goheen pressed Mike to say that Leonard would be all right.

"I don't know, Miss Anna," he told her. "We have to examine him, make all sorts of tests. Surgery, even if feasible, would be a risky thing on a man whose health is already poor. I wouldn't, at this minute, care to make any sort of prognosis."

"Will the paralysis last?"

"It can get better—or worse."

"He won't make an easy patient," said Doyle Goheen, who was not a man ready to offer judgment.

Mike nodded and stood up. "I've found that out already," he said. "And Bee doesn't promise to be of much help."

"Oh, she'd want to—"

"I meant only that Leonard will not listen to her. In fact, her presence seems to upset him."

"He's a hateful person," said Lucy firmly. "Everyone thinks so. Smart—as a lawyer. But—well—"

Mike smiled at the nice Goheens. Leonard Keel was known for his foul and slashing tongue. That these people would say as much as they had was indication enough of the man who had become his patient.

"Did Dr. Bowlin see him?" asked Miss Anna.

Mike's lips thinned. "Yes. And of course he will consult with me for the next few days. Unless . . ."

"Maybe Dr. Bowlin will want to send him somewhere else," suggested Lucy.

"That could happen," Mike agreed, "though I would not advise moving him just now."

He carried his dishes to the kitchen, bent and kissed Anna's cheek, and told her to get to bed. Then he walked to the chair where Meg still sat; he put his two hands on the arms of the chair and bent over her, toward her—to kiss her.

She drew back, away from him, her eyes wide, and she thrust out her hands against him. "Don't!" she cried hoarsely. "Don't touch me!"

At once, Mike straightened, and for a moment he stood looking down at her. Meg sat white and trembling, tense and shamed. She found her handkerchief and pressed it to her lips. Mike shook his head and went out of the room. Doyle Goheen followed him, but the two men said only a word at the door.

Anna reached up her hand. "Sit down, my dear girl," she began.

Meg stood up. "Don't talk to me!" she cried.

Anna reached up her hand. "Sit down, my dear," she said softly, "and tell me what is wrong . . ."

Meg did sit down; she even held her mother's crippled hand in her own, and she wept softly, pitiably. But she would not talk.

"You are in trouble," said her mother. "We all can see that. And we would want to help you, my darling. . . ."

"I—can't," said Meg. And it was all she would say.

Lucy finally came and told her mother to let the girl go.

"She's here with us. She will work out her problems, Mums," she said. "She knows we love her and want to help. That maybe is enough for now."

Her mother sighed. "I'll go to bed then, Lucy," she said wearily. "It used to be that I could do for you girls."

"You still can," Lucy assured her, turning the wheelchair toward the bedroom. She sent a reassuring smile toward Meg, who got up and started for the stairs.

"Thank you," she said to her father as she passed him.

CHAPTER FIVE

THEY HEARD nothing from Mike the next day, or the next. On Sunday, Meg asked Lucy if she had heard anything about Leonard.

"Only that he is critically ill and that the doctors are making tests."

Meg nodded. The two were walking home from church. There had been a light snow, but the sun was shining brightly, and the sky was a clear, frosty blue. "You haven't seen Mike?"

"No. Have you?"

Meg shook her head. "I like Mike," she said, as if examining her own feelings. "It's just—I just have a thing about men, Lucy. I'm sorry—"

"I know. And I have an idea you'll get over this feeling."

"I'll never, all my life, forget . . ."

"No, you probably won't. Nor shall I. But, Meg—"

Her sister nodded. "I made a fool of myself the other night."

"It puzzled Mike—and distressed all of us."

Meg said nothing. They spoke to three college students whom they passed; she and Lucy laughed at the antics of a small boy with a large sled. They walked on.

"Mike may be staying away," Meg said then, "because of me."

"Oh, I don't think so," said Lucy. "He's awfully busy, you know. Not only with Leonard just now, but with the hospital. He's talked about it, about not having any interns and wanting to set the hospital up so he can get some next summer. And he talks lots about assembling a staff of doctors."

Meg nodded. "He will have to have a good staff for a teaching hospital. That means dealing with the doctors and with the other faculty of the medical school, as well. Then

he will need resident doctors, technicians of various sorts
—orderlies, and aides . . ."

"Does he have to do all this?"

"He has to supervise it and deal with it personally in
many cases. He's Chief of Medical Services, and that is a
big job."

"Bonita . . . ?" asked Lucy.

Meg seemed really interested in the matter of the hospital. "Bonita is Chief of Services," she agreed. "Nursing,
o.r. duty, and care—that sort of thing. She assigns, directs
—and would train if they get a school of nursing."

"Will they?"

"I don't know. I'd say as of now that Mike would get his
teaching program in shape first and correlated with the
medical school. He's in charge of Bonita, too, by the way,
though she must be a great help. Do you understand about
the registry for intern placement, Lucy?"

Lucy laughed. "Not really. Though I try to look wise."

"You don't need to look anyway but as pretty as you
are."

The girls turned into their own street and started up the
hill. Meg explained about intern registration and placement. It was a center, she told, where senior medical
students or interns wanting to do additional service—perhaps in a specialty—registered their names and their
preferences; Mike had to declare his hospital as available,
and make a good thing of their advantages. He would need
interns!

"Besides all that, you know," Meg continued, looking at
Keels' house as they passed it. Bee was probably at the
hospital. "Mike goes to the university's central office several times a week. The medical school here, you know, is a
branch of the university. I can't decide if Mike enjoys
doing so much administrative medicine or not."

"Does he talk to you?"

Meg's cheeks colored. "I haven't let him," she admitted.

"If you like Mike and are interested in his work, I think
you could at least talk to him about the hospital," said
Lucy, turning into their own driveway. "Do you know
what I am going to have for dinner?" she asked.

"Turkey hash."

Lucy laughed. "That's for tomorrow. No, I'm going to
broil some steaks. How about that?"

Meg smiled at her. "I'll eat mine," she promised.

"You'd better!" Meg must have lost ten pounds during the past month.

In a day or two Mike dropped in at the Goheens', both casual about this appearance and apologetic about not having seen them sooner. "I'm so doggone busy!" he cried, collapsing into the green leather chair.

At once, Miss Anna must be told about Leonard Keel, though there really was not much to tell. Mike insisted that he was not acting "professional." "We're trying to build the man up a little, and watching things. If there will have to be surgery, a little time could be in our favor."

Would he stay for dinner? Lucy asked him.

"I'd love to, unless I get called away." He looked at his watch. It was four o'clock. "I came here with the thought of taking Meg for a buggy ride." He glanced swiftly at Meg.

Her cheeks flushed. "Oh, no!" she cried. "No . . ."

Mike shrugged. "Then how about my taking you and Lucy on a tour of the hospital? Have you ever been?"

"I haven't," said Lucy. "Have you, Meg?"

"Well—not really."

Mike stood up. "Then we'll go right now. It's quite something, you know."

"I'll keep Mums company," said Meg. "You take Lucy."

"No, *sir!*" said Lucy. "I don't know a heart-lung machine from a bedpan. You're the scientist of the family. Take her, Mike. By force, if necessary."

"I won't need force," said Mike. "And another time, we certainly must get that bedpan thing straightened out."

No one ever directly mentioned the fact that Anna could not be left alone for more than a short time.

Meg really wanted to see the hospital. Before Mike's return she had not really looked at the place, thinking that he would show it to her. So now, though obviously a little reluctant, she fetched her tweed coat and a red scarf and went out to the car with him.

Lucy stood at the door, watching them. "I hope Mike's careful . . ." she said under her breath.

"Are the streets slippery?" asked Anna.

"No." The streets were not what Lucy had been worrying about. "I think Mike wants Meg to work for him and with him. I was hoping he'd ask her just right."

"He will. Mike has always known how to handle Meg."

The new teaching hospital, built to serve the new medical school of the state university, had been the subject of comment, criticism, and praise since first its plans had been displayed to the general public. Even the professionals who heard about it, and who came to see it, had their questions. From the first, Meg had been interested, and when it began to seem that Mike would work there, she had accumulated every detail she could hear or read about the place.

Immediately she revealed her familiarity with the concept to Mike. "But I haven't seen it," she hastened to say.

"Why not? We used to explore buildings and houses under construction."

They had, too, walking along precarious planks, climbing ladders, risking their very lives.

"I knew you would show it to me," said Meg now, going in through the glass front doors.

He did show it to her—the great, circular building, its blue-paned windows, and the service cores in the center of each floor. They explored the whole building, from maintenance shops and laundry in the sub-basement up through the admissions, emergency, and business areas at street level, to the intensive-care rooms, with restaurant and quarters for accompanying families—the medical floors, the pediatric and orthopedic floor—all wards and operating room were like segments of a giant pie radiating from the central area of nurses' stations, floor labs, supply rooms, and food services.

Mike especially showed Meg the operating rooms, pointing out how much space they allowed the surgeons. Observers would sit on the floor next above, looking down through the domed glass ceiling. "As much of the recording devices and that sort of thing as possible is kept in adjoining rooms," he explained. "O.R. is for surgery, and only that, with as few warm bodies close at hand as can be arranged." He showed her how, above the operating table, a cylinder poured out a flow of sterile air, adjusted at the most desirable temperature and humidity. The used air was drawn off near the floor and not recirculated.

"It's an efficient system," he said. "Not more than one grain of pollen, not more than one microbe gets through in every hundred cubic feet of new air."

"How do you know that?" asked Meg.

"Because we test it. Our lab— Meg, I want you to work in our lab. Will you?"

"Oh, Mike . . ."

When he had shown her any of the laboratories, her eyes had burnished the brightness which had been about her ever since they first had entered the tall blue glass and silver steel building. But—"We should get home," was all she said now. "Lucy will expect us for supper."

"That's right." He would, he told himself, press for an answer later.

During supper—or dinner, as it was interchangeably called in those parts—Meg talked a great deal, and enthusiastically, about Mike's hospital. Lucy was grateful to see the girl again animated and interested in something.

"You're wonderful," she told Mike when he helped her change the plates for dessert. "I wish I'd baked you a lemon pie."

"I'll make do with cup custard and cookies," he told her. "And if I can get Meg to work for us—"

"Will she?"

"That I am about to find out."

So he asked her again, earnestly, if she would, please, *please* come to work with him in his lab, doing his personal research tasks. "I don't have the time or chance just now to keep at it myself as it needs to be done. All the daily checks, entries, tests—you know the sort of detail work I mean, Meg. I could get a boy or a girl to do some of the stuff, but I feel you will understand my project and have some ideas of your own. When I agreed to come here, I was promised I could have my own facilities to continue the research I want to do."

Meg put her spoon down on the flower-sprigged plate. "Are you going to stay here?" she asked.

Mike leaned back in his chair and looked at her. The cleft in his strong chin, the hollows below his cheekbones, were prominent. His blue eyes were intent. "I'll stay here," he said as steadily as she had spoken, "if I can get things properly set up here."

Meg half rose from her chair. "Oh, no, you don't!" she cried hotly. "You'll not make *me* the one to decide this important thing for you, Mike Tryon! You've no right to do that! Besides—" she sat down again, retreating into the colorless, dispirited person she had been for the past month—"I am not that good."

He protested. He talked to her. "You said, when I first came home, that you would do anything to keep me here," he reminded Meg. He told her that she could learn the things she didn't already know. But he was sure that she was just as good as he had estimated she would be. He said he needed her. He argued that she liked to do exactly his sort of work; she was trained—"What in blazes," he demanded heatedly, "is wrong with you, Meg Goheen?"

She began to gather the supper dishes on a tray. He took it from her. "Will you," he asked, "or won't you work with me?"

She followed him into the kitchen and took an apron from the hook. "No," she said.

"Will you tell me why not?"

She did not answer that.

So he kept trying. For the next hour he kept trying, but Meg would say nothing more on the subject. He got no sort of promise at all.

"I'm getting nowhere," he said finally. "And I've used every means I know. I've reasoned, I've pressed my need, I've exerted my fatal charm—"

He kissed Miss Anna, thanked Lucy for the supper, shook the Dean's hand. Then he took Meg's arm, feeling her resistance and ignoring it. "Chorley wants out," he told her.

"Chorley always wants out."

But she went with him to the front door. There he stood looking down at her. She was a nice girl in a red sweater; she had a good, clear mind— Why? "Meg," he said then, "could I have a date with you for next Saturday night?" He noted the way her eyes flared, the way her lips . . . "We could drive to the city," he continued, not seeming to notice. "I've discovered the most wonderful Italian restaurant there. You would flip over their veal parmigiano. Will you go, Meg? It's what I came all the way from India to do."

But Meg only shook her head. "I'm sorry, Mike," she said softly. "I truly am."

He studied her face under the lights which hung above the door. "All right," he said then, and, putting her aside, he went back into the house. "Lucy," he called while still in the hall, "will you go to St. Louis with me Saturday night —food, dancing—my charming company—"

Lucy came out to him, smiling. For the swiftest second her eyes flicked toward Meg. "Of course, Mike," she said warmly. "I'd be delighted."

On Saturday she was still delighted when Mike came to fetch her. She wore a dress the color of her eyes, and the soft brown fur jacket which the Dean and Anna and Meg had given her for Christmas last year. She sparkled at her every point.

Meg watched her tie a gauzy blue scarf over her golden hair; she watched Lucy go out along the flagstones to his car. To be as joyous as Lucy—her very shoes twinkled, and the way she had looked up at Mike . . .

But Meg had not seen the way Mike looked at *her* during the gay flurry of his departure with Lucy.

Miss Anna saw it, and Meg's father.

Meg missed her teaching. She should never have given that up—not without talking about her plan a little to Lucy and to her father. At least that. Meg was accustomed to being busy, to being among people, active. Now she wouldn't even take walks with Chorley. Her car scarcely left the garage; if people came to the house—students or other faculty in the evening—she was sure to take the first chance to escape to her room.

Lucy tried to keep her occupied and even interested in the things which she did. No, Meg did not want to work at the children's clinic. Lucy talked to her about her plans for the Christmas music at the church. She showed Meg how to do things for their mother, but Meg was not anxious for the minutes of intimate girl-talk with Mums which Lucy so treasured.

She performed the household duties which Lucy set for her, but one morning when she had dusted a single row of books in the Dean's study and was ready to start on a second row, she turned, poised there on the small ladder, and told Lucy that she knew what was going on.

"You're keeping me busy just the way you've helped Doshie keep Karen busy."

Before she answered, Lucy finished brushing out the fireplace. Then she said quietly, "I am trying to help you where you seem to need help, Meg."

Meg stood, book and feather duster in hand, and looked

down at her sister in her blue gingham dress, a blue scarf tying her pretty hair. "You try to help Karen, too," she pointed out.

"Yes, I do. Why not? With Karen, you and I have both thought that if she would let herself be helped, things would improve for her."

Meg considered this. "Am I like Karen?" she asked.

"No! You are older, and you should have more sense. This thing that happened to you—there should be no feeling of guilt such as Karen must have. It was a shock, of course."

It had been a shock, and Meg was still held in that state of shock. She was "not herself." She was often cross—and then contrite. It was difficult to cope with both moods. She often wept alone at night, and sometimes wept when a small upset offered her the occasion. She would have liked to stay in her room more than she did, and when forced to be with people, she was silent. And—Lucy hunted for a word. Patient. Meg struggled to be patient. As if she waited numbly for a great pain to run its course, to subside.

She made other efforts, too. Lucy agreed that she did. Meg had set herself a routine of daily tasks and performances to which she adhered stoically. She would get up at a fixed hour each morning, dress and eat breakfast, wash the dishes, talk to her parents. She would help Lucy with household tasks, dust books—even go to market, though she was not good at that and told Lucy to go while she did other things at home, where she could attend to Mums if she were needed, answer the phone and the door— She made an effort, which was noticeable to Lucy, to talk to the Dean at dinnertime and for a fixed period afterward.

This was good. Any self-discipline was good, Lucy thought. And she continued her endeavor to fill Meg's time, to divert her thoughts. One evening in mid-December, she succeeded in getting her sister to agree to attend a concert at the college. The Goheens always bought two season's tickets for the series, taking turns staying at home with Mums. Tonight the Dean would stay, with his usual jokes about being glad to get his girl to himself.

It was a bad night, snow blowing gustily; Meg decided that only students would be at the concert. She and Lucy wrapped woolen scarfs about their heads, put on boots and heavy coats, and started out.

"The North Pole's already been discovered!" their father called after them.

"We'll find something!" Lucy told him. He laughed, closed the door, and went back to the fire and the book which he was reading aloud to Anna.

The concert's audience was somewhat diminished by the weather, but the auditorium still was two-thirds full. No one had "dressed," and the smell of heated wet wool soon spread throughout the hall.

Meg and Lucy found good seats in the sixth row on the aisle, speaking to students, faculty, and friends, examining their programs— This performance would be by a dance group.

"It's going to be arty," declared Lucy. "It always is when they give long titles to the dances."

"Their bare toes will turn blue," Meg predicted with a small chuckle.

"It's warm enough in here— Oh, hello, Dr. Bowlin!" Lucy smiled happily up at the tall man.

"The beautiful Goheen sisters!" he greeted them. "May I sit with you?"

"Of course," said Lucy readily. "We'll just shove all this rummage over to another chair."

He helped her do it, putting his own coat on top of the heap. In the shuffle, he sat down between Lucy and Meg. "What this hall needs is a checkroom," he decided.

"Oh, people pile stuff on the table out in the entry, but then you have to wait hours to get your things out of the stack. We thought a chair might be available to us tonight."

"And it seems to be. Is this program going to be any good?"

"Maybe not," said Lucy. "There is always one poor one in the series. Still—we may be surprised."

He looked at his program. "Barefeet dancers," he decided, and Lucy laughed aloud. Then she explained why.

"That's all right," he told his companions. "Sitting where I am, I'm sure to enjoy my evening. How is your delightful mother?"

Lucy told him, and then she went on to ask the doctor how Leonard Keel was doing.

"Lucy!" Meg protested under her breath.

"But I want to know . . ." Lucy explained. "The doctor doesn't have to answer if I've overstepped ethics and things."

Tony Bowlin laughed. "I don't mind telling you how this patient is, Lucy. And Meg . . ." he slanted his glance toward her.

"At Lucy's age, she should be more tactful," Meg insisted.

"Oh, Lucy's just the right age! Couldn't be better. Well, my dear, your friend Leonard has big problems, most of them medical. From the bustle now going on behind the curtain, I don't think I'll have time to go into detail, but there are many factors. We've about decided to send Keel to a big center like Mayo's or Barnes."

"Mike says you're a fine surgeon," said Lucy. "Can't you operate?"

"I think he needs a specialist." Dr. Bowlin settled back and watched the stage curtains part.

The performance was neither as good as it might have been, nor as bad as they had feared. Lucy's occasional glance at Meg showed that she was able, somewhat, to lose herself in the program. She even laughed at a comedy number and clapped enthusiastically after a clever one.

Before the evening was over, Dr. Bowlin was called away. "I'm sorry," he whispered. "I was looking forward to pizza afterward."

The girls had been able to park in the lighted lot beside the college auditorium, but when they went out to the car, before they got in, Meg looked into the back seat, and she carefully locked all doors before they drove away. Lucy made no comment other than about the program which they had just seen.

"The Pennsylvania Dutch one was the best," she said. "One doesn't have to be naked and glistening to dance. I'm sorry Tony missed that one."

"You and he seem to have become great friends," said Meg, inching down the hill.

"He called me Lucy. And I like him."

"But he's still a doctor, and there are ethics . . ."

"You mean I shouldn't have asked him about one of his patients."

"Certainly not that particular patient."

"Because of the suggestion . . . All about Bee and him, you mean?" Lucy glanced at Meg.

"Yes, I do mean that," said Meg.

"But, Meg," Lucy attempted, "you know—and he'll find out—that I just can't be anything but honest and outspoken. I truly wanted to know how Leonard was doing. Dr. Bowlin took my question that way, I am sure. As for the other aspects— Well, he's made no secret of his interest in Bee. They've been seen together. I've seen them myself. And Doshie says Bee was all ready to divorce Leonard when he collapsed."

"Unless Bee told you that herself," said Meg sternly, "or Dr. Bowlin did—"

"Oh, heavens, Meg! Of course he didn't tell me any such thing. You heard everything he said, and I personally don't think he resented my talking about Leonard."

Meg was taking the long way home, going down into town and up the hill again. She would not ever, Lucy had noticed, drive past the college observatory.

"Tony will know," Lucy said again, "as you seem to have forgotten, that I am one to speak my thoughts frankly. And I like things to be that way, too!"

Meg sighed and nodded. "I've put a heavy load on you, haven't I lately?" she asked.

"Yes," said Lucy readily, "you have. I would always want to help you, of course, but I think matters should have been handled differently. There were things that should have been done at the time. I believe there may be —or should be—ways to help you now."

Meg held the car at a crossing light. "Do you think?" she asked tensely, "that it would have helped to have all the students at the performance tonight know what happened to me?"

"You are very popular with the girls. Tonight a half dozen asked when you were coming back to teach. They would have sympathized with you, they would have been angry, and sorry."

"And they would have *known*."

"Yes," Lucy agreed. "But, Meg, as things are, people know something has happened to you. Both Dad and Mums —Mike—Doshie—have asked me what happened. They love you and would want to help you."

"What would they do?"

"I don't know," said Lucy. "But there must be some way to help you! I'd do anything, if I only knew what to do." She was almost weeping.

"Lucy!" Meg brought the car to a stop alongside the curbstone. She turned and put her gloved hand on her sister's sleeve. "I am sorry," she said, "for the hard time I have given you. I've thought of going away—I've offered to go away—"

"No," said Lucy. "No."

"Perhaps things will work out. In time. I already know this: if anyone could help me, ever, it would be you, Lucy."

Lucy was not comforted. "That's fine for my intentions," she said, "but what can I *do?*"

Meg started the car forward again. "I don't know," she said wearily. "I don't know what I would be doing if our positions were reversed, if this thing had happened to *you* —as it more logically should have. You are the cuddly, pretty one."

Meg had said all that before, and often. Lucy could have screamed to think that Meg wished . . . She was still talking about the way she felt.

"Do you believe you would have felt better if this *had* happened to me?" Lucy demanded, hoping to end the surmise on this subject.

Meg shook her head. "I don't know," she admitted. "You're the pretty one, and the positions are not reversed. I was the one— Now, can't *you* find the brains to solve the problem?" She slid the car into the garage, but she sat there, her face set, her eyes staring before her. "*You* be the calm, efficient one!" she said. "*You* take care of me and my hurt!" Her tone was bitter. The words and the thought behind them slashed at Lucy like small knives.

She got out of the car and went into the house. She and Meg talked briefly to their parents. Meg then went upstairs, and Lucy prepared her mother for bed, talking about the concert and the people they had seen. She told about Dr. Bowlin and what he had said about Leonard Keel; she told how nice he was, and that he had been called away.

When, finally, she could go upstairs herself and take her bath and get into bed, Lucy was still remembering Meg's bitter tone. "You're the pretty one. *You* find the brains . . . *You* take care . . ."

Had Meg, all these years, wished she could have been the pretty Goheen sister?

She was pretty enough, and always had been. She had lovely black hair; her dark eyes were notable. She had a good figure and handsome legs— Meg was a handsome girl and, when herself, her vivacity added beauty to her face.

But, yes, all their lives people had said—as far back as Lucy could remember—"Oh, here's the pretty one! Here's Lucy! Of course Meg is smart. She makes top grades in school. . . ." Sunday school, day school, at parties, Lucy had overheard what was said, and sometimes resented it. Because she had had "brains" enough. She could do many things which Meg could not do. Her music—her housekeeping skills—but—

Meg was right. Meg was the clever one, and Lucy the pretty one. "Luscious Lucy" was the one whom the boys, and the men, had pursued. Lucy might even have better handled this tragic thing which had befallen Meg.

"Did I tell you?" Meg called from her room. "That dog—that night, you know—that dog was dead at the side of the road when I left . . ."

"All right, Meg," said Lucy wearily. "He was dead. I wish the whole thing could be that dead—just lying there where we—you and I—could go off and leave it."

Meg said nothing, and Lucy regretted the slightly sharp edge to her voice. But she was tired. . . .

What had she been thinking? Oh, yes, that she, Lucy, could perhaps have handled the assault, and its effects, better than Meg had done. If that were so, couldn't she find a way for Meg to handle it?

She got out of bed and went to the window to open it. The snow had stopped, and the sky was full of icy stars. Lucy stood for a long time looking at them.

When finally she went back to her warm bed, she told herself that, at last, she was glad Meg had told no one but Lucy. Secrecy *was* a help! Tonight the students who had spoken to Meg, their other friends, feared that she was sick, and they were concerned. But not knowing the shameful cause of Meg's "sickness," it was going to be easier for Meg to recover from it. One did not remember, nor gossip about, an illness.

And recover she would, of course. It would take time and patience, but with Lucy's help, encouragement, and even nagging, Meg would—

Impulsively, Lucy got out of bed again. She went across the hall, her bare feet silent. Meg lay on her side, and Lucy bent over her lightly to kiss her sister's cheek. "I am going to help you, Meg," she whispered. "I am going to . . ."

Meg stirred drowsily. "Go back to bed," she murmured. "You'll catch your death . . ."

Her breath smelled of whiskey.

In the nursery school where Lucy played the piano three times a week for games and song sessions, these last days before Christmas were very busy.

And of course she was busy at the church, too. In other years, she would have had Gloria, or someone, come in to be with her mother. This year, with Meg at home, Lucy felt freely able to leave, delegating various home tasks for Meg to do. She could iron and prepare lunch. . . .

She sent Meg on errands, too, urging her to walk and take Chorley. "I find you very useful," she told her sister.

Each morning she planned her day, and Meg's. "If you are going to be here, Meg," she would say, "I'll go to the church and work on my Christmas prelude—then I'll have my hair done. Can you manage lunch for yourself and Mums?"

"If it's not too complicated," said Meg. "I've already mastered the can opener."

"There will be a proper award in your Christmas stocking. Yes, you can have soup—or Mums would enjoy a sandwich from that beef roast. Slice it thin. . . ."

"Get along to your descants and your fugues," Meg told her. "I'll tend to things."

"You can put hangers in those new Christmas balls, too," said Lucy, wrapping a fleecy shawl about her head. It was a sunny day, with an icy wind blowing. "Don't leave Mums alone for more than fifteen minutes at a time . . ."

"Now why would I leave her?"

"I meant leave her while you go upstairs and make your bed. Or maybe carry the trash to the incinerator."

"All right, all right," said Meg. "I know the rules. And today I may even observe them."

"Fair enough," said Lucy. "I'll take your car, O.K.?"

Meg waved her on.

It was on that morning that tragedy struck their street. One would not have suspected such a possibility. The houses sat serenely along the curve of the rising hill, the yellow frame Goheen house, the Keels' handsome French Provincial, and the brick house of the Chambers family.

They all sparkled in the clear winter sunlight. A few dry leaves danced along the street, now and then swirling into rustling eddies.

Doshie Chambers, in an old cotton knit blouse and skirt of brilliant blue, her blond hair confined with clamps calculated to hold it somewhat close to her head later in the day, wondered when on earth Karen was ever going to get out of bed. Here it was after nine o'clock—the girl probably was sulking. The night before Doshie had had some things to say about the way she acted whenever she saw Dr. Bowlin. Last evening he had brought Bee home from the hospital and had sat in front of her house for a while, talking to her. Karen must cut a wedge out of Doshie's fresh chocolate cake and dash out to present it to Bee, and of course thereby get a chance to speak to Tony.

He was nice to the girl. Tony Bowlin was nice to everyone. But he certainly could see through that maneuver, and Doshie had told Karen so. All evening, Karen had moped. And this morning—

Doshie started up the stairs. First, she looked into Judith's room. It was tidy, but what on earth was the girl doing with a tennis racket *and* a ball on one of the beds? This time of year? Not that Doshie really cared. That amount of "litter" was nothing in a college girl's room.

Then Doshie went on through the bath which the girls shared and tapped lightly on the half-open door of Karen's room. She was smiling because she really liked the way this room had turned out when she had redecorated it a year ago. The ruffled white curtains at the window gave it a feminine look, but the straight brown draperies which were pulled across the wide glass took away all feeling of fussiness. The brown and white checked gingham dust ruffle of the bed . . .

Karen was in that bed, resting against three pillows, listening to the radio. She glanced up at her mother when she sat down on the side of the bed. "Can we turn that off?" Doshie asked.

Indifferently, Karen's hand went out; her finger pushed the lever, and the room was quiet.

"That must be Chorley Goheen barking outside," said Doshie.

Karen made no comment.

"Aren't you hungry this morning?" asked her mother.

Karen's long, straight hair fanned out across the pillows. It was not a "pretty" way for a girl to wear her hair. Karen's pajamas were old ones, faded from many washings. In these sulky moods, the girl made no effort to look attractive, though, really, she could be quite stunning.

"No breakfast?" her mother asked again.

"Oh, please . . ." Karen begged.

"Well, I defrosted some peaches," said Doshie, "and they are delicious. It's so lovely and sunny, and I had things to talk about."

"I'll bet," muttered Karen.

Doshie held her face immobile. "I don't like Karen," she was telling herself. "I don't like her at all when she is this way. Why should I bother . . . ?"

She smoothed her skirt down toward her knees. She had half made a decision to talk to Karen about Judith, to ask her— She spoke aloud. "I wanted to ask you what I should do about Judith," she said. "Sometimes I think I am too strict with her." She glanced at Karen, who was staring at the wall behind her mother.

"I thought," poor Doshie continued, trying to sound casual and friendly, "that you would know if I had made mistakes with you, Karen."

Karen turned on her side, away from her mother. "I don't want to talk about it," she mumbled.

Doshie beat her closed fists together in an extremity of frustration. For seven years she had been living with this girl and trying— "I am getting sick and tired," she cried now, "of people who don't want to talk about things! Meg Goheen, and now you— Why do you *do* this way?"

"Because," said Karen, "when I wanted my mother to be sorry for me, she just hated me!"

"That's crazy!" cried Doshie. Then she leaned forward to look at the girl. Why—she *was*—

Karen turned again to look at Doshie. "Yes, Mother," she said in an odd way. She sat up, she half turned, she felt under the piled pillows, and then, to Doshie's stunned, unbelieving horror, she was holding in her hand a small, square gun—a black gun that shone a little. Her hand shook, and she steadied that wrist with her other hand. She was pointing the gun straight at Doshie. "I don't want you tired any more!" she cried, her voice thin and shrill. "I hate you, too. I—"

Scrambling, Doshie backed away from the bed, holding

her hands before her. "Karen . . ." she gasped, her voice cracking dryly with fear. "Don't, darling . . . Look, dear! Listen to Mother . . ."

Karen, still holding the gun with both hands, seemed ready to get out of the bed on the other side. She put her feet down to the floor and sat on the side of the bed—afterward Doshie remembered that she had done this—and then she sort of huddled over and forward, hiding that gun—and it went off. It was an accident! Karen wouldn't have—shot herself! She wouldn't—have—

But she had shot herself. The air was faintly blue with smoke, and there was a sharply acrid smell. Karen made a small, gasping sound and fell back, one hand flung upward against the pillows—that hand held the gun. Her other hand was clutching at her stomach; it clutched, and then it relaxed. A round stain, a thickness, a redness, began to spread, to well up between her fingers. . . .

And Doshie screamed. She backed clear to the wall, away from Karen, and she screamed again and again. Then, beginning to shake, she went back and leaned over the bed, but she could not bring herself to touch the girl. She knew that she must do something. Even if Karen was dead, and with all that blood . . . Now the gun had fallen away from Karen's hand, but Doshie did not touch it.

She must call Louis, she thought. No—first she must call a doctor. She must—*Lucy!* Lucy would know what to do! She would call Lucy. Bee would not be at home, but Lucy was close . . .

Talking to herself—"Don't fall down the stairs," she said in a strange, thin voice. "Don't panic—you remember the Goheen number—dial it slowly and get it right—lean against the wall—don't faint."

Meg answered the phone. "What's happened, Doshie?" she asked at once.

"It's—Karen," said Doshie. "And it's awful! Is Lucy . . . ?"

"I'll be right down."

But Doshie wanted *Lucy*, not Meg! She sat down in a chair and shook harder than ever. She looked at the stairs; she must unlatch the door for Meg—then she should go back and try to do something for Karen.

The girl had on those awful old pajamas. . . .

Meg came very quickly. Yes, she said, she had run. Now they must be quick. She couldn't leave Mums for more than fifteen minutes. Lucy was at the church. "Doshie, get hold of yourself!"

She even shook Karen's mother, and soon Doshie was able to tell her—a little—about what had happened. Meg ran upstairs, with Doshie behind her; she pressed towels against that awful place and told Doshie not to lift the girl's head. She came downstairs again, and in the most efficient way she called the hospital. "This is Miss Margaret Goheen," she said. "This is an emergency. I must speak to Dr. Tryon *at once*. Please hurry. Yes, I'll hold."

White-faced, eyes staring, Doshie sat on the stairs and watched Meg. She tried to tell more of what had happened. It was Louis's gun. "He keeps it—he has always kept it in our bedside table. I hate it. He had no right to keep a gun where a girl like Karen could get it." No, they hadn't quarreled. Oh, of course Karen was never happy about anything, she—

Mike's hearty voice came through the phone, and Meg told him quickly, completely, what had happened. She was at the Chambers', Karen had shot herself after threatening Doshie. Yes, she seemed still to be alive. In the abdomen, yes.

Then Mike's voice again. Meg put the phone down. "He will send an ambulance," she said. "It will save time to bring her to the hospital where he will be waiting."

She looked at her watch. She picked up the phone again. "I have to call the police."

"Oh, *no!*" cried Doshie.

"If I don't," said Meg, "Mike will. He said I was to do it. Did you touch anything upstairs?"

"I couldn't," said Doshie. "I couldn't!"

Meg made the call. She told Doshie to get her coat while Meg ran back home and checked on her mother. Yes, she would come back, if she could.

She was back before the ambulance or the police arrived. Doshie said that she had caught Louis at his office; he would come to the hospital. "He wanted to know why I had let her do it," said Doshie, her voice rising hysterically.

Meg took her arm. "You hang onto yourself," she said sternly. "After you've left, I'll close the house and send word to Lucy to pick up Judy—"

Afterward, Doshie told Lucy that Meg had been as cold as ice.

"She got a lot of things done," Lucy pointed out.

"Well, yes, of course she did. But I thought, at the time, that what I wanted was for someone to have hysterics with me. And that would never be Meg."

Lucy said nothing.

The police came, the ambulance came. The stretcher went upstairs with the policemen; it was brought down again, and Meg buttoned Doshie's coat under her chin, gently drawing the metal clips from her hair. "You're to ride in the police car," she said, "and talk to the officer. This will let us get Karen to the hospital more quickly. Try to be as calm as you can, Doshie."

"Oh, Meg . . ."

Meg kissed her. "I know," she said. "But do it one step at a time."

"Don't tell your mother."

Meg laughed. "Of course I'll tell her. She has arthritis, but she's not stupid. Right now she's watching all this from the window."

"She—"

"We'll all pull for you, Doshie. Don't worry. Mike will be at the hospital."

It all became a blur to Doshie. She rode along the familiar streets, seeing only the back of the ambulance ahead of the police car. She talked to the policeman—there was almost nothing to tell. She had not touched the gun. She thought it was one her husband kept. . . . There had been no quarrel. Her other daughter was at school. Her husband—

The shining new hospital rose before them, a strange, round building; it looked enormous. The cars went around the drive—there were people in white—two men, a nurse —at the wide doors to take charge of the stretcher. The policeman detained Doshie until the stretcher was inside. Then Mike was coming toward her.

He looked big and capable in his white clothes. Doshie could only press her face against his shoulder. "I'm just scared to death," she told him.

He led her inside. "Shall I stay with Karen," he asked, "or with you?"

"Oh, with Karen!" She wiped her coat sleeve across her face.

Mike nodded. "Here's Louis," he said.

Down the corridor two men in baggy green clothing

were pushing a different stretcher—they must have moved Karen— There were doors, and a screen, and—

Doshie fell into her husband's arms and wept noisily.

Mike touched Louis's arm, and he too disappeared down the corridor.

"You can wait in here," said a nurse. "Mrs. Chambers, do you know your daughter's blood type?"

Doshie tried to think. "I should know . . ." she said. Her lips felt thick—she looked pleadingly at Louis.

"It's all right," said the nurse.

The room where they were told to wait was an office. Louis seated Doshie in the chair which faced the desk and wiped her cheeks with his handkerchief. Louis Chambers was a big man, handsome and dark. He capably held a big job for the state and tried to cope with his family as efficiently. The second assignment often baffled him.

The nurse brought two cups of coffee on a tray and asked if Mrs. Chambers would like a sedative.

"I'd like to know about my daughter," she said.

"Yes, of course. The doctors are examining her, and as soon as we know anything, we'll tell you."

Doshie nodded. "I know," she said dispiritedly. Louis pulled up a chair beside hers. "You should maybe have that sedative. . . ."

"What I should do is go out and find my girl. . . ."

"What happened, Doshie? What caused her . . . ?"

Doshie shook her head. "I'll tell you all I know," she said. "Last night I corrected her a little about being silly—*Louis!* Do you suppose Dr. Bowlin is taking care of her? He's the head surgeon, and she shot herself right in the stomach!"

"Then he'll take care of her. But try to tell me, Doshie."

"I am trying! But— Oh, I can't stay in here!"

"I can't either," said her husband. "Not with the door shut."

"Then let's go!" said Doshie, standing up.

They went out into the corridor. The nurse at the desk looked up at them. The curving hall was a busy one—nurses, orderlies, wheelchairs—a cart—Doshie and Louis passed doors—and came to one with a glass in it. "Emergency C," said gold letters on the glass.

Louis looked in, and Doshie stood on tiptoe to see. There was Karen on the table, her clothes off—a towel spread across her breast. Her hair was bound into a white cloth. There were men—one, two, three, four, *five* men—a white tube was taped to Karen's left wrist—a masked doctor, a tall one, was lifting her right arm high in the air. Another man stood farther down the table, his hands on his hips—he was looking down intently— Why, *that* was Dr. Bowlin!

"Where's Mike?" Doshie asked Louis.

"Shhh. He's around someplace, you can be sure. She looks little, doesn't she?"

"Karen? Yes, she does. Oh, Louis—she is such a troubled person. Is it awful to wish . . . ?"

"Yes, it is," said Louis. "Here, let's go back— Oh, there's Bee!"

And there was Bee, standing at the big desk writing something. She had dark-rimmed glasses on a ribbon—and she was completely surprised to see the Chambers.

"What on earth?" she asked, taking off the glasses, then putting them on again. She wore a long white coat over her dark skirt and white blouse.

Louis and Doshie together attempted to tell her what on earth . . .

Halfway through, she took their arms. "You two are in a state," she said. "Come down here—" and she led them back to the same office where they had first been told to wait.

"Don't close the door!" Doshie said loudly.

"I won't, I won't," Bea said reassuringly. "Wait here. I'll go to Emergency and see what goes on. You wait."

Louis and Doshie sat down and waited. Pretty soon Bee came back. "They'll be coming in here for some information," she said.

"Karen . . . ?"

"She's alive, but she certainly made a mess of her belly. Tell me what happened. Bowlin is going to want to do surgery."

She talked to them and let them talk. She gave them cigarettes and seemed to be entirely free for their affairs. Then finally a doctor, whom she introduced as the surgical resident, came in—his name was Garido, and she called him that—Dr. Garido. He called her Dr. Keel, with an emphasis which showed that he liked Bee. This young man had brought with him papers fastened to an aluminum board, and he told Karen's parents that their daughter would need immediate surgery. Would they consent?

Doshie showed signs of panic, but Louis reached for the board. "The man said immediate," he told his wife.

His name written, he asked if Dr. Garido had time to explain to them—a little.

Bee took the board and read what was written on it. "I'll explain to you, Louis," she said.

"Can I see her first?" asked Doshie pitiably. "She said I hated her. I don't. I don't!"

The young resident looked at her compassionately. "We'll bring her along this hall," he said. "She may not be conscious enough to respond . . ."

This satisfied Doshie. She signed the paper, then took her stand at the door while Bee talked to Louis—and to her—about spleens and things. Dr. Garido had gone off with his signed paper.

By then, Dr. Bowlin was up in the surgery suite consulting with Bonita Sturgeon about the work which he planned to do for the Chambers girl. Bonita herself was getting o.r. ready for this surgery; the floor was really busy that morning—two gall bladders, a hip to pin—the works. Tony was suited, but had not yet scrubbed, and he expressed himself rather fluently on the subject of pretty girls who played around with .38 revolvers.

"I wouldn't say this pretty girl was playing, doctor," said Bonita.

"But what would make her *want* to do such a thing?"

"Don't you listen to town gossip, sir?"

Tony glanced at the tall, rangy woman. "I may not have caught up on it all," he conceded.

So Bonita told him about Karen and Doshie; as she talked she took out surgical packets, checked on the instrument tables, and did a dozen tasks. She ended with the conclusion that the girl was unbalanced—perhaps always had been.

"All girls caught out in a necking area are not crazy, Miss Sturgeon," said Dr. Bowlin wryly.

"No, they are not. But Karen took this event—and her mother took it—harder than most girls do these days. They—dwelt on it. Both of them. Doshie vacillated—and how's that for a ten-dollar word?—well, Doshie did, between being afraid if Karen showed any interest in another man, and a wish that the girl would find some man who would marry her and get her off her mother's hands. And

Karen—well, she wanted to get away, too, I think, but she was too timid to make any bold moves."

"So she timidly shoots herself."

Bonita shrugged and went to answer the telephone. "That, or she was showing her mother something. Like I said, she's a bit on the crazy side. Hello! Surgery, Miss Sturgeon— Oh, *no!*" She turned from the wall phone to look at Dr. Bowlin. "All right," she said. "I'll tell him."

"Karen?" asked the surgeon when she hung up the telephone.

"No," said Bonita. "It's Mr. Keel. He's had an attack, or seizure . . ."

Dr. Bowlin frowned. "What about Tryon?" he began, then he snapped his fingers. Karen's emergency had caught the surgical staff with a full schedule. Tony had left Mike to do a cut-down . . . He started for the door. "Find Bee," he said over his shoulder as he went out.

Behind him, Miss Sturgeon shrugged and smiled.

Since his admission on Thanksgiving Day, Leonard Keel had been in one of the intensive-care rooms, or cubicles. Lately—this past week—Tony and Mike had been making plans to send the gravely ill man to a large medical center where surgery, or any other measures, might be tried in his behalf. Leonard was very sick, and he made a most difficult patient. Had Tony had no personal feelings about the man's wife, he still must have given a deal of consideration to the ethics of his profession which would force him to prolong Leonard's life in any way he could.

This morning, even as he approached Keel's bedside, his thoughts surveyed the whole situation. Should the life of such a man be extended? Should the doctor, any doctor, be placed in the position of fate deciding the length of a man's life?

The nurse and the attending resident moved aside for Dr. Bowlin to make his examination. Leonard's condition was indeed grave. He was breathing heavily and was obviously in pain. The surgeon's hands moved swiftly, his eyes were intent, his judgment—

Before he had finished, Bee came into the room. Tony glanced at her.

"A crisis?" she asked softly.

Tony nodded, straightened, and took his stethoscope from his ears; he put his hand on Bee's shoulder. "I must talk to you."

90

Behind him, above the oxygen mask, the very blue eyes of the sick man watched them go.

"I was down with Karen's people," Bee said because she could not bear to speak directly of Leonard.

Tony guided her into a small room, then unoccupied. Even in this new hospital it had already become the repository of gear not in use—a walker, some flower vases on the shelf, a stack of unopened wipes boxes, three envelopes which contained plastic syringes . . .

The doctor closed the door and turned to face Bee. She was not a pretty woman, but one always spoke of Bee Keel as "nice." Normally her smile was ready, her interest keen, her sympathy automatic. She was clever and friendly and—

Dr. Bowlin put his hand on her shoulder. "We are going to have to move him, Bee," he said firmly. "And at once. I'll go with him if necessary."

"But you're operating on Karen, aren't you?" she asked. "Garido told us . . . Louis and Doshie signed the release."

Tony nodded. "We must operate on Karen at once," he said, "*and* move Leonard."

Bee gulped. "He won't go, Tony," she said.

"He'll have to go!" Tony cried. Then he looked keenly at Bee. "Why won't he want to go?" he demanded.

"Because he'd like nothing better than to see you put in a spot where you'll have to operate or see him die."

"I'll not do either," said Tony grimly.

"Do you think . . . ?"

"It's an aneurysm, Bee," said the surgeon. "There will need to be tests, of course, but—"

"And then surgery."

"Probably."

"Oh, *Tony!*"

Tony started toward the door. "So we'll move him. You can tell him so while I take care of Karen."

Bee stood where she was. "An aneurysm," she repeated, her voice croaking in her throat. Then she stiffened. "But you, Tony—you simply cannot operate on him!"

He came back to her, and his hand stroked her hair back from her face. "If necessary, I could," he said quietly. "I'm a better doctor than you think, Bee."

"I know how good you are!" she cried. "But—"

"As I say," he broke in, "I'm a better doctor than you think."

Now it was she who walked away from him a step or two. "I know what you mean," she said. "That you think you could forget—and you probably could. But still, people will think—even I might think—and Leonard—"

"Let's go talk to Leonard about it," said Tony, opening the door.

But Bee did not move. "You can't," she whispered. "You can't."

"I think we must move him," said Dr. Bowlin. "Then I won't have to decide." He grinned down at her. "Refusing to operate might cause a bit of wonder, too, you know, my dear."

And Bee began to cry. "I don't love him," she gasped. "I —hate him!"

Tony shook his head at her. "Hush," he said sternly. "I've heard enough this morning about family hates— Besides, you don't. You couldn't hate anyone. Get yourself together. I'll talk to Leonard. There is very little time to lose for him or for Karen."

Bee watched him go down the short, curving hall, a tall figure in gray-green, his shoulders square, his stride quick and purposeful. Yes. Though loving her, Tony could indeed operate on Leonard and do a perfect job. But if that perfect job should save her husband's life . . .

She did not follow him to Leonard's room, if such it could be called. These small, pie-shaped cubicles in the intensive-care area contained a bed, a panel of switches, a small table, and little else. Even very sick patients sometimes rebelled at the austerity of their surroundings. Leonard Keel, who liked his luxury, had called his quarters "the cell" and the whole area "death row."

This seemed an especially apt name this morning, for Leonard, though conscious, looked much more like death than life. A big man and, in health, a robust, noisy one, now his body was wasted, the bones of his face were skull-like, his eyes were feverish. An oxygen tent had replaced the face mask.

Dr. Bowlin came to the bedside and took the sick man's wrist between his long, spatulate fingers. Leonard would have drawn his hand away, but the doctor held it firmly— as firmly as his gaze held Leonard's blue eyes.

"I must tell you, Mr. Keel," the surgeon said quietly, "that your condition has become such that we feel a heart specialist's care will be immediately necessary. We should like to go ahead with plans to move you at once. I believe Dr. Tryon has explained to you the nature of the aneurysm which seems to have developed, that it is dangerous, but that it can be handled."

He dropped Leonard's wrist and straightened the edge of the oxygen tent. The sick man seized the heavy plastic with surprising strength. He wanted to talk, and Tony bent over to hear.

"Hurt—like hell!" gasped Keel. "I want—you—to cut this damn thing—out of me!"

Tony shook his head. "I don't think so," he said.

"Are you afraid to kill me?" asked the sick man.

Tony's face was a mask. "You have an aneurysm, sir. It may not be so large that surgery will be the only solution. In the hands of a specialist . . ."

"You aren't one?" The tone of voice was nasty.

"I am not."

"I thought you knew every damn thing there was to know about surgery. That was"—the patient gasped, waited, then resumed—"why you—were brought here—"

Leonard Keel was a curator of the state university.

"I am a well-trained surgeon," said the Chief of Staff with dignity. "But my name is not De Bakey. And I don't think your aneurysm is large enough for the risk of my trying to make it seem that it is."

"You don't know how to do heart surgery?" needled Bee's husband.

Tony shrugged. "I've worked on an open-heart team. We have the equipment here. But as yet, Mr. Keel, we are not practiced enough here—"

"It takes practice, does it?"

"It most certainly does."

"And then, of course, *my* name is Keel."

"It is, sir. But that is not my prime reason for deciding to take you to Barnes."

"I won't go."

"And I won't do the surgery you may need."

"I dare you to, doctor," said the sick man.

Tony grinned down at Leonard. "I don't think so," he said again.

Leonard's eyes wandered to the corner of the room and came back to the doctor's handsome face. "Know you—in love—my wife," he gasped.

Dr. Bowlin nodded. "Yes," he said, "I am."

Leonard almost smiled. "Be—fool then—not to—" His head fell back; Dr. Bowlin glanced at the nurse who had come to the door, and he went out, saying that Mr. Keel was to be observed very closely, an exact account of the vital signs maintained.

On surgery again, he consulted with Bonita Sturgeon. "Will you send for Dr. Tryon?" Tony asked her.

"For Mr. Keel?"

"His condition is grave, but I want Tryon to help me with the Chambers girl, which we'll do at once."

He went to the scrub basins and kicked on the water. Within minutes, Mike joined him. The two men had become friends. Now Tony scrubbed, his head thrown back on his neck, his eyes half closed. He was thinking about the difficult abdominal surgery before him and about nothing else, Mike felt sure. He smiled at the cocky angle of Bowlin's cap. His own sat squarely on his blond head, and he was sure there was nothing rakish about *his* face.

"You know," he said, after Tony had said a little about the job facing them, "we have been asking for a variety of cases here, and planning on how to get them, but this job today was not precisely what I had in mind. How about you?"

Tony shrugged. "We have to care for emergencies."

Mike was counting. Garido had come to the third basin.

"We probably will, in time, get our variety of cases," mused Dr. Bowlin. "Surgery is busy with a fair spectrum today just by confining our admissions to the indigent. Cases like Karen's must be handled. . . ."

Mike glanced at Garido. "What's this I hear about Keel?" he asked Dr. Bowlin.

Tony nodded. "He's had a relapse. I'm sure of the aneurysm. I hope it's still small enough for control, but we have some lung involvement now. Of course his emergency was not exactly what I needed with a dirty gut to excise."

"What are you going to do about him? Keel?"

"I want to move him. If we can't, and have to, surgery seems to be my specialty. Though I might get Miller Hubbard from the Cancer Hospital."

"He's a good man," said Mike. "And I am ready to help where I can. Keel isn't what we've been asking for, either, is he?"

"Oh, no!" said Dr. Bowlin. "He's not a case any hospital

94

gets every day. But any delay will probably make it disastrous to move him."

"How big do you figure that aneurysm to be?"

"It ballooned this morning, but I'd say it is still under three inches."

"Pain?" asked Mike.

"Not too much yet. Lung distress, but—"

Mike nodded. "Then—"

"Yes. We should move him. If we delay, he won't have a choice of surgeons. He knows that and expects me to kill him."

"You wouldn't want to do the job, would you?" Mike asked, aware, as was Tony, that both the resident and the nurse were listening for the surgeon's reply.

"Medically," Tony said coolly, "yes, I'd do it, and would want to."

The two doctors moved into the operating room and studied Karen's chart, which the anesthetist held up for them. Mike shook his head.

"She made a thorough thing of it," Tony agreed. "I'll have to remove the spleen, I think. Probably trim up the liver, too. She'd had no breakfast. That's a small break."

"You'd really not be fool enough," said Mike softly, close to Tony's ear, "to chance doing surgery on Leonard Keel, would you?"

Dr. Bowlin's heavy-lidded eyes smiled at Dr. Tryon. "The odds would be against any surgeon in his case, Mike."

"But you . . ." Mike blurted.

Tony stepped up to the table, the nurse began to whisk towels away.

"These women," Mike continued, his tone one of angry protest, "certainly can make life hard for us men."

Tony held out his flattened hand, and the nurse slapped the scalpel into it. "We'll talk about that later," he said.

He did talk about it three hours later. Karen's surgery was over and the girl was installed in an intensive-care cubicle twenty feet from that of Leonard Keel. The two doctors, masked and gowned, had looked at their patients and talked to the Chambers. Doshie was still in shock. Mike prescribed a sedative for her and urged her to go home.

Bee was easier to handle. She was entirely aware of Leonard's condition and of Tony's problems. "How's that for one of your troublemaking women?" Tony asked Mike, savoring the cup of hot coffee which he finally could enjoy.

Mike nodded. "Bee's fine," he said, "but she still complicates your life these days, doesn't she?"

Tony smiled. "That seems to be everyone's opinion. It's not entirely her doing."

Mike snorted.

"Then take our little Karen," Tony mused. "There's no man being hurt in her case, would you say? Or even a cause for her hurt?"

"Only remotely," Mike agreed. He began to pull the jumper of his scrub suit over his head.

"You're losing all your south of India tan," Tony pointed out. "And speaking of women, what about your Meg Goheen, Tryon?"

"Is she my Meg Goheen?" asked Mike gruffly.

"She was at the party they gave for you. But now—What's wrong with that girl now?"

Mike shook his head.

"I saw her at a concert," said Tony. "She acted like a person in shock or a woman hypnotized. Of course I don't know her well and haven't known her at all for long—"

"But you've pegged it," said Mike, climbing into his duck trousers. He filled his coffee cup and sat down on the low bench beside Dr. Bowlin. An orderly came in with a paper for Dr. Tryon to sign. When he had departed, Mike resumed the discussion. "I came home," he said, "very anxious to see the Goheens. I truly love that family and have enjoyed them for the best part of my life. Meg, that first night, was entirely her old self—gay, vivid, challenging. A swell girl. She and Lucy—"

"Lucy is lovely," murmured Tony Bowlin.

Mike's eyes shone. "She is that! In face and in spirit. They've been, not entirely jokingly, my girl friends since they were—oh, six and eight. I've known them even longer. Meg especially has stimulated me. Her mind is a fine one. We always read things together, and argued, and agreed. All that seemed still present the night I came home. Then—just overnight—there simply was no Meg any more. These days she's like a—well—like a totem pole. She looks somewhat like one, too—carved features, a little paint—clothing. But Meg is not there."

"Have you talked to her?"

Mike laughed grimly. "I've tried. Results, zero. She doesn't want to be touched or talked to. She won't consider coming here to work with me. Maybe I'm the one who's disappeared."

"I don't think so, Tryon," said the other doctor. "I get the same impression about her. Have you discussed this with Lucy?"

"Yes. That is, I've tried. She closes the door, too, though in a different way. However, I am sure she knows what is wrong with Meg, and I am certain she is terribly worried. But she won't talk about it or tell me."

"I'd keep trying with Lucy. She'll give you a clue."

"I hope you're right. These blind diagnoses are no fun."

"No, they are not. And here I add to your trouble by complicating the Keel situation for you. I've asked you to assist me. Will you?"

Mike stood up. "Oh, yes," he agreed readily. "Of course I will." He stopped with his t-shirt half on. "Look," he said, "have you considered . . . ?" He broke off and finished dressing. Dr. Bowlin watched him, a speculative smile on his face.

"Are we going to get the rest of that question, doctor?" he asked finally.

Mike tied his shoe. "I was going to ask if Bee will understand, should you manage to save Leonard's life?"

Bowlin started to answer at once, then he closed his mouth and sat thinking. Finally he glanced up. "I am beginning to see what you mean about women, Mike. They do complicate our lives, don't they?"

Mike stood up. "Are you ready to eliminate the problem?" he asked.

Tony laughed. "Not in my lifetime."

"Nor mine," said Mike, going out of the room.

CHAPTER SIX

AN ATTEMPT had been made that day to keep Anna Goheen from knowing entirely what had happened at the Chambers' home. Karen had been hurt, Meg had told her mother. This much she had to tell to explain her trips to the house and the ambulance which Anna would surely have seen go past the front windows. The girl was being cared for, she said. Of course Doshie was upset. It took very little to upset Doshie . . .

Lucy came home from her morning's errands and immediately became involved in a flurry of luncheon preparations. Then, she decided, she would make yeast rolls. This would account for her various trips to the kitchen— if questions became too difficult.

Meg offered to read aloud to Anna while she rested that afternoon.

The Dean was in on the conspiracy. He came home from the college with a problem to discuss. He had this girl—

She had been admitted to the college because of her great popularity in her secondary school, her extracurricular activities . . . She had been selected, or had been a candidate, at least, for America's prettiest cheerleader and of course had been a queen of something or other—but, oh, dear, she was not a good student. What, he asked, were they going to do about the lovely creature? The college didn't have a team to cheer—

Anna patiently waited. She talked about the rolls, she listened to what Meg read aloud, she talked to the Dean about his cheerleader.

Then, when Lucy was putting her to bed that night—a half-hour early, Miss Anna pointed out—she showed that she knew enough about what had happened to Karen that she meant to know more.

"I want to be told the whole thing," she said firmly. "So far I do not suffer from arthritis of the brain."

Lucy laughed. "Of course you don't darling," she said. "Of course you don't."

"Then tell me."

"We all agreed . . ."

"That I was to be treated like an idiot. All right. Go out and tell your father and sister that I can make some decisions, too."

Lucy did go out and tell them. "She's pretty firm about it," she said.

The Dean nodded. "We saved her the flurry of the day," he pointed out. "So—you tell her, Lucy."

"I'll have to," said Lucy, going back to the bedroom.

And she did tell her mother what she knew—that Doshie had called Meg, and Meg had gone down. . . . "You know that, Mums."

"Of course I know it. She went down twice, and you went down after you came home. . . ."

"Oh, but I didn't do anything, because Mike—" Lucy broke off, pretending to be very busy selecting a gown for her mother.

"What about Mike?" asked Miss Anna.

"Well—well, you see, dear—he didn't want the bed changed or anything touched until he had seen it."

"Why?"

"I don't know."

"Lucy . . ."

"Well, really, I don't. He said it made a difference where the—the bleeding was—but I don't know what difference."

"All right, then, dear, tell me the whole story as you do know it."

Lucy sighed. "Doshie called Meg, and Meg found that Karen had shot herself, with Doshie sitting right there on the side of the bed talking to her."

"Shot herself? Oh, dear!"

"Doshie feels just awful, Mums. She says she had not said anything to upset Karen—that Karen, without any warning, except to say something about Doshie's hating her, pulled this gun out from under the pillow and shot herself."

"Where? And don't tell me in bed."

"Mums!"

"Well, I've been coddled all day, and by now I'm a bit crazy myself."

Lucy knelt down beside her mother. "Do you think Karen is crazy, too?" she asked.

"Who else is crazy?"

"Oh, I meant do you, too, think that girl was—"

"Of course she was. To try to kill herself. Or *did* she kill herself?"

"No. No. Dr. Bowlin operated and saved her."

"Where did she shoot herself?"

"We should have told you, shouldn't we?"

"Of course."

"Well, she shot herself in the stomach. The belly, the doctors keep saying. They like that word."

Anna laughed. "It's a good one."

"Doshie sent for Meg—Meg called Mike. He said to send Karen to the hospital and not to touch anything in the room. At the hospital, they said he was very particular about the wound—how it looked, its size, place, and so forth—before they did surgery, you see, and changed things. He explained to Meg that blood stains on the sheets or on Karen's clothing would tell the direction from which the blood came, whether the patient had been moved, or whether the blood on things was that of the patient, or—or—"

"Did he think that Doshie might have shot the girl?" asked Anna calmly.

Lucy stared at her mother. "She didn't!"

"I only asked . . ."

"Yes, and you are being pretty cool about it, too."

"Look, my pretty girl," said Anna. "I read dozens and dozens of whodunits. I suppose the police were called."

"Oh, yes. I think Mike gave them orders, too."

"He would. You say Dr. Bowlin saved her life?"

"Yes, but it was a big surgical job, from what I can learn."

"Will she recover?"

"I asked that, and the answer was that, physically, she should recover."

"And . . . ?"

"Well, Mike says he thinks he is going to insist on a mental evaluation. Do you know what that means, Mums?"

"I expect the doctors do."

"I took it to mean that she could just as well have shot

Doshie instead of herself—that she is, and may be, dangerous."

"Poor girl, poor girl," murmured Anna Goheen.

"Mike talked about her—I suspect he's said the same things to the doctors—in their staff meetings, or wherever they discuss cases. He seemed to be seeking causes and perhaps placing some blame—"

"When did you see Mike?"

"This afternoon while you were resting. He places significance on the *Playboy* magazines which Louis Chambers keeps on the coffee table in their living room. He said, and I agreed—I've heard her, too—he said that he remembered how, even several years ago, Doshie would talk about birth control at the dinner table. He said that, as the girls grew up, sex was as familiar a subject in that house as arithmetic."

Anna nodded. "I remember when Doshie used roosters and pullets and fertilized eggs for sex instruction to those girls. They weren't but children."

"It's considered to be the proper thing. . . ."

"It *is* proper at the right time and without the over-emphasis . . ."

"Doshie overemphasizes everything."

"She does," agreed Anna. "I presume she mentioned morality."

"She did. I remember the way she talked. But it was too much, too continuous."

Her mother nodded. "It was. And Mike is right. Those girls, when they first reached adulthood, had come to consider human sex as being a common, farmyard thing. You cannot preach freedom of sex without risking an interpretation of license."

Lucy brushed her mother's hair soothingly. Mike had remembered the chickens, too. "He went on to say that a girl, lightly experimenting with premarital sex, is not always prepared for the physical and mental repercussions of its consequences—that it can bring her world tumbling down about her ears, which it certainly did for Karen."

"And Doshie," said Anna sadly.

"Yes, of course. And Judith, too."

"Judith has a boy friend," said Lucy's mother, with rising interest.

The brush paused. "No!"

"Well, of course she has. She told me. She wants me to let him come here—"

"But—"

"Doshie should let her bring him to their house. And I shall tell Doshie so. It's right for Judith to have boy friends, to see them in her home, and not meet them outside. Doshie should want to know these boys."

"Oh, Mums . . ."

"I'll talk to her. And maybe Mike can use some of his evaluation on her, too."

"You'd better talk to him, perhaps."

"I shall."

Lucy got her mother into bed and was ready to turn out the lights when Miss Anna again spoke of the day's tragedy. "This is a terrible thing, Lucy," she said mournfully.

"Yes, dear, it is. Doshie has a hard time ahead of her."

"Is she staying at the hospital?"

"No. Mike won't let her. Of course she's there as much as he will let her."

"You went to the hospital while Meg was reading to me."

"She didn't want to go. And I thought one of us should tell Doshie—well, that we were ready to do anything we could."

"Did you see her?"

"Yes. She was—crushed. Louis was more calm."

"Of course. And Mike talked to you."

"Yes, he did. You know, he's really wonderful, Mums."

"I know it. I tried to talk to Meg about him today."

"Oh, Mums," Lucy protested softly.

"I am as concerned about her as I am about Karen, Lucy, dear. Our girl is in trouble."

Yes, thought Lucy. Yes, she is.

"Have she and Mike quarreled?" Anna asked.

"Oh, no, Mums," said Lucy quickly. "I don't believe they have. For one thing, who would ever quarrel with Mike?" His tall presence, his handsome face, his sunny hair, his earnest blue eyes . . . His kindness, his—

"You girls," Anna was saying, seeking a comfortable spot for her shoulder, "have always looked on Mike as a god."

Lucy laughed. "You should see him at the hospital, Mums, in his white clothes, tall as trees, coming toward you; he walks with long strides, and the light shines on his hair. You'd think he was a god, too."

"No doubt, no doubt," murmured Anna. "How is he getting along at the hospital?"

"I should think fine. He seems to be in great authority."

"I meant—is he going to get his interns?"

"I'll bet on it. He has a way about him—you should see the nurses; every one of them is in love with him."

Anna laughed. "Just like the Goheen girls, eh?"

"Well—"

"You know what I think? I think Mike may have proposed to Meg, and she turned him down."

Lucy shook her head, her soft hair flying up and out. "Oh, no, Mums!" she cried. "She wouldn't do that."

But even as she spoke she knew that Mike could have asked Meg to marry him—and under the circumstances, she definitely would have said no—and been deeply shaken by the development, too.

Her mother was watching her. "All we know," Lucy forced herself to say lightly, "is that she wouldn't go on a date with him."

Her mother's eyes twinkled like blue stars. "So he took you. And you liked it?"

Lucy pouted. "Well," she said ruefully, "I wish he had had other reasons for asking me. I felt at the time, and even more now, that I shouldn't have gone to the city with Mike when I knew he'd rather have Meg. I should have—"

"When I was young and at a premium," said Doyle Goheen from the doorway—he had overheard the last part of their conversation—"girls took their chances where they found them. That's how your mother got me."

Anna's laughter was as merry as Lucy's, and the Dean's rumble joined in warmly—so warmly that, for the briefest second, Lucy almost succumbed to her wish to confide in her parents. She would tell them about Meg's "trouble" and get them to help. . . . But, swiftly, almost too abruptly, she went out of the room. Anna gazed solemnly at her husband. "Sometimes, Doyle," she said anxiously, "I feel that Lucy may be in more trouble, greater trouble, than Meg."

Doyle Goheen found something to adjust in the window draperies. "And what trouble is that, my dear?" he asked.

Anna sniffed. "I didn't marry a stupid man," she said with vigor. "So—who is this in my bedroom?"

He chuckled and came over to the bed and took her gnarled hand gently in his. "I'm just nonstupid enough," he told his wife, "to know that I—that we—cannot live their lives for our grown daughters. The best we can hope for, my darling, is that they will let us share the lives that they choose for themselves."

"But lately . . ." Anna protested.

"Lately a door has been closed, yes. If we are patient, it will be opened again. Or perhaps another door. Meanwhile, we wait, and watch, and are ready."

"We could . . ."

"Perhaps we could help them. Certainly, we would try. But only when we are asked, dear. Only then."

Had Mums asked Lucy if she had talked to Mike about Meg? Lucy couldn't exactly remember, there had been so many wayward and disturbing currents in last night's bedtime conversation. Lucy did not like having to be so careful of what she said. . . .

But it was a good idea to talk to Mike about Meg. Heretofore Lucy had avoided it. Or perhaps Mike had? Anyway, she couldn't think of a single reason not to talk to him. Of course, she couldn't, specifically, but she could ask him for suggestions as to how to get Meg back into the flow of life. These days she was like a woman carved in stone. There was no response!

The idea was quickly and easily put into action. As soon as she could—breakfast out of the way, Mums up and dressed—Meg asked to make the beds upstairs and straighten things—would she, please, darling?—Lucy picked up the telephone, dialed the hospital number, and asked if she might speak to Dr. Tryon, please? This was Miss Goheen speaking.

The voice at the other end said, yes, Miss Goheen, she would try to locate Dr. Tryon. Would she hold?

"I'll hold," said Lucy contentedly.

It took five minutes, perhaps even a little longer. Lucy waited. And finally Mike's rich voice boomed in her ear. "Hello! Tryon here."

"Oh, Mike," breathed Lucy.

"It's Lucy, then," he said.

"Yes. Of course. Because I want to ask you to come to supper this evening. Can you?"

"Party?"

"Goodness, no. It's baked beans."

"Then I'll come. Time flexible?"

"Sure, with beans."

"I'll be there. Thanks, Lucy."

"O.K. How's Karen?"

"Holding her own. This will take time, you know."

"If you say so, I know. I'll see you, Mike."

"Sure."

Lucy hung up the phone and considered her dinner menu. The beans, of course, with a chunk of pork loin baked with them. A good green salad. Rye bread or brown bread? Perhaps whole-wheat muffins and tart plum jelly. She'd make the lemon pie which Mike loved.

Meg said nothing when Lucy told her that Mike was coming for supper.

At four that afternoon, she set the table, then said she was going to the library and would take Chorley.

"They won't let him in there . . . Or will they?"

"Chorley is a well-read dog," said Meg, taking the poodle's leash off the hook.

"Don't get to reading and forget the time."

Meg shook her head and lifted the green bag of books which she planned to return to the library. "I'll be back in an hour," she promised.

It was a chill, misty day, but Chorley was happy to go for a walk, even on a leash. He greeted everyone they passed with a wide grin and lay down obediently on the tiled floor of the lobby, where Meg fastened his leash to the hook which held the doors open in warm weather.

"I mustn't forget I have Chorley with me," she said to herself as she went into the library. "I mustn't forget . . ."

She had found that she must make such reminders to herself. She could, quite easily, become so bound up in her stony aloofness from people that she forgot herself as a person. And it was not fair to a dog—or to Lucy—for her to let the animal lie forgotten on the lobby tiles, or permit Lucy's dinner to be delayed too long.

"I mustn't forget . . ." said Meg, going from the desk to the stacks. She would select her books and not sit down to look at anything. That way—

At five, Mike came in from the hospital saying that he had walked down. He got paper towels from the kitchen

and wiped the moisture from his hair; he hung his raincoat on a hook. He kissed Lucy's cheek, took a cookie
from the brown jar, went to kiss Miss Anna Go-*heen!* and
then he sat down at the piano.

"It's only fair to warn you I am going to play," he
announced.

"Did you ever learn *Anitra's Dance?*" asked Lucy innocently.

Mike made a face at her. He played for twenty minutes
or so, talking to Miss Anna as he did, and to the Dean
when he came in. When Lucy's muffins began to perfume
the air, he went back to the kitchen.

"Where's Meg?" he asked forthrightly, perching on the
stepstool. His finger delicately lifted a bit of crackling
crust from the crock of beans which Lucy had set on the
cutting board to "rest" before serving.

"She took Chorley to the library. If she doesn't come
within ten minutes, I'll call and have her sent home. She is
pretty forgetful these days."

"She's pretty something these days," Mike agreed.
"What's wrong with that girl, Lucy?"

"I was going to bribe you with lemon pie to tell *me.*"

Mike looked at her, puzzled. "Don't you know?" he
asked. "How long has she been this way?"

Lucy bit her lip. If she could only tell Mike the whole
thing! "Well," she said slowly, "its been a couple of
months."

"Since I came home."

Lucy sighed. "Yes, but—"

"I don't think I've said or done anything, Lucy."

"Well, you'd know," Lucy told him.

"That's right. However, the girl must have had some
severe trauma."

"That's a hurt."

"It's a hurt—a bruising hurt. For a while there, she
seemed panicky—"

"You're smart, Mike."

"I'm a doctor, and I love Meg. Now, let's see what we
have. She suffered a trauma—we don't know what?"

Lucy looked into the oven.

"She still doesn't talk about it," Mike continued, "but she
no longer runs. She has forced herself to endure the fact
that people are around her. She isn't exactly in communication with us, but she endures our presence."

"That's right," said Lucy. "She sets herself a schedule and works to stick to it."

"Does anyone ever get through to her?"

"Sometimes. But then she does run away."

"Mmmmm," said Mike. "And of course she is drinking."

Lucy's eyes flared. "How did you know that?"

"You said I was smart."

Lucy agreed. "Mums knows she does, too. It hurts Mums."

"Of course it does. Have you told Meg . . . ?"

"I've protested, but I don't push her too hard, Mike. Or should I?"

Mike ran his fingers through his thick hair. "I don't know, Lucy. If the girl would talk to me, or if we could get her to see someone she *would* talk to—" He glanced at Lucy, who was shaking her head. "I'm greatly disturbed about Meg," he concluded.

"Oh, yes!" breathed Lucy. "And if we could only— You will try to help her, won't you, Mike?"

He shrugged. "I certainly will," he agreed. "If I can. Just how . . ."

"I don't know, either," Lucy confessed. "You could see her as often as possible, maybe."

"*You* see her every day."

"I know that. But I'm not you."

He laughed, stepped to the floor, and put an arm around Lucy's shoulders. "That's good!" he told her.

"Meg's good, too, when she's herself."

"Yes, she is. And I'll see what I can do. The drinking's no help, probably. What about sleeping pills?"

"I don't think so. At first I gave her a couple."

Mike swung on her. "When *at first?*" he demanded.

Lucy backed away, her fingers spread across her mouth.

"You've promised not to tell, haven't you?" he demanded roughly.

"I—she came home one night—in a state. As I say, I haven't wanted to push her."

"For fear she'd leave. All right, Lucy. I'll still do what I can. Do you think I should go after her?"

"Maybe. It's dark." Lucy took the car keys from their hook. But before Mike could get his raincoat, Meg's step and voice were heard from the back porch.

"Don't shake, Chorley!" she was enjoining the dog.

Lucy got dinner on the table by the time Meg had taken her coat and books upstairs and had come down again. The meal went well, the food was delicious. Mike told Miss Anna and the Dean as much as he could about Karen Chambers.

He ate two platefuls of beans and four muffins—he greeted the lemon pie with an enthusiasm which made even Meg smile. "I hope you baked two," he told Lucy.

"Well, I didn't. And you couldn't hold it if I had."

"Oh, yes, I could," Mike assured her. "Look—no belt. And this sweat shirt has miles of room."

"You'll make do with one piece of pie," she told him sternly.

"But I can come back for a cold bean sandwich tomorrow?"

"Yes," she agreed seriously, "you may do that."

"It was the pie and the cold beans," Mike told the family, "that made me decide I would stay on here at the hospital."

"Oh, *Mike!*" There was pleasure all around the table. Mike was looking only at Meg.

"Are you going to get your interns?" she asked him.

"Yes. And I've cleared the way for the research I want to do."

"But that is simply great!" cried the Dean. "We all are glad, Mike. I hope both you and the medical school—and the hospital, of course—will find it a good decision."

"What sort of research are you going to do?" Anna asked him.

"I have two or three projects. One is how to be sure Lucy makes me a lemon pie twelve times a year. The second is to establish enough evidence to let me get medical examiners for this state and rid of the politically appointed coroners that now handicap us."

"Our coroner is elected," said the Dean.

"You bet he is. And the one in the next county, too. *He's* an undertaker. *We* happen to have a so-called doctor. He couldn't make a living at his profession, so he must be pretty bad. And I learned the other day of a woman who got the job after her husband's death. Last month a man fell down a well shaft, and she decided he had had a heart attack, with no examination, no autopsy— She just said he had an attack and fell."

"If he didn't have one . . ."

"An autopsy would have shown that, Miss Anna. And his family then could have collected accident insurance as well as workmen's compensation."

"Oh, dear. You are worked up about this, aren't you?"

Mike laughed and sat back in his chair. "I'm worked up," he agreed.

"But getting rid of coroners isn't your first interest," Meg told him.

"No," Mike agreed. "It isn't. Oh, I'll work at it. I feel very strongly on the subject. I look at the position of coroner from a scientist's viewpoint; I don't think this delicate field should be entered for any other reason than science. I don't think we should have undertakers or druggists or anyone who can't do an autopsy, and interpret it, one who overlooks valuable evidence and often unwittingly destroys the same, who has no knowledge of, or respect for, modern laboratory facilities.

"But you're right, Meg. I'll get most worked up about my third research project, which is in the field of viruses, and I am counting on you to take charge of my lab on that."

Lucy saw Meg's face light up for a brief second. "Oh, yes!" she cried. "Meg could do that."

"Indeed she could and should," said the Dean loudly.

"It's the sort of thing she's always wanted," Anna assured Mike.

"And it's what she schemed to do before you came home," said Lucy brashly.

Mike was still looking at Meg, but by then she was again stonefaced. "Lucy's joking," she said stiffly.

"Why, I am not!" cried Lucy, determined to reach Meg. The way the girl had fired at Mike's suggestion . . . "You studied biology and messed around with smelly frogs and stuff—your hands smelled, too. And every now and then you would say, 'When Mike comes home—' By home, she meant the whole United States, Mike—and she meant she would go into your lab, wherever it was, and run things. Which probably could have meant running you, too."

Mike laughed. He would give Lucy an "E" for her effort. "I'd like that," he told Meg. "How about it?"

"She should do it," said Meg's mother. "It is absolutely the right thing for her. And it's a good thing she gave up her job at school, because now—"

Mike leaned forward. "What's this?" he asked. "When did you give up your teaching job, Meg?"

"Didn't you know that she had?" asked the Dean.

"No. When did you do it, Meg?"

She sighed and said something about his wanting some more coffee. But Mike was not to be turned aside. "You were teaching when I came home. I remember telling you that your skirt was too short for a schoolteacher, and you said— Why in the devil did you quit, Meg? Or, if you did quit, and have been available all this time, why aren't you already working with me?" He spoke roughly, his voice was raised.

In another time, Meg would have answered him in kind. She would do what she pleased, she would have said, when she pleased, and she was not about to ask Mike Tryon what she could do.

In another time.

Mike had expected to strike some sort of spark, Lucy felt sure. But it did not work. Meg dropped her chin upon her chest, and her fingers rubbed along the handle of her fork. "You'll need to get someone else for your lab," she said, her tone cold. "I definitely will not work there."

"You'll have to earn your living somewhere, won't you?" Mike demanded, leaning across the table toward her.

She did not look up. "I plan to find something," she said —still in that low monotone.

Mike sat back in his chair, but he continued to look sternly at Meg, his head tilted to one side, his mouth pressed tightly closed. His eyes studied her concernedly, consideringly. That's the way he probably looks at a patient, Lucy decided. Mike was so absorbed that it seemed, for a minute, that he would not respond to Doyle Goheen's attempt to change the subject.

But then Mike glanced at his host. "You asked me about Leonard Keel," he said, noticeably picking up the subject offered to him. "Well, I'll tell you, sir. He's another problem, and a large one. The man needs a heart center's care. His need became desperate two days ago; we were set to move him, but he also began to show signs of picking up a pneumonia. God knows where he got that! We have him in complete isolation, under oxygen—"

"Only a doctor says 'a pneumonia,' " commented Lucy.

Mike glanced at her and smiled. "We are trying to get a

specialist," he continued, "an artery specialist, to come here to consult, and perhaps operate on Keel. We have the equipment, but those chaps like to stay with their own crews, and they keep busy—so busy that a gap of thirty-six hours means that several of their own patients must be put off. That means our chances for a specialist aren't good. The pneumonia may take a week to clear up; by then Keel could not survive moving, we feel sure. So it seems that Bowlin may have to do the job."

"Is he able?" asked the Dean.

"Oh, yes, sir. Entirely able. As a surgeon, that is. To date he hasn't done much heart surgery for us. He doesn't yet have his own crew organized and trained. . . . Then, I'd think he would be handicapped by the personal complications which exist."

"Poor Bee," murmured Lucy, who was refilling the coffee cups. "She's such a darling."

"Yes, she is," Mike agreed. "And a first-class doctor, too. I wish she had stuck with her career instead of marrying Leonard Keel, though her career gave her something of a wallop only this morning."

His audience was interested, and he noted that Meg's head had lifted.

"I am speaking out of turn, of course," he warned. "But the situation offers some interesting possibilities."

"We won't gabble," Lucy assured him.

Mike smiled at her. "I knew that before I spoke. Well— you see, Bee does some pediatric surgery—tonsils, heman-giomas—things of that kind. This morning she was taking out tonsils, and her patient—an eight-year-old girl—suf-fered a third-degree burn from a hot metal gag which was put into her mouth."

"Oh, dear!" cried Anna.

Mike nodded. "You bet it was oh dear! Things really popped around there. The resident nearly had a stroke. He did go into mild hysteria. The patient's family are the precise sort to sue the hospital, the surgeon, the instru-ment nurse— Just let some lawyer get hold of them and talk to them. We can only pray he won't be smart enough to sue the circulating nurse."

"Was she to blame?"

"Yes, she actually was. And remember that promise not to gabble! Bowlin's taken her off o.r. duty, of course, because it was her job to have a basin of water available with which to cool sterilized instruments—and one was not in place this morning."

"Was the child . . . ?"

"She was burned, Miss Anna. Which makes for a sore mouth and throat, apart from the usual tonsillectomy soreness."

"Were the parents told?"

"Oh, yes. They are ignorant people; they hardly are able to comprehend why a gag is used—but they'll understand one was used, and that it was too hot, that it burned their little Mirabelle—and they'll talk about it. That's where the lawyer will come in."

"Looks as if Bee might need Leonard," drawled the Dean.

Mike nodded. "If they don't name the circulating, the others have a good chance to come out of this. But it was a nasty thing, all around."

By talking this way he had won some attention from Meg, but directly after the meal, when the family rose from the table, she went upstairs and stayed there.

"You're going to have to help me wash the dishes," Lucy told Mike, fetching him from the Dean's study, where her parents were settled. "Meg's run out on me."

"I'll help you," offered the Dean.

"I'd rather have Mike," Lucy assured him pertly. The Dean laughed. "I hope my feelings shouldn't be hurt."

"They shouldn't be. We won't be long."

"Meg sulking?" Mike asked, following Lucy back to the dining room.

"I told you—when pushed too far, she runs away."

"How far is too far?"

"She knows. I don't. I am really worried about Meg, you know."

"Why not? I am, myself."

"I know you made her that lab offer this evening in an effort to help her."

"Like fun I did. I need her. I had asked her before— and then she told me that she had a contract with the college. Now—you were right. She did train with the thought of helping me. We used to talk about it."

"I know you did," said Lucy. "And she used to glory in the advantage which her education gave her over me. In our bid for your interest, you know."

Mike smiled, but only faintly. "She used to do a lot of things," he said, "that she doesn't do at all now."

"I know. That's why I wanted to talk to you."

Mike carried the heavy tray to the kitchen. "When I considered coming back here to work," he told Lucy, "a big item of my consideration was that I would have Meg to help me in my lab. My work is such—just anyone couldn't carry on in a way to relieve me for my duties as Chief of Medical Services. Her refusal will present a real problem to me."

"Then you really do want her help. I mean, you weren't only being kind to her."

"I'd like to help her, all right, but— She was interested, Lucy."

Lucy put on her apron. "I know she was," she said.

"If she's the scientist I think she is . . ." Mike mused. "In science, you know, pretty one, and certainly in medicine—there's not too much room for personalities."

"Oh, Mike, she doesn't feel . . ."

He nodded. "I'm just poison," he said. "But I suspect other people—other men, maybe—are poison, too. The thing is, she should be able to forget the people with whom she works in her interest in the work she would be doing."

Lucy thought about that. She scraped plates and filled the sink with hot suds. "About personalities," she said, offering Mike a dish towel, "aren't you concerned about Meg—because she *is* Meg?"

"Oh, yes," he agreed. "Yes, I am. The girl could be sick, Lucy. Do you think there's a chance we could get her to the hospital for a check-up?"

Lucy shook her head and put a glass into the drainer. "No chance at all," she said.

"But—"

"I've suggested it to her."

Mike polished the glass.

"You say medicine has no room for personalities," mused Lucy. "But earlier you mentioned the personal angle which makes things hard for Dr. Bowlin, and Bee, and of course Leonard. . . ."

"There still isn't room for such things," Mike pointed out.

"No, but they are there, just the same. And don't a lot of people have such angles to cope with? Your child who was burned—the fact that her parents are ignorant and vulnerable to the bad lawyer—"

"I see what you mean. And of course you are right. We all do have personal problems."

"That's right. I see it everywhere. Even among the little nursery-school children whom I teach to sing. There's one child who tells me he can't sing—that his Daddy sleeps in the daytime and he can't be noisy."

Mike chuckled.

"It complicates his school life," Lucy assured him. "And there's a young man in the church. He's been offered an advance in his job, but it involves travel; he thinks he can't take it because his wife is afraid to stay alone at night."

"That girl needs a spanking."

"She does. We can see that she does, but the nice young man— Then, of course, there are the Keels and the problem presented by the fact that Bee and Tony love each other."

"I think they really do."

"So do I. And so does Leonard."

Mike nodded. "He told Bowlin that he'd be a fool not to operate and kill him."

"Oh, Mike."

"He said that. And Tony intensified his hunt for a specialist."

"Honestly! *People!*"

"Which was the subject of this thesis, wasn't it?"

"If I know what thesis means. Yes, it was. Then—we mustn't forget the Chambers family, must we?"

"I don't believe we can. Because there is such a clash of personalities in that family . . . Doshie keeps saying that she always treated her girls as intelligent."

"She did. Mums said that she wouldn't allow them to talk baby talk."

"And she gave them sex instruction when they were four."

Lucy nodded and worked for a silent, thoughtful three minutes. Mike caught up on the drying and watched the girl. She was thinking so intently that he could fairly see the wheels spinning.

Lucy was thinking. She was wondering if she could discuss Meg's case with Mike by doing it hypothetically. Their talk had got away from Meg. So if she would seem to talk about girls like Karen—and Judith— She would give it a try!

"You take a girl," she said, "who thinks she knows all there is to know about sex. She's been taught in her home and at school—maybe she has studied enough science—and if you would ask her, she'd say she understood exactly what the birds and the bees were up to. She would be quite calm and aloof about it, seemingly accepting the development as a natural phase of life, something due to be experienced as one's years went along." Lucy's blue gaze lifted swiftly to Mike's face. He was listening. She hoped she was not being too clumsy. If she were, she would give the whole thing away—

"All right," she said. "Then—all of a sudden—just like that!—this smart girl gets violently exposed to the thing for which she had thought herself prepared—and—well—it is violent—and shocking—and—well—she experiences shock. I've used that word too much, but it's what I mean." Oh, dear, she was being clumsy! And she probably had told Mike Meg's secret, and—

But Mike thought she had the Chambers thing still in mind. "I may be wrong," he said gravely. "I wasn't at home at the time. But my impression has been that Karen was not subjected to forcible rape. Was she?"

Lucy gaped at him. *Karen?* She'd not been talking— She clutched at her poise and self-control. She'd been pretty darned hypothetical, it seemed.

"Oh, *Karen,*" she said aloud. "No, there was nothing forced—she had been dating the boy—they had gone steady for several months. The shock to her came when she found herself pregnant and had to tell Doshie."

"I see," said Mike. "And Doshie—"

"Well, she just blew up all over the place. She insisted on a wedding. One minute she wanted it done in the next state and a notice put in the paper. The next she wanted a wedding in church, and she got that, though Karen did not want it. She carried lilies, I remember, and cried during the ceremony. And we could all see Doshie's sigh of relief when the minister pronounced them man and wife."

"The marriage didn't last, evidently."

"Oh, no. The boy—he was just a kid. He kept playing high school baseball—they lived with Doshie and Louis—and Karen lost the baby in the fifth month—and, well—the boy's family engineered the divorce. It was a great mess. But, since then—instead of Karen's going back to school or getting a steady job—she's been depressed. She's quarreled with Doshie—it's been hard on Judy, who was growing up."

"And now," Mike concluded, "though I suppose Doshie's intentions have been the best . . ."

"Oh, they have been!" agreed Lucy. "Meg said she was overprotective—"

"Well, whatever she was, or failed to be, the situation now has become a matter of psychiatric help for Karen. . . ."

"Will Doshie . . . ?"

"Lucy, my darling, Doshie is not going to be in control of that girl. Not for the time, anyway. We find Karen to be a deeply disturbed person. The shock of the initial experience may have been the first cause, as you suggested. We can't risk further bungling."

But Lucy had been talking about *Meg,* not Karen! Were the cases so alike? Was Meg also "greatly disturbed"? Would "further bungling" cause Meg— Would Lucy's own well-meaning and loving intent cause harm instead of help to her sister?

Mike was saying something about the state authorities. Lucy turned her troubled face toward him. "You don't mean the police?" she asked. "Do they have to be involved? In Karen's case, I mean, of course."

There was a flash in his blue eyes. Later she was to remember it.

But that night—he watched Lucy transfer the remaining beans to a smaller casserole. "The police are the instruments of enforcing the state's authority, dear. There are laws about guns, you know. When someone is injured from a gunshot, it becomes a possible crime."

"Oh, but she—"

Mike smiled at her. "Yes! She was disturbed," he agreed. "She shot herself. But she could just as well have shot Doshie—and killed her. Therefore Karen is considered to be dangerous, and when she recovers from her injury and the surgery, she probably will be moved to a state institution where . . ."

"Oh, that would kill Doshie!"

"She would be upset. But I think Doshie is not so easily killed. Meanwhile, of course, we'll do some work on persuading her—and you, it seems necessary—that such a transfer, the availability of such care, would be a good thing for Karen."

"How?"

"Well, they do some very good work. Their rehabilitation record is excellent. They almost certainly will be able to do for Karen what her mother could not do."

"You mean she will recover? Mentally, I mean. Or—well—you know what I mean!"

Mike laughed. "It takes doing, sometimes. But, yes, they'll seek to adjust Karen to the point where she can handle her own problems."

"Maybe Doshie should go along."

"I am going to suggest some psychiatric adjustment to Doshie. But I've no way of forcing her."

"She's meant well, Mike."

"I know that, and I'll tell her only that her sense of direction needs guidance. There's Judith coming along, you see."

Yes, Lucy did see. "Doshie herself says she doesn't know just what or how to do with Judith. Oh, Mike, you bully Doshie! Will you?"

He laughed. "I'll do what I can."

"I think," said Lucy, vigorously scrubbing at the bean crock, "that if Doshie will let her alone, Karen will get well."

Mike shrugged. "These things, you know," he explained, "almost always—not only in Karen's case, but in almost all cases of mental shock and disturbance—recovery nearly always depends on what the patient is able to do within herself and for herself."

Lucy rinsed the bowl and gave it to Mike. "That is the last dish," she told him. "Thank you for helping."

He had helped. He had given Lucy an answer to her questions. If she now could *use* that answer and pass it along to Meg. For surely, surely, Meg could help herself!

CHAPTER SEVEN

AN HOUR LATER, when Mike went back to the hospital, he saw Tony Bowlin's low sports car parked in the Keel driveway. He whistled softly—if Bowlin had been there long, the neighbors would have plenty to talk about. Not that they needed anything. But still, with her husband so ill, Bee should be more discreet.

Within minutes, as he walked along, Tony's car passed him, so perhaps the call had been a short one. Perhaps he had brought Bee from the hospital and gone into the empty house with her. The hour was not late. . . .

Tony had not brought Dr. Keel home. He had eaten dinner at a restaurant, and then had stopped at Bee's on impulse. Bee would still be upset over the tonsillectomy mishap of that morning. Tony must find out how well-versed she was in forensic medicine. Their hospital was a new one, and he had already talked to the o.r. personnel on the subject. He and the Administrator had decided that they must prepare themselves for trouble, whether it developed or not.

Bee was glad to see Tony and offered him a drink. "Though you shouldn't stay," she said.

"I shan't. I came to talk about the gag mishap this morning. We have to decide what to say, if anything, about that."

"Mhmmmmn," said Bee. "I hope the neighbors understand why you are here."

The Keel living room was blue. Bee was bundled into a large, fuzzy white robe, and she sat in one of the blue armchairs beside the fireplace. Tony fixed his drink and took it to the other chair. Hung on the chimney breast, there was a painting of bright flowers, and against the blue shutters of the wide window ivy, growing from a series of white pots, made a delicate, bright tracery.

Tony sighed. Someday, he had hoped that he and Bee
. . . He smiled across at her. "I can say the devil with the
neighbors!"

She shrugged. "They get the message without your saying a word."

He had not touched her.

"I came about Mirabelle," he said again. "And to tell
you that I think we have Leonard's pneumonia about
cleared up. That means, in a couple of days, I am going to
send him to Barnes." He sipped his drink, the ice cubes
tinkling.

Bee rubbed her fingertips together. "He won't go,
Tony," she said, her tone weary.

"He'll have to go. And this flare-up has shown us what
we already knew—that it is not safe to delay surgery."

Bee leaned her head back against the blue brocade cushion, and her eyes studied the man seated across from her
—Tony Bowlin, lean and brown and exciting. Six months
ago he had come into her life. She was the one member of
the new hospital staff who knew the town and the university people as well. She—and Leonard—had undertaken to
make the new Chief of Staff feel at home. They had
entertained; Bee had taken him to the city and introduced
him to the medical people there; she had shown him the big
hospital complex.

She and Tony had interests in common. His passion was
fly fishing and Bee was good at that; she took him to
Leonard's cabin on the Bourbeuse, she took him to the
bank of their own river—this involved a picnic lunch and
a long afternoon in the sun and shade of the riverside.
They talked. They liked the same music, disliked the same
sorts of books. They disagreed earnestly about politics and
agreed joyously on food. Dr. Bowlin was a kind and
thoughtful man; she had never had this from Leonard.

In the hospital, the surgical chief made full use of Bee's
abilities; he admired her as a doctor as well as a woman.

One morning in July, on the golf course, he had stood
up to Leonard Keel when the attorney had endeavored to
put on one of his famous scenes, attacking the "new doctor"—and indeed all doctors—in his best sardonic vein.
Leonard had found himself well matched, and Bee was
jubilant.

Her friendship with Tony warmed. "Why did you ever
marry such a character?" Tony had demanded of her.

"I was young—and had been the sort of sheltered girl to whom brutality can seem glamorous."

"Does he mistreat you?"

"He can no longer hurt me, whatever he says."

"You deserve better than that." And Tony had set out to show her something better. Bee was a wonderful person; she deserved—

The town talked. Leonard talked about the situation, too. "I think I've lost my wife," he told a half-dozen people.

"I hope he's right," was Tony's comment when this was repeated to him.

Bee made plans to divorce Leonard.

And then—Leonard had become ill—desperately, almost hopelessly ill.

"He is going to make you operate," Bee told Tony this night. "And you are not to do it. It is too much to ask of you."

Tony finished his drink and rose. "I have Leonard's consent for surgery," he told Leonard's wife, "and if we can't move him, I am afraid I shall have to operate."

"Tony—"

He smiled back at her from the hall. "Don't worry," he said.

That same evening, after putting her mother to bed, Lucy had gone upstairs to her own room and found Meg drunk. This was the first time . . .

Lucy knew that she often took a drink at bedtime. But to find her sister sprawled across her bed, her hair and clothing disheveled, her face—

Lucy was torn between panic and disgust. At first she closed the door of Meg's room—she would not have a thing to do with such behavior.

But by the time she herself was ready for bed, in red-piped white pajamas, her hair tied away from her face, Lucy was sorry for Meg. She endeavored to rouse her, and did get enough mumbling response that she could undress her, wash her face, and get her into bed. She then searched the room and confiscated the two bottles of bourbon which she found. Next morning perhaps they would have a showdown.

Now she smoothed Meg's dark hair and felt heartbreak for her sister. That same evening, she had, though obliquely, talked to Mike about Meg. Now, and soon, she must come right out and demand his help. It might be necessary to tell him why she so desperately needed help. If so, she would tell him—as much as she had to.

The next day she went to the hospital to see Karen if allowed, to sit for a time with Doshie, and to ask at the desk if it would be possible for her to see Dr. Tryon.

No, it was a personal matter. . . .

As she waited, she saw a man come up to the desk—he was called "Doctor"—he seemed familiar, but she was not sure. She didn't think she would forget such a person, because he was most attractive, perhaps forty years old, with a strong, hard-bitten face, the skin of it as brown as Tony Bowlin's. His brown hair was smoothed back on his head, and there was a streak of gray— He had a crisp, determined manner. Lucy became so intrigued with the stranger that Mike had to touch her arm to get her attention.

She laughed in confusion, and explained.

Mike nodded. "The competition around here gets worse and worse," he declared. Then he lifted his voice. "Miller," he said to the man who was bending over some papers on the counter. He looked sideways at Mike, then straightened and came toward him. "Lucy," said Mike, "this is Dr. Hubbard. Miss Goheen, Miller, and what are you doing in my hospital, interesting my girl?"

Dr. Hubbard held out a long, lean, hard hand to Lucy. "You know, of course, that one could not avoid Tryon's girls." His voice vibrated. Lucy liked him!

"I've raised Mike from a pup," she said. "I know all about him, good and bad. Are you on the staff here, Dr. Hubbard?"

"No. I teach in the medical school here, but I hang my staff hat at Engert."

Engert was the state cancer hospital.

"Oh, but that's close enough," said Lucy. "Mike must bring you to the house. And your wife, too, of course."

"When I get one," said Dr. Hubbard, his gray eyes smiling. "Thank you, Tryon. You have good taste."

Mike made a huffing sound and took Lucy's elbow. "Theoretically I am a busy doctor," he told her, guiding her down the hall.

"He's nice," said Lucy, looking over her shoulder. "Have I seen him before?"

"I don't know, but I'll lay a bet you'll see him again. He evidently thinks you're nice, too."

Lucy gave a little skip of pleasure, and Mike chuckled. "If you came to see me . . ." he suggested.

"I didn't. I came to see Karen, and Doshie. Then—I thought I'd ask a favor of you, Mike. If you weren't too busy—" her pretty face sobered—"I—I needed to see you."

"Well, maybe I needed to see you. I like my girls to wear woolly pink sweaters," he told Lucy. "And I like to take them away from guys like Miller Hubbard . . ." He bent over and looked intently into Lucy's face, then his finger tipped up her chin. "Hey!" he said. "What's wrong?"

She began to twist her fingers together. "Oh, Mike," she said. "I was only pretending back there at the desk. I pretended with Doshie, too. But I'm afraid this pretending isn't going to be possible much longer, and—"

"Something's wrong," he said. He pushed against one of the flat doors. On it his name was painted in gold letters. Just DR. TRYON, but somehow that looked more important than a longer title, and—

Lucy stumbled a little as she crossed the threshold. She looked about her curiously; she would want to tell Mums about Mike's office. It was—nice. The carpet was dark blue, the desk silver gray, on the wall there was a crayon study of a dancing woman.

Mike stood against the wide window and watched her, his forehead puckered with concern. "What's happened, Lucy?" he asked gently.

She looked up at him, her eyes dark behind their thick lashes. "Oh, Mike!" she breathed.

"Sit down . . ." He led her to the long couch; she sat down on it, and he sat beside her. "Tell me."

"It's Meg," she said. "Last night—when I went up to bed —she was drunk, Mike. Sodden, foolish drunk! And this morning she looked awful, and felt awful. . . ."

"Of course. Did this happen because I—what was your term?—because I pushed her too far last night? About her working with me here, you know."

Lucy pleated her fingers together in her lap. "No-o," she said. "I think it was because she wanted dreadfully to do what you asked. And—she couldn't."

"Why couldn't she?" Mike kept his voice quiet.

Lucy just shook her head.

"Any reason," he said, "must be in her mind."

Lucy glanced up. "Suppose it is?" she asked. "Isn't that as bad?"

"Yes," he agreed. "Yes, it is."

Will you help her, Mike?"

"Of course," he said quickly. "But how, Lucy? I mean, what can I do?"

"Oh, there would be ways. If you would come often to the house—and maybe take her places."

"She won't go. I've tried that."

"She let you show her the hospital. I think she'd go—the three of us. Nothing elaborate. Times when Dad could stay with Mums. Or, I'm planning to ask Doshie to sit with her —Mums thinks that would help Doshie."

"It would. And I'll try to drop in often, and I'll try to take Meg places. I'll agree that she needs to think of something besides whatever it is that is troubling her. But I'd sure as taxes like to know what *is* troubling her."

Yes, and he had a right to know, but—just now, at any rate— "She has something on her mind," said Lucy lamely.

"I can see that. How long has she been this way? I mean, were there signs of it before I came home?"

"No."

"I couldn't be to blame . . ."

"Oh, you're not! That's why I asked you to help. Meg has always been crazy about you."

"All right. So she was her normal self when I came home. And—what happened then, Lucy? At that time?"

"She—" said Lucy. "She changed. She cried a lot, then she withdrew into a box, or shell . . ."

"And she began to drink."

"Yes. But last night was the first time . . ."

"I asked you about sleeping pills. Are you sure . . . ?"

"I don't think she's taking any, Mike. She told me she drank so she could sleep, but—"

Mike got up, went to the window, and looked out at the hospital grounds. It was a sunny day, with a brisk wind tossing the trees. "All right," he said finally. "If you've promised Meg you won't tell me what happened to her."

"I—" said Lucy. "She asked me to promise."

"I figured that. And I'll try to work around it. I'll see

what I can do, because it so happens that I'm crazy about Meg, too, Lucy."

"I know."

He came and bent over her. "And about you," he said softly.

A raindrop tear slipped down Lucy's cheek. His finger-tip caught it and wiped it away. "We'll think of ways," he said. "I'll drop in—there's my cold bean sandwich for this evening. I'll try to get her to walk Chorley with me. Another time we'll go to see Doshie—and Bee— You can run out of mustard at suppertime . . ."

"Mustard?" asked Lucy, half laughing, half crying.

"For your famous hot dogs. Of course."

"There really is something—if you could get away," Lucy told him. "Next week—there's to be an important dinner in the city—a party—at the cathedral. At the hotel, that is. It's for the new dean, and Meg was on the commit-tee who chose him—she really should go—and would, under other circumstances. Now she's saying it's too much of a drive for two women alone—she means herself and me—and she won't plan to go."

Mike went around his desk and looked at his calendar. "What day?"

"Thursday. There's a reception—cocktails, I suppose—and then the dinner. Those things are always fun. We welcome the dean and his wife, and he gets to know the church people."

"Do you and Meg usually go to these things?"

"Yes. And, well, I thought—of course it would mean half of the afternoon and late into the night—maybe there would be someone else . . ."

Mike smiled at her. "I rate a twelve-hour break," he said. "I'll try to plan it, Lucy."

She stood up. "Oh, Mike, if it would only work—"

"It's worth a try," he said. "You be getting Meg into the mood."

"She's contrite today. Maybe if I'd ask her now . . ."

"You do that. And I'll be around for that sandwich this evening."

It was managed, though not too easily. Meg at first flatly refused to consider the trip. Yes, she then admitted, she supposed she still was on the standing committee—but—

well, perhaps she could go— It did seem to mean so much to Lucy—

Lucy enlisted her parents' help in the project. They said they would welcome a long evening alone. "Our honeymoon cottage gets a bit crowded at times," they told their daughters.

Lucy did not stress the matter of clothes. The dinner was to be held at the hotel across the street from the cathedral, and it would be beautifully staged, but delegates would come from all over the diocese. There would be tweed suits as well as glittering dinner gowns and cocktail dresses. Lucy's blue suit with the lamé blouse, and Meg's oyster-white wool, would be just right.

If Lucy could hold her sister to their plans until they were on their way . . .

It was not easy. Beginning Wednesday night, Meg developed a dozen reasons for her to stay at home. She had a run in her last pair of sheer stockings—she had a headache— Didn't Lucy think Dad had a cold? (He had sneezed once at dinner.) The weather—

The weather was perfect, and Lucy stayed right with Meg. At two o'clock of that afternoon, she and her sister dressed. There were aspirins in Lucy's purse for headaches— Besides, they would have a doctor along.

"Oh, Lucy . . ."

"Mike needs to get away from the hospital," said Lucy, "to get clear away where he can't be reached by telephone. He'll have a wonderful time."

Meg finished dressing. Would they need hats?

"No. There's to be no service at the cathedral. It's just a party."

There were other small items—which coat Meg would wear—where she would sit in the car. Lucy made a thing of insisting on sitting next to Mike. "After all, I arranged this whole safari. Meg, you take the window."

Meg had been planning to sit in the back seat. . . .

On the drive, Lucy chattered about the changes which the new highway had made in the trip to the city. She and Mike reminisced about other trips, in other times—and before they had gone fifty miles, Meg was arguing a point or two.

When he picked them up, Mike had found Meg looking white and a little grim. But the main thing was: she was there, on the way to the city, and the party. She looked nice—not as pretty as Lucy, whose cheeks were pink and her eyes shiny with excitement and pleasure in this achievement, but Meg looked all right.

"One of us should stay with her," Lucy told Mike when they came into the hotel and Meg announced her intention of going straight to the little girls' room.

Mike caught at Lucy's arm. "Let her alone," he advised. "She'll hunt us up if she feels the need."

"All right." But Lucy still thought she needed to go up to the little girls' room, too. And she did go, to find Meg talking with almost her old animation to a group of women she had found there and whom she knew.

She and Lucy knew a lot of people who were at the party. It would not have been practical, really, for the three of them to stay in a group. The Bishop wanted to talk to Mike about India. The dean's wife, who had a sixteen-year-old daughter, asked Meg about the college; Lucy talked to some of the women who were acting as hostesses at the cocktail hour. Regularly, she sought out Meg—

"She's being actually gay!" she told Mike triumphantly, pointing out her sister across the room.

"Let's join her," said Mike.

The room was crowded, a dozen people spoke to them and detained them, but eventually they came up behind Meg, who was making a group of people laugh hilariously over her account of the way a parish dinner could be in her own small town.

Meg looked wonderful. Her eyes shone, and her cheeks were flushed. She gestured with the glass which she held in her hand, and sipped from it, and talked—

"The Bishop visits us once a year," she was saying. "Not more often, thank the dear Lord!" From a passing tray, Meg exchanged her glass for a full one. Lucy began to frown.

"There must be a service, of course," said Meg, "for confirmation. And there must be a dinner. He tries to evade the dinner; he changes the time of his visit—but, before the service, or after the service, our church will not be denied. We give him a *dinner!* Now, in our town, there are places where one can eat professionally." She too laughed merrily at the word. "But I mean it!" she insisted. "We have a country club, we have two decent restaurants, we could use the cafeteria at the college. But, no! St. Swithin's in the Fields must put on its own dinner. And in the cellar, if you please." Meg drained her glass.

"All right, all right," she conceded. "We proper Episcopalians do call it the undercroft. But it still looks like a cellar and smells quite a bit like one, too. The reason we hold the party there is because the children can come, and the theory is that the Bishop wants to see the children. Which well may be, but I doubt if he appreciates their racing and running and shouting about the hall, their— Well, let's forget the children. We have a dinner to set up. And of course we must do the Bishop proud. There must be a head table. And we won't go into the jockeying that goes on about who is to sit at that head table. The Bishop does, we all agree on that! And of course our plain white tablecloths aren't good enough, so someone brings a white lace cloth—in the cellar, mind you—and someone else puts a pink bedsheet under the lace. And a third woman proudly produces a pair of candlesticks—these are butane-fired, of all things, so forget the pink wax tapers. There is a flower arrangement—

"Some loyal member thinks the plain white tablecloths of the faithful should also be adorned, so she brings in a stack of bright plastic place mats—in all the liturgical colors—which she scatters down along the tables. The rector's wife says they look awful, and takes them off. This precipitates a battle which should be told about in Crécy!

"Now! It is my belief that the Bishop should always come to the church the night before his official visit if he really wants to know how his parishes are getting along! He—"

"Let's get her," said Mike to Lucy. "She's stoned."

By the time Mike could put his hand on her arm, Meg was telling about the food brought in covered dishes to the dinner, and her listeners were convulsed with laughter.

"Do you realize what seven casseroles of green beans can look like?" she demanded. "And do you want to be the one to say whose casserole should be placed to the front of the serving table? Do you . . . ? Oh, hello, Mike."

Mike smiled at her. "There's someone I want you to meet," he told Meg, his grasp firm upon her arm.

They got her away, but very soon dinner was announced, and Meg was the one to lead the way to the dining room. She didn't want Mike "pawing her," and he dropped his hand from her arm. "Lucy," said Meg, "why don't you sit with your friends? We certainly see enough of each other at home."

Lucy fell back a step, and Meg marched into the big dining room—a gold room, indeed, that night, with golden candelabra, golden and crystal chandeliers, golden bowls of flowers. She went unerringly, proudly, the length of the room, pausing just once to steady herself by the back of one of the gold and brocade chairs—then she went up the three carpeted steps, and along the table—

"Mike, *stop* her!" cried Lucy. "That's the head table . . ."

It was the head table. The new dean would sit there, the Bishop—and their wives—the speakers for the occasion—and Meg.

The dean spoke to her, the Bishop did—her chosen chair was between theirs. Lucy, in agony, saw the Bishop's wife—a sweet woman whom the whole diocese loved—unobtrusively leave the dais and, indeed, come to a chair at the same round table where Mike and Lucy stood helplessly watching Meg and wondering what they could do.

"Tell her!" Lucy said to the Bishop's wife.

"It's all right, dear. The dean will enjoy Meg."

"No, he won't," said Lucy grimly. "Oh, Mike . . ."

"I'm afraid she would make a scene," Mike told her. "Maybe now is the time for some prayers of our own."

"I hope they bring her coffee, but quick!" said poor Lucy.

She could not eat her own dinner, which was an excellent one. She watched Meg, thankful that wine did not seem to be on the menu. The dean was talking to Meg. "He must be a saintly man," Lucy told Mike.

"He's kind, of course. He and the Bishop both will recognize her condition. And there is your coffee."

Meg even drank some of it. She ate some of her dinner, too. And talked—a bit loudly, and much too lengthily. She gestured with her hands. . . .

And when the speakers took over, Lucy's prayers were answered. Meg slumped back in her chair and began to look sleepy.

"We'll get her out the minute this is over," Mike told Lucy.

"If we can. Now, if she'll just sit quiet . . ."

Meg did. In fact, by the time Mike came for her, she was only very tired.

Lucy had fetched her coat, and she had Mike's car

brought to the hotel's side door. Mike was gentle with Meg, and tender. She sat docilely in the middle of the front seat and dropped her head on his shoulder for the first forty or so miles. Now and then Lucy would speak, Mike would reply—Meg said nothing.

Then—"I miss going through the towns," Lucy was saying. "These superhighways get awfully monotonous. I'd rather—"

"I made a fool of myself," said Meg unexpectedly.

"Oh, dear Meg . . ." Lucy began.

"Yes, you did," said Mike bluntly.

Meg lifted her head. "I feel sick," she told him.

"You'll wait until we come to a turnout," said Dr. Tryon.

Lucy handed her sister a Kleenex.

"Were you ashamed of me?" Meg asked her.

"Yes, we were," said Lucy, borrowing from Mike's book.

Meg sobbed. "I'm ashamed of myself. Why didn't someone take me away from that table? Everyone watched me."

"Yes," said Mike.

Meg sobbed again.

When they reached the turnout, she said she didn't want to stop, she just wanted to get home. "But don't worry," she said loudly. "I won't take a drink. In fact, I don't plan to drink ever again. If I can be like that— I didn't drink so much."

"You drank too much," said Mike.

"You mean I can't hold it." Meg sat thoughtful. "All right. That's settled. And another thing—I'll stay at home. Rather than play the fool again in public, I'll stay in the house. I won't go out of it again." She put her head down again on Mike's shoulder and slept.

"That wasn't exactly what I had in mind," Lucy murmured to Mike.

"Don't worry."

Lucy sniffed. "I'm sorry I got you into this. Though what I'd have done if we'd come down, just the two of us . . ."

"Someone would have helped you."

"I'd have died."

"Michael, the lifesaver," he drawled.

Lucy smiled at him feebly. "You've been wonderful," she whispered.

"Will your folks be up?"

"I don't think so. It's after eleven."

They were not up. There was only the light at the front door and in the hall. Lucy unlocked the door; Chorley came from the kitchen, yawning and stretching. Mike brought Meg in, half carrying her. Lucy led the way upstairs, turning on lights as she went.

When Mike came down again, the Dean, in his bathrobe, was in the hall. "Meg sick?" he asked.

"You might say so, sir," said Mike.

"Ah-huh!" said the Dean. "Good night, Mike."

"Good night, sir. Hang on to the dog, will you?"

"I'll do that. Will Lucy need help?"

"No, sir." The Dean suspected what went on. "Meg is—is all right now. She fell asleep on the way home, and she was—groggy."

A spark flashed in the Dean's eye; Mike grinned, lifted his hand, and went out to his car. The Dean turned out the lights and went back to his bed. Groggy, indeed!

But it did make a man, a father, shake his head. To go to a church dinner— Their church was liberal, but surely not that liberal. . . .

Upstairs, Lucy changed from her own good suit to a robe, and then she went in to help Meg. She found her sister sitting on the side of her bed; she was weeping drearily.

"I'll help you undress," said Lucy, getting a gown from the chest of drawers.

Meg was docile and sad. "I am so ashamed," she said over and over. Lucy made no comment. She was trying to estimate how many hours of sleep Meg's troubles had caused her to lose since last October.

"I wish you could get a good look at yourself," she said to Meg, and harshly for Lucy.

"I am looking at myself," said Meg. "And I don't like what I see."

"Well, I should think not!" said Lucy, picking up Meg's shoes and putting them into the closet. She came back to the bed. "Get to bed now," she said more gently. "We'll talk tomorrow."

Meg was weeping again. Lucy bent over and kissed her cheek.

She left the doors open. Perhaps shame—perhaps any

feeling—would be harder on Meg than the iron-still stoic endurance which had held her for the past weeks. Lucy turned out her light and determined to sleep, but how could she with the sound of those muffled sobs . . . ?

Despair could be bad. Karen had despaired. And what if Meg should try suicide, the way Karen had done? Lucy stiffened in her bed. But it was true! Karen had brooded and been ashamed . . .

Oh, dear, oh, dear! As silently as she could, Lucy slipped out of bed and went to the door of Meg's room. Meg lay as she had left her, still weeping.

What could Lucy do to prevent her sister . . . ? She had been trying to do things for Meg. Tonight—poor Mike. Lucy had really got him into a mess. He had been so kind —and so firm with Meg. He had looked so fine in his dark suit, and Lucy had, with the best intentions in the world . . .

Hell paving. That's what she had been doing—and probably what she would go on doing. Hoping that she could help Meg, and prevent—

Shivering, Lucy crawled into bed again. Poor Doshie still thought she could have done something to prevent Karen's— Could she? Could she?

The next day, Lucy was tired, and she had a dozen things to do. Meg, to her relief, came down for breakfast looking pale, but dressed, and even ready to offer to help Lucy.

She could, said Lucy. "It's my morning at the school, and I should try to find Mums a new housecoat. If I could eat lunch downtown . . ."

"Go ahead," said Meg. "I'm no good at housework, but I'll try. What is there to do? Beds, dishes, lunch—what else?"

"That will do it," said Lucy. "I'll put a wash through while I'm getting Mums dressed. Then I'll take off."

"Fine," said Meg indifferently. "Lucy," she said then, "about last night . . ."

"I'd rather forget last night, if you don't mind."

Meg nodded. "I don't blame you. But I would like to repeat the promise I made. I won't drink any more."

"All right, Meg."

"I really don't drink so much . . ."

Lucy disappeared down the steps to the basement. She really did want to forget the session in the city. She filled and started the washing machine and went up to dress her mother. She told Anna about the party. Yes, Meg had seemed to enjoy herself. The food was good—stuffed chicken breasts, asparagus—cherries jubilee—

She went upstairs to change into a suit, she came down. Meg said to take her car—which, once she was out on the street and looked at her watch, put Lucy a good half hour ahead of schedule. Not quite enough time to do any shopping, but enough that when she went up the hill and around the road, she could stop at the Observatory and, sitting in the car, somewhat organize her work with the children.

The day was a gray one, but not really cold. Lucy didn't need the heater if she closed the car window. Doing this, she realized where she was, and her hand went back and across to lock the car doors.

Curiously she looked across the cleared space to the old shingle-covered Observatory. The wart, the college girls called the small, round building. And this was where—

Not since that night had Meg been willing to drive along this road. The place looked peaceful enough. The roadside grass was brown, dry. There were still some leaves in small, rusty heaps. The branches of the tall trees reached upward like pencil scribblings against the sky. Down the hill there was a fine view of the town and the river—

But here, in this quiet place where squirrels ran about and flipped their plumed tails, and a downy woodpecker hammered against a tree trunk, was the turning point in Meg Goheen's life. Lucy, too, could feel some of the sinister quality of the place. Here had happened so much that was violent, and tragic, and final.

To be a gay and joyous young woman, then turned so swiftly into one who was desperate with pain and shock, and—and—lately, numb endurance. And how long would Meg endure this thing which had been put upon her? For weeks she had seemed not to try to get over her tragedy. But hadn't she? Had not mute acceptance, wooden endurance of pain, been the only way to survive it? If not, what other way was there? At least, Meg had struggled for pride. She avoided people and the chance that they would do something or say something that would tear open the wound which she was hoping might heal. There were times, of course, when she had tried to escape memory—

Could Lucy blame her?

But how long must she suffer so? How long must she

encase herself against hurt? Would memory last her whole life? Must she, for her whole life, find ways to dull that memory and to cover it over? Surely it would not take so long! Pain, it was said, was soon forgotten.

Mike said Meg's help must begin with her wish to help herself. Or, in talking about Karen, he had inferred that. Was he counting on Meg's being clever enough—and she *was* clever! Meg had a brilliant mind! Surely, and very soon, too, she must find a way to build a new life for herself.

When she had first suggested leaving home, and had repeated the offer a time or two since, Lucy had protested against departure. But maybe she was wrong. Lucy, sitting there that morning thinking about it, was ready to decide that she had completely bungled things with Meg.

If Meg went away—far away—and found herself a job, a whole new set of friends—people she didn't know, and who had not known her—

But, good heavens! No one here in the Heights knew what had happened! No one but Lucy and the man—that awful man!—and, of course, Meg herself. Meg's own behavior did make her friends suspect that something had happened. Doshie had mentioned it. Mike asked about it. Mums and Dad—others, too, were concerned.

Why, they asked, had Meg given up her teaching? Why didn't she play golf any more? Or go bowling? Why wouldn't she play duplicate bridge, as she had done for three years? Was the girl sick?

And being told nothing, they answered their own questions. Yes, she must be sick. She looked bad. A breath or two of what else they were saying had reached Lucy. People—Meg's friends—were concluding that she had suffered a nervous breakdown.

Had she? Was she still suffering one? Lucy didn't know enough about the illness, nor its symptoms—but Meg *was* suffering—from shock.

And anything as big as a nervous breakdown must be started by something that could be called shock. A woman disappointed in love, a man faced with failure, and—Meg.

The familiar terms were all there to be used. Shock. Attack. Violation. More hateful ones, too, were apt. Thinking of them, Lucy must nod her head until the blue scarf slipped from her hair and had to be brought up again and tied into place.

What had happened to Meg happened to other women —to young girls, to women in their homes. One read about such things in every newspaper, just as one read about murder and dreadful accidents—drowning, an airplane crash. All crippling events, if not fatal ones.

One read, shook his head, perhaps clicked his tongue against the roof of his mouth— Was each of these tragedies as great a personal shock as had been Meg's? Did families suffer, and friends wonder—and the person herself find life ruined?

Or was it special with Meg, that life should have stopped short for her, that she—?

Yes, of course it was special. Meg's pride had been ravished as well as her body, and such an experience was devastating, to be borne, perhaps, but not soon to be forgotten. Recovery to a normal way of living could not come quickly. Not for Meg.

She had always done things well, had always been in control of her life. She had made good grades at school, she had played games well, she had been popular. Failure of any sort was unfamiliar to her. She could have no basic understanding of her will's being overruled, her wishes being opposed and denied.

Not lately, but a time or two at first, Meg had said that logically this attack should have happened to Lucy. That it could have happened to her, inferring that Lucy was the prettier young woman, that she was more desirable to men.

It was not a good and solid argument, but Lucy might do a little thinking on the subject. What if the attack *had* been made on Lucy Goheen, back there in October? What would she had done, what would she be doing now, what would she want—to help her through the experience?

Would she, too, have tried to destroy all evidence of its happening? Would she have tried to suppress all thought of it? Or—

Lucy knew what she would have wanted. She knew it loud and clear. She would have wanted all the love and assurance available to her. She would have gone directly to her father, her mother—to Meg, and to Mike, for their sympathy and understanding and their help. She would not have liked the experience, the shame of it—but the enveloping warmth of their love would have helped her and in time would have healed her.

In Meg's case—she had told only Lucy, and it was only Lucy who could help her. Lucy had tried to be kind. She had tried to be wise. But was she giving Meg the love and unquestioning loyalty which Meg had a right to expect?

Oh, Lucy had listened to Meg; she had spent sleepless nights suffering for her and with her. She had attempted to argue her sister into resuming her normal way of life. She had enlisted Mike's help and they had bullied Meg into going to last night's affair, where she did not want to be and where—Lucy had been cross with her. Putting her to bed at the end of the disastrous evening, she had been blunt instead of wrapping her in love and sympathy.

Meg must know that Lucy did love her, but Lucy should say so over and over. She should praise Meg and encourage her. She had done some things for the girl, but not enough—not nearly enough. And she would do more.

She would really try to understand Meg and to be sympathetic about her situation. Or, which might be more important, she would just be sympathetic to the girl and love her.

Last night, for instance, she could have slept with Meg, put her arms about her, let her sob out her grief and frustration, knowing that, above all else, she had Lucy's love.

These opportunities did not present themselves too often, but when they did—

Besides that, Lucy would talk more specifically to Mike —and to Mums and Dad. Those three were wise and tolerant. They would accept the fact of Meg's problem and would stay with her in any attempt she might be willing to make to solve it.

Lucy would encourage a few friends, enlist their help. She would let them come to the house, she would see to it that Meg saw them and give them a chance to get her back into bridge playing and the redesigning of the golf greens.

Lucy, glancing at her watch, bent forward and started the car. She should be getting to the school now. The squirrel flipped his tail at her as she passed, and a nuthatch ran down the oak tree.

The church and the school were two blocks down the hill. There the rector, Father Finlinson, was out in front trimming the shrubbery with a pair of hedge clippers. He was a tall, lean man, kindly and understanding. If Lucy could only coax Meg to talk to him. She could even tell him her secret and know that it would go no further.

Could Lucy herself perhaps talk to the rector? Because she needed help, too.

She parked the car and gathered her music books, the kazoo which she had brought with her, the envelope filled with black-paper musical notes which she had made and cut out on Sunday afternoon—the whole notes, the grace notes, the sharps and flats. Watching her, the Dean had said she was cutting out paper dolls, and he was going to appeal to the new psychology professor at the college.

Could Lucy perhaps go to that man and ask *his* advice? She had met him, and she was pretty sure he would leer at her and decide that she was the one involved—which would be hard to take, but Lucy might try it.

Then—who else was there? Well, there was her father's friend and crony, Donald O'Hara, attorney at law. There, too, she would find the protection of privileged communication if she would present Meg's problem to him, but Mr. O'Hara would insist on trying to find the rapist. . . .

Lucy sighed and hung her coat on the rack in the school hall. The children were being noisy that morning. She would have no further chance to think—but she needed no more time. Any of these people, if approached, might offer some help. So—she would use them and their help.

That afternoon, when Lucy went home, Meg came out to the drive to help carry in the groceries which she knew Lucy would have bought. "Doshie is visiting," she told her.

Lucy glanced at her. "Trouble?"

"With Doshie there is always trouble."

"Is she upsetting Mums? I mean, did Mums get her nap?"

"She lay down for an hour. I fed her shirred eggs for lunch."

Lucy almost dropped her bag of oranges. "*You* shirred eggs?" she asked.

"I did," said Meg. "You have a whole row of cookbooks. I can follow directions. The kitchen may be considered a laboratory . . ."

Lucy shook her head. Then she looked more keenly at her sister. There was something about Meg . . . "How'd they turn out?" she asked. "The eggs?"

"We ate 'em. But we decided that you were the cook of the family."

"Good. I wouldn't want to lose my job. But, thanks, Meg. I really appreciate what you did."

Meg nodded and held the door open for Lucy to go in. "A man called," she said.

"Oh? Who?"

"He said his name was Miller Hubbard, and that he would call back."

Lucy put the meat and the ice cream away. She took off her coat. "He's a doctor I met at the hospital," she said.

"Probably wants a date."

"He's nice. You'd like him."

Meg sniffed. "I'll stay with Mums while you have the date," she offered. "Mums says she is getting used to my awkwardness. She finds it interesting to see what I'll do next."

Meg *was* in a different mood—a better one, and Lucy would not question it, even if she had the time. "Let's go in and take over Doshie."

"They are in the study."

They were in the study, Doshie on the couch, Mums in her wheelchair beside the small table where she kept her quilt-making supplies. Dr. Bowlin had fitted her hand with a brace which made it possible for her to hold a needle. She lifted her face for Lucy's kiss. "It's nice to have you home again, dear," she said.

"I hear Meg's been cooking."

Her mother laughed. "That isn't why I'm glad."

"I know. Hello, Doshie. How is Karen today?"

Doshie sighed. She wore a yellow sweater and brown skirt, and her hair was rather wild upon her head. Lucy stifled a sigh of her own. She supposed Doshie's problems also could take a little love and sympathy.

"Karen's doing all right," said Karen's mother. "They let her sit in a chair today. But, of course—" She lifted her shoulders and smiled wryly.

"Today Doshie is worried about Judith," said Anna Goheen.

Oh, dear. "I haven't seen Judith lately," Lucy said lamely.

"Nobody sees her," said Doshie. "She has a boy on her mind."

"Oh, yes, I did hear that she had a boy friend," said Lucy. "Who is he?"

"I loathe the term," Doshie said bitterly.

"Well—I'm not fond of it, either. Mums, what did one use to call a boy when he got interested in a girl?"

"A beau," said Anna, fitting a pink patch to a white one. The new brace helped a lot.

"We called 'em dates," said Meg.

"We called 'em boy friends, too," Lucy countered.

"You, maybe," said Meg.

Now this retort was a change! Lucy risked a smile toward Meg, who was sitting in her usual low chair and ready to smile, though uncertainly, back at Lucy. For goodness' sake!

"Who is the boy?" she asked again.

"Oh, he's Franklin Perry," said Doshie. "He's a town boy. He's Judith's age, but still attends high school. I think he plans to enter the university next year."

"Why, I know him," said Lucy. "He works at the paint store part-time and goes to our church. He wants to learn to play the organ. So far he's terrible, but I tell him to keep trying."

"And you let him practice," accused Doshie.

Lucy tucked the red velvet cushion between her shoulders. "Well, yes, I do, Doshie. The boy is earnest . . ."

"I discovered that Judy went to the church with him yesterday. That's why I came here today. To tell you—"

Lucy whistled soundlessly. "To tell me I couldn't let him practice?" she asked.

Meg was watching her; so was Mums.

"Well, something like that," said Doshie. "I know you would want to help me."

"If you need help, yes, I would," Lucy agreed. "But telling Franklin he can't . . ."

"Oh, it's not his practicing. I want you to tell him not to take girls with him into that empty church—"

Lucy's eyes sparked. "What empty church?" she asked.

"Well—"

"You should know more about our church, Doshie. It is never empty, except maybe in the middle of the night. The parish hall adjoins it, and the school is there. The Girl Scouts meet in the undercroft, *and* the Boy Scouts! Somebody practices on the organ, or the junior choir has a

138

rehearsal, or a bunch of women are polishing the altar brass, or—"

"All right," said Doshie. "And they see Judith go in there with that gangling boy—"

"Most boys of eighteen do gangle, dear," said Mums. "Judith has cut her hair, Lucy."

"Oh, has she?" cried Lucy. "Does she look nice? I'll bet she does if it shows her cute kitten-face."

Doshie sighed. "I thought you would help me," she said wearily. "You must know how terrified I am about Judith."

"Why?"

"Oh, Lucy!"

"Well, I mean it. Judith seems a very nice girl."

"A very nice girl who happens to be sneaking out to keep dates with a boy."

"Why does she sneak out, Doshie?" asked Mums.

"I told you. To see this Franklin Perry. He's tall and thin, and he wears black-rimmed glasses, and I don't know what appeal he has. But the minute my back is turned—"

"In the first place, you do know what appeal he has," said Lucy. "And isn't Judith going regularly to her classes at the college?"

"Well, yes, but—"

"She sees young Perry after hours—in the late afternoon or evenings. He doesn't have a car, I happen to know."

"No but—"

"Why does she have to go out to meet him? Why don't you let him come to your house?"

"Every evening?"

"If that's what they want, yes."

"Louis would have a fit."

"Oh, Louis. Besides, he isn't home every evening. And when he is—you could let the kids have the family room and the kitchen. Not just Franklin, but all the kids who want to come. And you should make them want to come. If you'd provide some sources of fun . . ."

"Oh, Lucy, these days . . ."

"Yes, I know. You're tired after your trips to the hospital and your worries about Karen. But Judy could get the records and the Cokes and the snacks—if you'd tell her—" Lucy sat forward on the deep green couch. "Doshie," she said, "have you ever sat down with Judith and had an entirely frank talk with her about Karen?"

"Well, I've seen to it that she knows . . ."

"I don't mean the sex part. I mean a talk about what is happening to that girl now. You might even mention your loss of communication with Karen, and how it has brought hurt to the girl as well as to you. You could show Judith what Karen has lost."

"If she ever had it," said Doshie bitterly.

Lucy looked to Meg and Mums for help.

"There's no reason why Judith couldn't have the things Karen has lost," said Mums quietly. "I think Lucy has given you some good advice, dear."

"Oh, she'll think I'm trying to keep her at home."

"Well—"

"She knows I am suspicious of her."

"And that you don't trust her."

"Mrs. Goheen, if one of your girls had got into trouble —" Lucy felt the hair rise on her forearm—"wouldn't you have worried about the other one?"

"Perhaps, but I'd do everything I could to help the other one. And I'd hope that she would know that I trusted her."

"I trusted Karen."

"Karen is one problem. Judith is another."

"And one I probably won't solve either," said Doshie miserably.

Meg sat straight up in her chair. "Personally," she said briskly, "I can't see why you don't let life be simple for the child, but if you can't, why don't you ask Father Finlinson to help you with Judith? A while ago you were telling us how kind he has been, how wonderful he is with Karen, that he gets her to talk and even to laugh."

"Oh, yes, but that's with a patient in the hospital," Doshie pointed out. "And he has been good to her. Now that she's crazy." Her face settled into lines of protest. "He never did much of anything for her when she appeared to be like other girls."

"Oh, Doshie!" cried Lucy.

"Did you ask him for help?" demanded Meg.

"The whole town knows Karen's story."

"But you are not members of his church. What could he have done for the girl? Come to her in a way to show that the town talked about her, that he believed the stories and didn't trust her?"

"You said for me to talk to him about Judith."

"That makes it different," said Meg. "I was suggesting that *you* go to him with *your* problem."

Doshie sat thoughtful. "You mean, I have more troubles than my daughters. Well, I—"

Lucy sat back in the corner of the couch listening, hearing, and watching Meg. There was a change in her. Whatever it was, whatever it meant, Lucy must be careful not to do anything . . .

She had been surprised when Meg brought up Father Finlinson as a solution to problems so soon after her own planning to talk to the clergyman. He probably could have helped Meg, and the psychologist, and Mike, could have helped her as well. But more likely, appealing to them would not have helped.

Meg would have suspected, she would have known that Lucy had talked to them, and the knowledge would have crushed her completely. She would have— What would she have done? Left town was the most probable move.

This afternoon, talking to the rector about the music for Sunday's service, Lucy could have spoken of Meg. Then she would have come home, found this slight change, this new willingness on Meg's part to join in a conversation with others—only to have the good priest blunder in and show Meg— Yes, Meg would run.

Even Mike. Because he was a doctor and would not reveal what she told him, Lucy could have talked more freely to him than she had done. And he—he had always loved Meg—more than he loved Lucy, the younger sister had suspected. For years the two girls had joked extravagantly about their plans to "catch Mike." Mike knew it, and had played the game with them. Was he ever as serious as they were? Lucy thought that was likely.

Now—suppose she had told Mike the whole story about Meg? He would have been angry and certainly shocked. He would have been kind. But would he have, ever again, considered Meg as a desirable woman whom he might marry? Lucy did not really know how men felt about these things.

If there had been, ever, any seriousness for him in the girls' contest, wouldn't this revelation have hurt Meg's chances? Lucy had not, until this minute, considered that aspect. But wouldn't it change things?

And if it did change things, wouldn't the balance tip toward Lucy?

She put her hand to her cheek, which was hot. Doshie and Meg were still talking—her thoughts had taken only seconds, for all their important turn. She leaned forward and straightened a book which lay on the small table.

No! she told herself. Even if Mike were revolted at what had happened to Meg, he would not turn to Lucy. She would not "get him" in that fashion—not unless he loved her, had always loved her, and wanted her for his wife.

And certainly not if he guessed at the methods which she had used, or might have used, pretending that she wanted to help Meg.

The telephone rang, and Lucy went quickly to answer it. Glad to get away from her thinking for a minute which she decided to extend; she had the groceries to put away, she must freshen herself after her long day. She must begin her preparations for dinner. . . .

And, doing those things, she must, against her will, continue to think.

About Mike.

Poor Mike. The dear man had come home expecting to find two friendly and even loving girls waiting for him. He expected to be swept up, immersed, in their frank rivalry for his attentions. He was ready to enjoy that, and he even might have been ready to decide. . . .

But almost at once, he had found himself ignored as a desirable man, especially with Meg. The truth, of course, which he didn't know, was that all men had lost their desirability with Meg.

As for Lucy? Well, she had been busy these past two months. But of course she loved Mike, and she wished things could have proceeded in a more normal fashion. Even now, if he would ask her, she probably would say yes, she would marry him. But the shine was gone, and the fun. There would be no triumph, no excitement.

Because Meg no longer cared . . .

Didn't she?

Until last October, all had been fair in love and war. Now Lucy could probably get Mike by fair means, or not so fair.

And it would not be fair, pretending that she wanted to help— Did she want to help Meg? Or complete her destruction?

Scrubbing potatoes to put into the oven to bake, Lucy thought forward a bit to that destruction. It would not be —nice.

And did she want Mike at such a price?

Did she?

Mike . . .

Of course she wanted him! Since Lucy had been fifteen, she had dreamed of loving Mike Tryon and being loved by him. The thought of being in his arms . . .

Yes, she wanted him. In any way she could get him.

The declaration there made startled Lucy. She opened the cupboard door and looked at herself in the mirror which she had fastened there. She touched her yellow hair and the corner of her red lips— She didn't look like a witch!

But she must be one. And wasn't it a good thing that men only guessed to what lengths a woman would go to get one of them?

Lucy closed the door again. Well, she did love Mike. And she had feared, for years, that Meg's brains would have more appeal to him, a brainy man. But now—with Meg in her desperate protest against all men, defending the privacy of her own person—

Lucy ran cold water into the sink and began to wash the salad greens which she had bought that afternoon—bibb lettuce, iceberg, chicory—endive . . .

She filled a wire basket with the crisp green leaves, and then carefully, quickly, she carried it to the back door to swing it out over the calacanthus bush. Chorley pushed his bulk between her and the door jamb, and for a minute or two she stood there—he'd be wanting to come in again. It was beginning to mist a mixture of rain and snow.

Again, Lucy was asking herself how she would have felt, how she would have behaved, had the disaster been hers instead of Meg's. And—she took the next step—though wishing she could stop thinking at all—had it been Lucy, attacked and left ravished, what would Meg have done about her, with her, toward her? Would she have taken advantage of her sister?

No, Meg would not.

As things were, she had not used the event to her advantage at all. As kind, though puzzled, as Mike had been to Meg, she had not once played upon his sympathy.

All she had done, what she had done, was to cherish her

own pain, and figuratively, though somewhat literally, too, she had groveled about on the ground among all those scarlet leaves hunting for some remnants of pride with which to clothe her shame and go on living.

Chorley came back to the house shaking his coat free of water as he passed Lucy.

"I could have got *that* wet with my salad basket!" Lucy told him, returning to the kitchen.

While she was still working with her greens, Doshie called good-by from the front hall, and Lucy answered her.

"Shall I take Chorley out?" Meg asked, coming to the kitchen door.

Lucy shook her head. "He went out, got damp, came in."

"Mums wants to play cribbage."

"You play with her. I have these things to put away and dinner to start."

Meg disappeared. Lucy, looking around, verified the doorway's emptiness. What had she been thinking about? Oh, yes. Meg's pride. And about Mike. Whether he loved Meg or Lucy and—

The greatest facet of Meg's tragedy could well be the loss of her desirability to Mike. She believed in that loss. It could be a bigger reason for her despair than even the terror of what had happened to her. That "happening," she felt, had lost Mike to her—and she despaired.

Now this could be laughable reasoning, and old-fashioned—Victorian. But it was not puritanism. No. One could read about—in the Bible, in James Joyce or Mailer—and know about—in London, New York, and Laurel Heights—other moralities. But for the Goheens, and perhaps for Mike—they had their own standards of behavior.

Lucy's mother disapproved of drinking and would have no liquor in her home. Yet people seldom refused an invitation to the yellow house on the hill.

"Keep yourself precious." So the Dean and Anna had taught their young daughters. "Keep yourself precious for the man you will love and marry."

Yet no girl was ever so popular as clever Meg, except luscious Lucy with her wide blue gaze!

Meg had wanted, fastidiously, to remain "precious," and for Mike.

That was why she had been so anxious that he not know what had happened.

And Lucy had almost told him. Perhaps she had told him—which certainly was not her privilege nor her right to do. And now she must do no more. If she could not find a way really to help her sister, she should leave Meg alone. She must not spread the destruction by talking about it to lawyers, and ministers, and friends.

Meg could herself go to those people. She knew that they could and did help others. She had told Doshie to seek such help for herself and Judith.

Lucy nodded her head vigorously. Yes! She should stay out!

She heard her father come into the house; within minutes Meg again came to the kitchen door. "I'll set the table," she said. "Did your Dr. Hubbard call?"

"Yes," said Lucy.

"Did he want a date?"

"Yes," said Lucy.

"Are you going?"

Lucy reached for a pan from the shelf of a low cupboard. "I asked him to call back tomorrow. I'd need to see how things were then."

"What things?" asked Meg. "Where? And with whom?"

"Well—Mums, of course."

"And with me. If that's it, you go ahead. I'm all right. That is, I think I shall be. You're to go. Only—"

Lucy turned to face her. "Only what, dear?" she asked.

Meg smiled wryly. "Stay away from those cocktails. One can't trust the things!"

She disappeared into the dining room, and Lucy busied herself, slicing the roast. . . .

"I wish someone had warned me about them," said Meg, coming back to the kitchen for the salt and pepper shakers.

"Warned you about what?" asked Lucy, preoccupied with the amount of meat she would need.

"Cocktails," said Meg. "And things. Things like running away. Heads in the sand. And just—things."

Lucy gazed at her, her eyes a very dark blue. "And now you know?" she asked curiously.

"About cocktails, I do. Yes. I know about them. Though not much else. So don't count on me for too much." She went away.

Lucy put her slices of meat into the pan of bubbling gravy. She brought a package of frozen peas from the refrigerator. Meg came back to the door.

"Lucy . . ." she said timidly.

"Yes."

"It isn't easy for me to talk about—things."

Lucy nodded. "I know. It isn't easy for me either."

"For *you?*"

"Yes," said Lucy, dropping the cube of frozen peas into the steamer. "Yes," she said. "I keep telling you that you are not in this thing alone."

"Have you said that?" asked Meg. Lucy glanced at her. Meg stood in the doorway, her face thoughtful, puzzled. Then she sighed. "I'm going to try, Lucy," she said, her voice faint.

Lucy came across to her. "To listen to me?" she asked.

"I'll begin there." Meg leaned forward and kissed her sister's cheek.

Lucy gave her a little spank. "Let's not get sloppy," she urged. "Look! Tomorrow night, will you go with Dr. Hubbard and me?"

Meg stepped back. "No!" she cried. "No."

Lucy shrugged. "All right. It was just an idea. He asked me to go bowling, and you're good at that."

Meg began to walk away. Her face was confused. "No," she said in a smothered voice. "You go. . . ."

"Dinner will be ready in ten minutes," Lucy called after her.

Meg answered something. Lucy went to answer the ringing telephone. It was Mike calling.

"How's Meg?" he asked.

"All right," said Lucy guardedly.

"Really?" he demanded.

"Yes."

There was a pause. "Good," he said then. "I thought I might get over for supper, and I still may drop in later. You could save some dessert for me."

Lucy laughed. "Oh, I will," she promised. "It's Jello and oatmeal cookies."

"Lucy!" Mike cried in pain. "You wouldn't do that to me?"

"I'm afraid so," she told him.

"Then," he told her firmly, "I guess I'll have to find me another cook."

146

Lucy was still laughing when she went back to her dinner preparations. She put the cookies on a plate and set out sherbet dishes, to be filled later with the Jello.

Another cook, she thought. My goodness, she told herself, didn't it ever occur to you Goheen girls that Mike did *not* come home to marry one of you? He must have known a few ladies in all the places he's been—Boston, England, India—

She took her bowl of salad greens from the refrigerator and reached for the bottle of oil. Somehow she didn't think Mike had found another "cook" in India. . . . She reached for the vinegar, poured it carefully. Or in Boston . . .

He had come home. . . .

She went into the dining room and gave a five-minute warning to her parents.

Mike had come home. All over the world, just about everywhere, there were hospitals and medical schools where he could have worked. But he had come here, the only place where the Goheen girls lived. . . .

Meg came back to the kitchen, her face composed. "Did Dr. Hubbard call again?"

"No. It was Mike."

"Oh."

"He won't be over. He doesn't like our dessert."

"Not as well as lemon pie," Meg agreed, carrying the salad into the dining room.

Dinner was put on the table, the family assembled, grace was said, and the Dean made his usual little speech about leftovers being what made a roast worthwhile. His daughters smiled at him fondly.

"How was your day, Father?" Mums asked him.

"Just terrible," he answered cheerfully. He served her plate—the Dean liked to serve the plates from the head of the table and would gladly discourse on the sense of power this task gave a man. "The provider, the one who nurtures his family . . . I have a real problem," he declared.

"You always have several problems, don't you, dear?" asked Anna.

The Dean filled another plate. "Yes," he said consideringly. "I suppose I do. But this one—" He handed Meg her plate. "Do you remember the spastic we decided to admit last year?" he asked her. "We decided it last year, I mean, of course."

Meg frowned in an effort to remember. "Oh, yes," she said then. "She came this fall—I remember. She walked with the aid of two canes. Not a pretty girl."

"Not a pretty girl at all. And not of a good disposition, I'm afraid. But we decided we should make some concessions for her handicap, and we admitted her. We assigned her to a roommate who was ready to cooperate—but, oh, dear! Here you are, Lucy, my darling. And now Father gets what's left!"

His womenfolk laughed softly. He always said that, too.

"What's gone wrong with your problem girl, Dad?" asked Lucy.

"Oh, don't call her that!" he protested.

"I'm sorry—"

"She's a girl with problems, all right," said her father, his eyes twinkling at his younger daughter. "We've been quite patient—she gets priorities with the elevator—the washrooms, I understand—even in the cafeteria line— We are all sorry for her. But her roommate has told us that she simply cannot live longer with Kathleen. The girl won't bathe or change her clothes. She accuses her roommate and other girls in the dormitory of stealing her things. Did I say I had a problem? Of course we are all sorry for the poor thing, but—"

"That's your problem," said Meg, putting sour cream on her potato.

"Eh?" said the Dean.

Meg nodded. "Sure. You can't help anyone so long as you're *sorry* for them. The thing to do is to treat them as if you didn't need to be sorry. You'd crack down on another girl who was personally dirty. You'd investigate any accusations . . ."

The Dean sat back in his chair. "You're right," he agreed. "You're dead right. I'll have Miss Canda on the carpet tomorrow. So—what else is new?"

Each of her family was watching Meg. It had been weeks since she had spoken so vigorously, and— She must have known they were looking at her, but she gave no sign.

"Doshie was in . . ." she told her father.

The matter of Doshie's distress was then handled. The Dean said Judith was a nice girl and seemed hungry for friends.

"For opportunities to communicate," said Meg.

Mums sighed audibly with relief. Meg glanced at her, but said nothing.

Lucy asked if Doshie had brought any news about Leonard Keel. He would have to have surgery, Anna said. He refused to be moved, and when they called in a specialist, Leonard insisted that Dr. Bowlin should do the work. The specialist agreed that he could. . . .

"But Leonard is taking this stand to put Bee and Tony on the spot," said Lucy. "I must say that I think Tony Bowlin has behaved admirably throughout this ordeal."

"According to Doshie," Anna said, "he spent some time with Bee at her home one night last week—which was not discreet. The neighbors saw his car in their drive. And he must have opportunities to see her at the hospital."

"She's probably lonely, Mums. Leonard doesn't want her in his room."

"He doesn't have company of any kind," said Meg.

"Oh, but his wife—"

"I am sure Bee would do nothing at such a time to offend public opinion," said Mums. "I'm provoked at Doshie for telling this. She wants people to be kind to her."

"And they are," said the Dean, "as I am sure they are kind to Bee. But it does seem too bad that, here at Christmastime, there should be such a superabundance of scandal. When it centers—or whirlpools, rather—among our friends and neighbors, the peace of my home—and I am sure of theirs—is undermined and threatened. I resent this. I know I am old-fashioned, but I do wish—"

Meg leaned across the corner of the table toward him. "Dad," she asked earnestly, "what *is* scandal?"

The Dean put down his fork and touched his napkin to his lips. His eyes studied Meg's face—the dark, somber eyes, the pale ivory skin, her sensitive mouth—

"Is it," she asked, "disaster improperly handled?"

Her father pursed his lips. "Disaster invited perhaps?" he said.

"Oh, no!" cried Lucy. He must not say such a thing to Meg.

"If it is not invited," said the Dean, "it becomes, not scandal, but disaster only."

Meg sat back in her chair. "That can be thought about," she said.

After dinner, Meg offered to wash and wipe the dishes.

"We'll do it together," said Lucy.

"But if you have a date . . . ?"

"I don't. That's for tomorrow night."

"I wanted to help. . . ."

"You may help. You do help."

Meg sighed. "I know," she said with an effort that was visible, "that I have put an intolerable burden on you." She turned to face Lucy. "And have planted a mine under this nice home and family."

Lucy frowned. She shook the suds from her gloved hands and turned to look closely at Meg. "I don't understand, dear . . ." she said.

"You should. You surely see the long and tempting fuse which I have planted. Anyone can find it and light it."

Lucy shook her head. "I still don't understand."

Meg leaned forward and kissed her cheek. "Let's not give Dad anything more terrible than disaster," she said.

Lucy turned back to the glassware in her sink. Had Meg guessed that Lucy had been planning to talk . . . ? Had she, unwittingly, said something?

Should Lucy now tell Meg that she was not going to seek advice from others?

No.

She just would not do it.

CHAPTER EIGHT

CHRISTMAS CAME at the end of that week, and on the day after, Bee Keel was served notice of a lawsuit which had been filed against her for the injury done the child on whom she had performed a tonsillectomy. The charge was lengthy and involved, but to the analytical mind of the hospital's Chief of Staff, it said only that Dr. Keel's mind had been on other things, that she had been careless—negligent was the term.

"We can lick this sort of suit," Tony told Bee.

"But not the gossip which caused these people to file it. Oh, Tony—"

He shook his head at her. They were talking, two doctors, in the hospital corridor.

"I am glad there was occasion for gossip," he said softly.

"Law suits hurt a hospital!"

"Not too much if we settle quickly out of court. We can, now."

"If Leonard hears about it . . ."

"He need not hear about it. You won't tell him. . . ."

Bee took a deep breath. "I don't tell him much of anything. . . ."

"He's not in good shape today, Bee. You might look at him."

She did look at Leonard; he was in great pain, and she quickly hunted Dr. Bowlin. "Leonard . . ." she gasped.

The surgeon nodded. "Yes," he said. "There is such a great amount of back pain that it means we are going to operate."

"Not you!"

"Hush. You think about what you want to be for the next few hours—the wife, bolstered by her friends, sitting in a waiting room, or—"

"Don't talk that way to me!" Her voice rose hysterically. "If that thing dissects—the man can be dying!"

"Yes. He can be. He is. As he has been dying since Thanksgiving. Do you want to watch the surgery?"

Bee walked away from him, fighting for control. "I don't want him to die!" she cried tensely.

"He may not."

"He will. He will. And by doing it, he will destroy us both. Because, if you operate . . ."

"My dear," said Tony softly, "you are only making my job harder." He signaled to a passing nurse, a young woman, crisp and attractive. Bee would not let herself collapse before Miss Egger as she might have done with an older, more motherly nurse.

"Help Dr. Keel," said the surgeon. "We are doing emergency surgery on her husband *stat*."

"Yes, doctor," said the nurse.

Bee straightened. "I'll take care of myself," she said. "You are needed on the floor, Miss Egger."

The nurse looked at Dr. Bowlin for her orders. He nodded. "Will you observe?" he asked Bee.

"I will not. I disapprove of the whole thing."

Tony smiled a little to see the way she walked along the rest of the corridor, head up, back rigid, step firm.

"Get Tryon up to surgery at once," he said to Miss Egger as he passed her. He was walking fast.

Almost at once, Mike came up to surgery, ready to protest Tony's decision that he should assist the surgeon. "You have more capable men on the staff. Surgeons . . ."

Tony was into his scrub suit. "But you understand the situation better," he said gruffly.

"That's a handicap," Mike told him. "I don't think you should operate."

"Neither does Bee."

"But now you are going to do it anyway."

"I don't have any choice, Mike. And I would like to have you across the table."

Mike kicked off his shoes. "All right, doctor. Leave some hot water for me."

The resident in surgery came in, and another surgeon. Two surgical nurses and the o.r. head. A good circulating. The time was six-thirty in the evening, and the big hospital was as taut as a fiddle string.

Mike came to Tony's side at the basins. "Is Bee observing?" The tiled, bright room was repeated in the long mirror.

"No," said Tony. "She's in the house—but I don't know where."

"Is someone with her?"

"I designated a nurse, and she set me down."

Mike smiled. He scrubbed his arm, his wrist, his palm. . . .

The wall phone buzzed and an orderly answered it. "Dr. Bowlin cannot come to the phone," he said. "I'll take a message."

Tony glanced at Mike. If Bee . . .

It evidently was not Bee on the phone. "Well," the orderly said, "I'll see. No, ma'am, you can't talk to him."

Tony lifted his dripping hands from the basin. The nurse enfolded them with a towel.

Standing still by the wall phone, the orderly said, "There's this dame, sir. She says she's the wife of some professor, and she has a hobby of watching operations; she's heard that you are doing a special one . . ."

"Good old grapevine," murmured Tony.

"Well, can she, sir?" asked the orderly.

Tony thrust his hand into the first glove. "No," he said.

"Anything else, sir?"

Mike chuckled.

"Just no," said Dr. Bowlin, cracking into the second glove. He went into o.r.

"Hobbies," growled Tony when Mike followed him.

"The wife of what professor, I wonder?" said Mike.

"Drama. She's asked before."

Mike glanced up at the ceiling. Through its dome could be seen the circling benches; they were well filled. "If she'd be up there, you wouldn't know it."

"I'm glad that hasn't occurred to her."

"It may have. She probably gets a lift out of asking you in person."

"Even when I say no?"

"Even when." Mike shook his head. "What it must be to appeal so to women!"

"You should know."

"Not me. I'm like a stork. A strictly one—er—dame man."

"Ah-hum. If only you could decide on the one dame."

The nurse finished tying Mike's gown, and the two men stepped to the table. Their patient was ready; the anesthetist's report was not good. Dr. Bowlin extended his gloved hand, for the first instrument. "This is going to take some powerful retracting, gentlemen," he told his assistants. "Keel is a big man, and we are going in deep."

They worked. Dr. Bowlin was not a talking surgeon. Now and then he murmured something to Mike. He would say a sharp, clear word to the instrument nurse or to one of the surgeons who were cauterizing and tying off. He indicated bleeders, a place for a clamp. . . .

Steadily, tension mounted in the quiet room. The lights were blue-white, the temperature a bit high for comfort because of the patient's condition. The circulating wiped Dr. Bowlin's forehead, came around to Mike—she had to stretch on tiptoe.

"Damn!" said Dr. Bowlin. Their artery had indeed dissected itself, forcing a mass of blood between the coats of the vessel.

"You'll have to close up," whispered Mike in Tony's ear.

"Who says?"

"Man, it's the only safe thing to do!"

Tony lifted his head and shook perspiration from his eyebrows. The head spoke sharply to the circulating. She came running with her towel.

"Safe for whom?" asked the operating surgeon. He considered the problem before him—the opened abdomen, the great, dark, pulsating tumor. . . .

"Buckets of blood," said one of the young doctors.

"That's right," agreed Dr. Bowlin. "You have your suction ready, I presume."

"Yes, *sir!*" said the man.

"As I see it," Tony said to Mike, "I have two patients here."

"You do," Mike agreed. "And the one on the table is going to die—which will be pretty awful for the other one, doctor. Perhaps I know better than you do what the town will say—and the patient's wife—your professional colleagues, too, perhaps. The risk is too great, man!"

"So, in my place, you wouldn't do it."

Mike made a sound, but actually said nothing.

"That's it, then," said Tony, talking to Mike as if they were alone in the room. "Here I stand, with this problem before me. It is a tremendous risk to solve it— A risk of another kind if I don't. But in listing your awful judges, you left one out, doctor."

Mike's throat muscles contracted and relaxed. The

nurse mopped at his brow, but her eyes were on what she could see of Dr. Bowlin's face—his brown forehead, his intent eyes . . .

"As I see things," he said softly, almost as if he spoke to himself, "I have only one thing to consider. I came into this o.r. to restore our patient to good health. I may not be able to accomplish that, but I shall have tried. And having tried, my conscience will rest easier than if I had not tried to fulfill this obligation."

For the first time, Mike thought of the students who were, at that minute, learning to be physicians.

Tony's hand was like a rock. Delicately, almost daintily, he lifted the great artery and sutured it above the tumor. Then he fished for, found, and secured it below. "There's your bucket of blood," he told his young assistant.

And bucket it was. The enormous mass did not sustain lifting it up and out. The surgeon waited impatiently while the field was made clear, then he began the still more delicate task of creating a bypass, a bridge.

Mike admired his skill and marveled at it, but afterward his only comment was on the remarkably short time it had taken, from skin to skin.

Tony Bowlin glanced at him; he sat limply, his head back against the wall. "A man should weigh three hundred pounds, all of it muscle," he told Mike.

"Did you eat dinner?"

Tony frowned. "I don't remember."

It was now ten o'clock. Keel was back in intensive care, the surgeon's report had been written. Dr. Tryon went out into the hall and came back. "I hadn't eaten either," he explained when the tray came in. Hot coffee, glasses of milk—sandwiches—a stack of sandwiches, two wedges of pie. . . .

Tony accepted the coffee and drank thirstily. "Don't think for a minute," he said, "that I didn't recognize the complications of that job tonight."

"I know you did."

"So did Keel. That's why he forced my hand. The man—"

"He's known for his refinement of cruelty, you know. And perhaps I was mistaken. The town might not have resented his death. In any case, you're not apt to meet up with just this set of circumstances again."

Dr. Bowlin considered the statement. "The patient's age,

his physical makeup, his history—his clinical picture—those were the only things I should have needed to think about. With hindsight, I can say that."

"You did consider only the medical problem."

Tony glanced at him. "Oh, Mike," he protested. "Oh, *Mike!*"

"Have you talked to Bee?"

Tony smiled grimly. "I sent her home. She thinks I'm wonderful—tonight."

"But—aren't you?"

"Time will tell."

Of course, Keel still could die. Did Tony mean that? No, he did not. He—Mike took a deep breath. "I'll go look at him."

When he returned, Dr. Bowlin was gone from the small lounge. "I think he went to bed, sir," said the duty nurse.

"I hope he can sleep," said Dr. Tryon.

"Yes. He looked—so tired."

The next time Lucy saw Mike for more than a glimpse or two—once he had come to the house while she was at choir practice—it was the afternoon of the Sunday when he had driven Doshie and Karen to the State Hospital. Dropping Doshie at her home, he had seen Lucy, in slacks and an old red jacket, a hood tied under her chin, out in the front yard taking down the Christmas decorations—the door wreath, the cedar rope which enwrapped the slender white columns of the porch, the luminaria bags which had lined the curving walk from door to street.

"Hold it," he said, going toward the house. "I'll come out and help you."

"You're too dressed-up," said Lucy.

He told her where he had been—though she already knew that—and he went inside. In there, Meg was stripping the Christmas tree, and he probably would stay where it was warm.

Poor Doshie. Lucy wanted to know—she sighed and went to fetch the garden cart into which she would put her bags of sand. Doshie had so wanted her girls to be modern, to be advanced. As they grew up, she had seized upon and used all the possibilities of permissive training; she had talked frankly to the girls; she had wanted them to experiment with life. And Karen had done so; she still would—

whether voluntarily or not. Shock treatment. Even LSD was a possibility.

Now, of course, Doshie did not want Judy to experiment at all. She must not try a thing. Her mother wanted—she said she wanted—the girl to make a B average in college, then to marry a nice boy and be comfortably middle-class. As if she despised all those things.

Did Doshie think of the Goheens' regulated life as middle-class—something to be despised and accepted only as a compromise? If so, she was wrong!

There was so much good in their lives. The Goheen girls had led lives enriched with books, music, and travel; they had first-hand knowledge of pleasure as well as of pain and sacrifice. An illness like Anna's could require a deal of learning along those lines. They had acquired the satisfaction of unselfish service, and could make it the basis of a good future.

Doshie had given none of those things to her girls. Just that they should live, experiment, marry—and end up "middle-class." Or in a mental institution.

Lucy, taught self-discipline and all the other conventions, had lost some things. Of course she had. The world was so crowded today that no one could have it all. But she and Meg had had a full life, teaching, helping others—doing the things they liked to do.

Lucy enjoyed baking a tender cake. Meg had been happy with her golf, her slides and serums. And she would be again.

Yes! They had led a full life.

Of course, Karen's had been full, too.

Judith's would be.

What filled the cup seemed to make all the difference.

Chorley jumped into the garden cart, tipped it, and spilled sand all across the grass. Lucy squealed and ran after the scampering dog.

Mike stood on the doorstep and laughed at her. He had exchanged his suit coat for an old jacket of the Dean's.

"You'll ruin your trousers," Lucy told him.

"It's happened before."

"Tell me about Doshie," she said when he came close to her.

"You know about Doshie. What are you going to do with all this stuff?"

Lucy fetched a small shovel and came back to retrieve

some of the sand. "After I bury Chorley . . ." she muttered. "Where was Louis today? Why didn't he go with Doshie and Karen?"

"They felt safer with a doctor along."

Lucy snorted. "You could have sent a nurse. That Louis . . ."

"Now, Lucy, don't be hard on him. He had some crisis come up—a road caved in, I presume. Or perhaps it was just male evasion of emotion."

Lucy straightened and pushed a lock of hair out of her face. "Do men avoid emotion?" she asked curiously.

"Well, certainly they do."

"Mmmm," said Lucy. "I never knew that."

"I won't even ask what else you don't know."

Lucy made a face at him. "How did Karen take—the trip? And Doshie."

"Exactly as you would expect. Karen was not disturbed. She's been that way, you know. Just accepting what is done for her."

"Does she know . . . ?"

"Oh, yes. The psychiatrist—and others—have talked to her—with little or no response. As for Doshie—well, she too ran close to form. She was—is—ashamed. And apologetic."

"Should she be?"

"Oh, not that her daughter is ill, and that she will be sheltered in a state institution. I've pointed out to her that Louis can pay for Karen's keep."

"Did that help any?"

"It helped Doshie."

Lucy frowned. "Pride, I suppose."

"No, martyrdom. The money—"

"Oh, for heaven's sake, yes!" cried Lucy. "That would be self-punishment for her. What a woman she is!"

Mike laughed. "Yes, she is one. Poor thing, she has endured a lot."

"We've talked it over in the family, you know. We don't think she understands what has happened to her."

"That's protective, Lucy."

"You mean, she doesn't want to understand. . . . *Was* she to blame, Mike?"

"That Karen went wrong?"

"No-o," said Lucy, rubbing her mittens free of sand. "That she didn't handle the things that followed."

A car full of students came up the hill. The girls were singing, *I love a Dean, just like our Dean, our love, our pride, Goheen!* Lucy waved her hand to them.

Mike leaned against a tree trunk and filled his pipe. "It is my considered medical opinion," he said pompously, "that, even remembering the adventures which led to Karen's pregnancy, Doshie's only fault lay in the fact that she probably gave her daughter some ancestry of imbalance."

Lucy thought about that. She rolled up the cedar rope, she took the shovel back to the garage and brought the stump of a broom with which to sweep the stoop and the walk. She was thinking deeply.

Mike took the broom from her. "Now what?" he asked. "Are you going to burn this stuff? And the Christmas tree? Inside, I had to high-step like that cat on that roof. Meg had glass balls all over the place."

Lucy nodded. "I know," she said, her tone preoccupied.

"I asked you . . ."

Lucy smiled up at him. "I'll put what's left of the sand into a box in the garage," she said. "And stack the greens down at the back end of the lot. We'll put the tree there, too. Meg will bring it out. And then we'll add our evergreens to the big pile we'll burn on the church parking lot on Epiphany. That's always fun. . . ."

"It sounds hilarious," drawled Mike.

Lucy looked at him, then she laughed. "I'm sorry," she said. "I was trying to look back among my ancestors to see if there was any imbalance. That's quite a word, you know."

Mike gathered an armful of cedar rope and started down the hill. "I wouldn't examine the ancestors too closely," he called back. "Though I remember a certain Aunt Betty who used to visit you—"

"There wasn't anything imbalanced about Aunt Betty," Lucy assured him. "Of course she mistrusted the night air—"

"And threw wads of cotton down the toilets—"

Lucy giggled. "Oh, yes, she did, didn't she? We always had to call the plumber after a visit. He got so he'd ask, 'Has Aunt Betty been visiting?' "

"But she wasn't imbalanced," drawled Mike, giving Lucy the help of his strong arm to climb the steep lawn again. "Why the check?" he asked. "Do you have any evidence of some imbalance being around now?"

Lucy bent over double to pick up the wreaths. "Well, Meg," she gasped. "Lately, she's been— Though I wouldn't call it imbalanced!"

"Neither would I," said Mike, starting to push the heavy cart. "But there are other names to call her. She's bad-tempered, and a long step to being a soak. . . ."

"Oh, Mike, no!" cried Lucy.

He stopped to turn and look at her. "Why else would I ever carry your sister up to bed?" he asked.

"I know," Lucy agreed. "And that was bad. But it was only for a short time—now she's stopped all that."

Mike looked dubious.

"She has!" Lucy insisted. "She was so ashamed to know what she had done. And since I'm with her constantly, I know that she hasn't drunk a drop since that night. Though, of course, she's still—" She walked away from Mike.

He followed closely at her heels. "She's still not herself," he said. "I've noticed that. And I may as well tell you—I don't like the new Meg."

"But you did like the old Meg."

"I sure did," said Mike vigorously. He left the garden cart at the garage, took two of the wreaths from Lucy's armful and again they went down the hill. "You girls," he said, "both of you—I had decided that there was no fate for me except bigamy—a return to Mormonism, or something. I've been trying for years to figure out some more legal solution, and have had to conclude that I must have you both, or nothing. That problem," he assured the laughing girl, "that indecision, has kept me pure as well as unattached for all these years."

He dumped the wreaths and stood for a minute looking down at the tree-covered grounds of what had been his grandfather's home. "I plan to build a new house there someday," he said softly, "and live in it. If you girls marry me, you would be close to your mother . . ." He turned. "Of course you two may have other plans?"

Lucy laughed, but she frowned, too. "Meg's not herself!" she said earnestly. "You must know that."

"Yes," said Mike, "I know it. Is there some reason?" He spoke casually, but he was watching Lucy most intently. And Mike—intent . . . Horizontal lines furrowed across his wide forehead. His deep-set blue eyes were steady; curving lines bracketed his firmly closed lips . . . His thumb was hooked into the narrow belt he wore, and his strong arms strained the sleeves of the Dean's old jacket. Here and now was Lucy's chance. She could talk to Mike about Meg, tell him—

She turned and gazed down at the trees of Judge Tryon's "place"—oak trees, an old ginkgo, wide-spreading—

"There must be a cause for the change in Meg," Mike prodded her.

Lucy sighed and looked then at her hands. One of her mittens had a hole in it. "I suppose there is," she said hesitantly. "But, you know, Mike—" Swiftly her eyes lifted again to his face. "I think Meg, like Karen, seems to need help in handling the results of what has happened to her more than—"

"Great Scott, Lucy!" Mike shouted. *"She's* not had a baby!" Then he bent forward. "Or has she?" he demanded.

He straightened and his hand caught at her shoulder. For Lucy had gone dead white. He told her that she had. And she well may have. Just to remember that first terrified month—not talking about it, but both she and Meg counting the days and weeping with wild relief when they were sure that nothing like that was going to happen. . . .

"I didn't mean to shock you or frighten you," Mike said in deep concern.

Lucy managed a faint smile for him. "It was a shocking suggestion. . . ."

He tousled her hair. "Let's go clean up the rest of the mess," he said, taking her arm.

Lucy leaned against his strength. "Oh, Mike," she begged. "Can't you *make* her go back to work?"

"I've asked her to work with me, Lucy. I want her, I need her—but she won't do it. And she was pretty flat in her refusal. I have concluded that I don't seem to rate with Meg any more. I certainly hope I still do with you."

Lucy hugged his arm. "You do!" she cried. "I adore you, Mike Tryon!"

"That's good," said Mike, picking up the handle of the garden cart. "We'll be married at Easter. Where do I dump this?"

Lucy showed him and watched as he endeavored to dump the sand directly from the cart into the box. Of course he spilled some and she fetched the broom and the shovel. "Will you try harder," she asked, "to get Meg to work? She needs it so badly. She's—well—lost just staying at home. And I keep thinking that if Karen had worked at some job, stayed with it, liked it, forgotten herself in it—"

Mike squatted down to sweep the last of the sand into the shovel and peered up over his shoulder at Lucy. "You still talk as if—"

Lucy felt her cheeks flame, and she put her hands to them. "Oh, no!" she cried. "It's just that they both had problems, and—"

"Mhmmmn," said Mike. "And you think Meg needs work of a kind to make her forget herself."

"Yes! Much more than Karen ever did."

Mike stood up. He put his hands on Lucy's shoulders and backed her against the garage wall. "Now you listen to me, Lucy Goheen!" he said sternly. "And I am dead serious!"

He looked serious, his eyes, his mouth. "Answer me this one question," he said. "*Can* you tell me what has happened to Meg? Specifically and exactly?"

Lucy gazed up at him, her own eyes wide and dark. But she shook her head from side to side. "Can't you make her tell *you?*" she asked, her voice husky in her throat.

Mike released her and looked defeated. "I don't know that I'd even try, Lucy," he told Meg's sister. "Meg is a dignified, reserved girl. I've always admired that in her, and I wouldn't want to be the one to threaten her reserve."

Lucy bit her lip against a swift stab of jealousy. He was right. Even at her gayest, Meg was like that, and everyone admired her. "She loves you, Mike," she said earnestly.

Mike whistled softly and stepped away from Lucy. He looked shocked—or was he angry? Hadn't he known . . . ? "You wouldn't dare tell me," he said roughly, "that I am the only one to help Meg?"

He paced the length of Meg's car, came back. "That would be insupportable, Lucy!" he said. "It would be enough to make a man hate a woman!" He turned on his heel and walked away again, clear out to the drive. Lucy watched him. He was not the only one who could help Meg. Of course he was not. But he certainly was one who could help her!

Looking even more angry—even his short yellow hair

seemed to bristle—Mike walked the length of the drive all the way to the street. He stood there for a minute, as if he debated what he should do—or say. He caught at a branch of the tree and broke it off between his strong fingers, then whipped it against his trouser leg. Finally he strode back to Lucy.

"Tell me," he said gruffly, "do you think I am at all like Tony Bowlin?"

Lucy looked up at him, completely puzzled. Why should he ask . . . ?

"Tell me!" Mike urged. "*Am* I like him?"

"Why," said poor Lucy, "I don't know, Mike. I mean, I don't know Dr. Bowlin well enough to say. . . ."

"You know him well enough!" Mike assured her. "And I happen to know that *he* admires *you*. He calls you the Ivory Soap girl."

"Oh, Mike!" cried Lucy. "I thought you were being serious."

"I am being serious," he assured her. "Now, this Tony — Don't you know him well enough to realize that the man risked everything—I mean *everything*—to save Leonard Keel's life?"

Lucy was still puzzled. What did Tony Bowlin and Leonard Keel have to do with— "Did he really do that, Mike?" she asked. Which wasn't the question she wanted to ask at all.

"Did he save him?" asked Mike. "Oh, yes, he did, Lucy."

"I meant—did he risk everything?"

"Yes. Yes, he did that, too."

Because he had been the only one to—

"Why?" asked Lucy.

Mike was exasperated. "Now," he demanded, "what do I hitch that 'why' to? *Why* did he take such a risk? *Why* did he save that man? In what way was there risk? And what risk did he run, anyway? I could answer them all, if I thought you really needed to know. But tell me this: Do you think I am the only one who can save Meg? Help her, rather."

"Maybe not," Lucy conceded. "But she loves you, Mike. And she trusts you."

"As you do."

"Oh, yes, Mike. Of course!"

He tried to smile. His finger lifted a lock of Lucy's

shining hair and tucked it up under the hood she wore. "What am I supposed to do?" he asked. "Put her to work? But she won't. She has said she won't work with me. Am I supposed to marry her? Though she won't do that, either."

"Oh, Mike . . ."

"Look, my girl." He stood towering over Lucy. And she thought, men live in a different world. Why do women keep trying to draw them out of it and into the little puddles of small female affairs? Why not be content if their eyes will smile at us, if their big hands will support us, if—?

"What on earth are you thinking about?" Mike asked her.

Lucy jumped. "Oh—about how nice you are. And how lucky Meg and I are to have you ready to—"

"O.K. O.K.," he cried, silencing her. "I've another question for you. It's this: Suppose I were ready to sacrifice myself to save Meg. And both words beginning with *s* need a deal of expansion and definition. But suppose I *were* ready to go to an extreme to save her? Who then is going to save my pretty Lucy?"

Slowly, painfully, her heart turned over in her breast. Her eyes dark and wide, Lucy stared at Mike. Which one of them *did* he love?

"Oh, for Pete's sake!" he cried—as if he were reading her mind. And he probably was! "Love complicates entirely too many things. If one but tries to keep it separate, if one tries to make a place for it alone . . . You say Meg loves me and trusts me. But, can't you see, Lucy, that if I took one step toward invading her privacy, I could destroy the trust and such love as she now may have for me?"

"But you wouldn't," said Lucy firmly.

"I don't know, Lucy. And perhaps I should take the risk. I'd hope I could be something like Tony Bowlin—that I could put my love for Meg—and for you, my darling—to one side and act as a man should to help anyone.

"You see Tony, motivated only with a wish to help his patient, could forget himself; he could forget Bee, whom he truly loves. He really does love her, Lucy! But he still, wanting to help Keel, could forget who Keel was. . . ."

Her face troubled and sad, Lucy went to hang the shovel on its hook. "If you won't help Meg," she said in a smothered voice, "and I can't find a way to do it—" she turned to face Mike—"what," she cried, "is going to happen to that girl?"

Mike took a deep breath. "If you are as serious as you sound, Lucy, why don't you ask that question of Meg?"

CHAPTER NINE

IN LAUREL HEIGHTS, childhood held no visible terrors. The college town was, on the whole, a living testimony to the unspectacular virtues of life in the Middle West. Stealing apples had not yet given way to the flash of switchblades. But—children were born, they got sore throats, they fell out of those apple trees. . . .

And Dr. Beatrice Keel felt that she must rise at seven, look with no enthusiasm at the tepid sunrise, eat her breakfast, and at seven-forty-five pick up her little black bag and go into the garage. Her car stood right there beside Leonard's longer, more gleaming black one. She got into the seat of her green car and pushed the button under the dashboard.

"I still get a kick out of that door," she said, chuckling. She backed out into the drive, then into the street, closed the garage door, and turned the car wheels toward the hospital.

At that hour, the streets of the town were still empty, but Bee on her thirty-fifth birthday could check off the houses as she passed them. She had cared for the children who lived in half of them; right at the minute mothers were feeding their babies formulas which Dr. Keel had prescribed. In this brick house a child was recovering from the fever which she had cured by her choice of medication. In that apartment house were at least three young brides drinking coffee who had been Bee's earliest patients—two of the girls' lives she had saved. A little girl on a porch waved at the doctor's familiar car, another driver honked and shouted good morning to her as the two vehicles passed each other.

At eight-o-two, she pulled into the hospital parking lot; she got out, picked up her bag, and walked into the building. A patient with a leg in a cast nodded good morning to her, and a young nurse smiled hello.

Up in her office on the third floor, a white coat replacing her tweed one, Bee found a dozen messages on the blotter of her desk. Some were phone calls, some were transcripts of admissions, all were about children. A pediatrician could only expect a lot of phone calls, and certainly could never be sure of what would turn up in the way of hospital cases.

Even as Dr. Keel was making the calls—to the floor-duty nurse, to several homes—Myrtle Payne, her nurse, brought more messages. Most of them were routine. A boy had coughed all night, a girl had a heavy chest cold, four children had sore throats. . . . The doctor spoke in an undertone, always calm and assured.

One child sounded as if he had measles. Bee promised to make a house call there. One seemed to have only an allergy to school. Bee handled all these things by telephone. That finished, the doctor left her office and walked to the pediatrics ward. There was no hospital smell of ether or alcohol. The walls were painted with some overcute children and improbable animals. The doctor's approach scattered a flock of white caps at the desk, and she picked up her stack of charts. Miss Payne took them from her. It was nine-o-five, and Bee was running a little late. But even so, she must answer the phone twice. Then she could go into the nursery, where her day's work really began with the examination of the new babies which the obstetricians were ready to turn over to her and her staff. Some of these babies Bee would have as patients for the next fourteen years.

The doctor washed her well-manicured hands with an antibiotic soap; the nurse put her into a wrinkled gown and tied a mask over her nose and mouth. "Watch the hair-do," said Bee automatically. She went into the first of the glass-partitioned rooms. In an incubator, the glass sweating, was a one-pound-four-ounce premature boy, kicking his red legs and crying. Her eyes smiling at the mite, Bee let the nurse put her into rubber gloves.

She thrust her hands through two openings in the side of the incubator and began her examination. She spoke cryptically to Miss Payne, who made notes on her chart board. "Except for his weight," Bee concluded, "he seems to be doing fine."

She then went into the next room where seven babies were making a noise in their new world. Bee examined each one, expertly and precisely running her fingers over

167

the small bodies. She noted the color of the skin, and the breathing, the movement of arms and legs. With her stethoscope, she listened to the small hearts and the sounds of the lungs; her hands felt of the abdomen, and she ordered X-rays for one baby whose stomach seemed too full. "It's probably nothing," she told Miss Payne, "but we must check."

She thoroughly examined each child, inch by inch, moving the legs, and even observing the shape of the feet. This was all done with the swift skill of a professional. After each examination she washed her hands. Then, removing her mask, she toured the maternity ward, chatting with the mothers, telling each one that her child was fine!

Out at the floor desk again she asked the name of the preemie. The two young nurses looked at each other, obviously confused. "All right, all right," said Dr. Keel. "Another gift of God. . . ." She went across to the elevator, glancing at her watch. It was nine-forty-five.

She got out of the elevator, still thinking about babies born out of wedlock, but ready to look forward to the variety of cases which she would find on this floor. Literally, a pediatrician got everything in the way of medicine. In a private room was a little boy with tubes in his nose and a tube in one arm—ten days ago he had been struck by a car. When his internal injuries threatened peritonitis, he had been brought to this hospital and Bee.

She spoke cheerily to the boy and asked how he was feeling.

The child did not answer; his eyes were still stunned with the hurt which had been done to him.

"The chart says he had a good night," said Miss Payne.

"Good," said Bee. "There is a neurological examination ordered for today. Will you bring that report to me as soon as it is ready?"

"Yes, doctor."

She next examined a boy recovering from pneumonia, and said good-by to still another who was going home after a bronchial attack. "Call me," Bee told the mother, "if anything unusual comes up."

The mother beamed at her. "I will, Dr. Keel," she promised. "Oh, I will!"

Bee went on through the ward, checking on this child and that—comforting one who cried for her mother, speaking firmly to a troublemaker. . . .

Finished, Bee looked again at her watch. "I'll take ten minutes to look at my husband," she told Miss Payne.

"Yes, doctor. You have a meeting—"

"At eleven. I know." Bee stepped into the elevator. She had already done a "day's work." But she loved being a doctor, she loved any small part which she played in eliminating the dread diseases of childhood. Still a young woman, she had seen polio rubbed off the slate, and would soon see measles. . . .

She stopped at the desk to look at Leonard's chart before going to his room. He was doing well, but he still made a difficult patient. Studying the statistics on his record, she felt a hand fall lightly on her shoulder. She knew, before she turned, that it was Tony. She trembled to her heels. . . .

"Could I talk to you a minute, doctor?" said the surgeon, a smile in his eyes, his face still. "No cause for alarm."

Bee followed him to the tiny lounge off surgery. He closed the door behind them.

"What's wrong with Leonard?" she asked gravely.

Tony shook his head. "Nothing. His recovery is slow but steady. We are taking him off intensive care today."

"That's very good."

"Yes, it is. And it seems that in a matter of a couple of weeks—"

"I'll have to make arrangements for his care at home."

"Well—"

Bee went over to the window. The view from it was uninspiring on this still, gray winter's day. "I planned to tell you this," she said in a strained voice. "Within a short time, I planned to say it."

"Bee!"

"Let me say it, Tony," she said. "Please let me say it!"

He was silent. Without looking around, she knew how he stood there, in his white clothes, against the flat gray door; his chin tilted up, he would be looking down at her, his eyes half closed. His eyebrows were only dark tufts, his ears were small and closely set to his head, his skin was brown, weathered. . . .

"I feel," she sighed, "that I owe it to Leonard to give you up, Tony."

"You owe it to Leonard," he said, "to be a martyr."

"No. No."

"But you know that I love you." He was coming toward her.

She turned. "And I love you, Tony!" she gasped. "I do love you!"

"Then—" He put his hands on her shoulders, and his eyes smiled at her.

"It isn't fair," she said, still hurrying the words, "that we should fall in love—too late—"

"But, my darling, I've waited for this time. And it isn't late at all."

She braced herself against his charm. He was so warm, so understanding. "No," she said firmly, "we can't—"

"I'll change your mind," he promised.

She nodded. "I know you could," she agreed. "But I am going in to see Leonard. I'll tell him that I won't divorce him—and having done that, I shall have to stick to my word. I won't be able to weaken—"

Tony drew her close to him, he held her head against his breast and stroked her hair. "Don't do it, Bee," he begged.

But without speaking again, she freed herself and went out of the room.

"Is Mr. Keel worse?" asked one of the nurses at the desk.

"No . . ." said the other.

"Dr. Keel looked so sad. And she'd been talking to Dr. Bowlin . . ."

In the early afternoon of a warm day in January, Mike stopped at the Goheen house to announce that it was the day for the January thaw, and he wanted a girl to take a drive with him.

"Do you have a girl around here, Miss Anna Go-*heen?*" he asked. Both Lucy and Meg were in the living room, where their mother had elected to rest on the couch. They watched Mike, smiling. Lucy wore a blue denim housedress and was sitting at the desk. She had already told Mike that she was "setting up the books" for the new year.

Meg had been reading aloud—she wore a dark red tweed skirt and a white blouse.

"I have two girls, Dr. Tryon," Mums answered his nonsense.

"Mhmmm. An embarrassment of riches. I even suspect you're something of a girl yourself."

170

Anna giggled. "Well, I used to be something . . ." she admitted. "But I wouldn't feel safe taking a drive with you."

"I hate smart women." He turned to Lucy. "And *I* shouldn't feel safe driving in broad daylight with a blonde. So Meg—"

"Oh, Mike," she said, holding her finger in her book.

"You're dressed for it. Especially if you have a sweater to go with that skirt. And while you're getting it, put a bit of powder on your nose, my sweet. It adds a certain something to a drive in the early afternoon."

"Mike, you are a nut!" cried Lucy.

But Meg had risen— If she came back with her sweater . . . Briefly, Mike held up his hands to Lucy; the second and third fingers on each one were crossed.

He was teasing Chorley, making the dog leap and bark, when Meg came downstairs again, wearing a red sweater, her hair tied with a twisted red scarf.

Mike made no comment, just said " 'By, now," to the women left behind. "Have hot crullers and mulled cider for our return," he told Lucy.

"I never mulled a cider in my life," Lucy laughed, hearing the front door close.

"I'm glad Meg went with him," said her mother.

"Oh, sure," Lucy agreed, turning back to her books. "Suppose you close your eyes, Miss Anna Go-*heen,* and try to go to sleep. I can't add with you chattering at me."

Her mother smiled and looked wide-eyed at the picture hung on the wall at the end of the couch.

"Where are we going?" Meg asked when Mike got into his own car seat and fastened the belt.

"University."

She laughed. "All that, for twenty miles?"

He nodded. "It's a beautiful day. But—"

"Too hot for Suez," said Meg.

"For the likes of you and me," Mike answered her, "ever to go—"

"Who is the Cake Parsee?" she asked.

Mike nodded. "I'm glad you remember your Kipling, my girl."

"I asked . . ."

"Oh, well, it's the bursar. I want more money."

"Who doesn't?"

"Now that's a fair question. Are the elm buds swelling?"

"They are," said Meg. "And the forsythia is popping out. Both will get their silly noses frozen. Why did they build the medical school twenty miles from the university?"

"Oh, there was no room on their campus, and land prices were prohibitive. Someone gave them land for a hospital in the Heights."

That someone had been Judge Tryon. He had also given a half million dollars for endowment. The hospital had become a teaching one for the medical school, and—

"Will your interview take long?" Meg asked.

Mike considered. "If he says 'no,' I'll be right out. If he says 'yes,' I'll do some arguing with him."

"Arguing?"

"Oh, sure. Once they agree to spend money . . ."

Meg nodded. "I can see that. Will I have time to stop at the bookstore? I want to get a sweat shirt."

Mike glanced at her. Meg seemed in a good mood. "An orange one?" he asked.

She nodded. "With a wildcat's head. That's the kind."

"I don't think you're the type, Meg."

"Well, sure I'm the type. But I was getting this for the little boy who is helping me put rocks around the edge of the flower beds."

"He's the type?"

"Oh, definitely. You see, he used to throw rocks at Chorley—and I would pick them up and put them in a heap. He got curious and asked me why I was doing that. I told him I wanted to edge the flower beds. Now—he's helping me."

Mike nodded. "They have shirts with the cat's tail on the back."

They drove along, talking nonsense, but making a great deal of sense to Mike, at least. Meg sat well over in the far corner of the seat, but she was friendly and fun to be with.

They played a game, often done in their youth, of matching rhymes from Kipling. Meg caught Mike and laughed gaily at his disgruntled face. When they reached the university, she elected to stay in the car while he talked to the bursar.

"The students are worth watching," she told him.

They were, too. All kinds, shapes, sizes, and sorts—most of them taking advantage of the warm sunshine. A youth in

172

suntans and unbuttoned white shirt frankly slept on the bricked terrace of the administration building.

Mike was gone forty-five minutes and came back circling his thumb and forefinger to Meg.

"How could he refuse?" she asked him. "The name must be magic."

"Not as magic as you might think. Let's walk to the Union."

"And the bookstore."

"And the bookstore. But first I crave a Coke."

Meg went along with him, and they talked of various things—graham cracker and marshmallow cream sandwiches, long hair on boys—and on girls—the cost of a college education—almost anything but Meg herself. She seemed grateful and relaxed into almost her old manner with Mike.

Finally, back in the car, their purchases heaped in the back seat—the sweat shirt, an enchanting marionette for Lucy, and a half pound of Mum's favorite Anna Claires. . . .

"She shouldn't eat anything so rich as those chocolates," Meg confessed.

"I'll slip them to her, and Lucy needn't know."

"Fooling Lucy is beyond even Mums."

"Mhmmmn. Now, let's see. I always lose myself getting off campus."

"Today will be no exception," Meg told him, "unless you really want to go to the stadium."

Mike swore mildly, backed and turned the car.

"Now you're headed wrong on a one-way street."

"I told you I hated clever women. Suppose you drive."

"No, but I'll tell you how."

"To Penang instead of Lagos . . ." muttered Mike.

"Did you eat mangosteens in India?" Meg asked him.

"In Burma. They gave me a stomach ache. But then, almost anything did give one— Meg, I have a desk for you in the lab, and I've ordered lab coats in your size. And I want you to show up Monday morning for work."

"What time?" she asked.

Mike glanced at her. "Eight o'clock. You'll have to have a sort of physical."

She made a face.

"It won't be bad. Blood count, chest X-ray— I think you

should do it, Meg. You're going to have to get some sort of job, aren't you?"

She laced her fingers together in her lap. "Yes," she said softly.

"Of course you are. You're too big a girl to sponge on the Dean. And you shouldn't push Lucy out of her job. Besides, I need you at the lab. And they don't need you at home."

"I'll be there," she said quietly. Her face, her whole person, seemed to relax—as if she were relieved to have the thing done.

Mike would still play the thing casually. He came into the house with her, and Lucy did have hot doughnuts for them. He told briefly that the trip had been a success. The bursar had given him some money and with it he was hiring a cheap test tube washer. . . .

"You're going to have to read aloud to yourself, Miss Anna," he turned to tell Mums.

A half hour later, when he departed, Lucy followed him to the door. She hugged his arm. "I love you, Mike Tryon," she whispered.

"And I love your doughnuts. . . ."

"You have sugar in the corner of your mouth."

He chuckled and went out to his car. Lucy leaned against the door frame to watch him drive away. She was so glad, so *glad*. . . .

Meg was glad, too, or seemed to be. She didn't talk much about the decision. She made her appointment, and on Thursday she went for her physical examination, looking white and tense, but she came home, obviously relieved. "I was nervous about the blood test," she told Lucy quietly.

"But it was all right."

"Yes."

On Monday she came down for breakfast, dressed for the day's work, and departed in much the same way she used to drive off for school.

"She'll love it," Lucy told her mother.

"She'll be working for Mike?"

"Oh, yes. But they have a big laboratory."

They did have. Meg's domain was a small room off the main lab. She had her own desk, sink, and files. There were a dozen girls who worked in the main lab, and half as many young men. The girls were of all sorts, and so were the men. Typical—a too-fat girl, a young man who thought he was a born comic. . . .

Meg did her work for Mike, and did it well. Mike was pleased with her work, but he found her far from able to get along with the technicians in the main lab—or with any of the young hospital personnel—medical students, technicians, nurses—aides.

"They're not all fools," Mike told her.

"They can sound like it."

One of the lab girls had announced her engagement that morning—a week after Meg had begun to work. The girl had been pretty "high" and the hospital jokes to her and about her became a little broad. Meg showed her distaste.

"The bride-to-be is a whiz at preparing tissue slides, Meg."

"She's silly today."

"O.K. Give her a day to be silly. If she's in love—"

"Some of the things said to her— Do men have to be nasty, Mike?"

"No. But aren't you being a little silly yourself to pay attention? Or even listen?"

"I suppose." Meg bent over her microscope.

That was the one flaw Mike found in her performance. If she would just relax, make friends—as the old Meg would have done. There were people working in the hospital who were ready to be friendly with her. But Meg—

She did her work, and very well. Really, she seemed relieved and content that she could work, keep regular hours, and be busy. Within her first week, after a half dozen concentrated sessions with Mike, where he was all scientist and the doctor in charge, she had the project organized and details scheduled. Her records were meticulous and complete. Besides this crisp efficiency, she looked the ideal of all lab-research workers. She stepped briskly, she worked intently, a slender, dark-haired girl, capable and efficient.

But not friendly. Not friendly at all. Among all the doctors, students, nurses, and other personnel, she made no friends at all. And this troubled Mike. That Meg should come so far, and then refuse to take another step. Meg had used to make friends with everyone! A gay word, a warm response—

But now she seemed alone in the crowd and determined

to stay that way. Puzzled, Mike vowed to complete the solution of the mystery which Meg had become.

He tried to find ways to get her back into circulation. He used that term in thinking about her. He would come into the lab late in the morning and suggest that they go together to the cafeteria for lunch.

"I'd rather have a sandwich and milk here," she would say, not looking up from what she was writing in tiny, print-clear script in the log.

Or—he would catch her in the hall and try to draw her into a conversation with others. He met with no success.

He brought people into the lab. Men. Tony Bowlin, who was having a rough time those days—and Miller Hubbard, who was a very swell guy. Lucy liked him; perhaps Meg would.

She was courteous to these people, and professional in her conversation with them. But she would not let that conversation become anything but professional. It was as if she wanted to shut herself off from any promise of personal interest in anybody, or from anybody's interest in her.

He thought of talking to her about this, but he had still said nothing when the day came that he had occasion to roar at her because of a scene she made one morning in a crowded elevator.

He heard about it in the doctors' lounge, he heard about it again at coffee break. He came to the lab at noon and asked Meg, "What happened this morning?"

She had a pipette in her mouth and did not answer him at once. Then she said only, "Oh, there was this man . . ." She put the pipette back between her lips and bent her head over the flask in her hand.

Mike shut the door into the main lab and came up behind her. "I want you to talk to me!" he said roughly.

Meg turned on the stool. "What about?"

"I don't know until you tell me what happened."

"You've heard some sort of tale."

"I've heard several tales. Among them that you think you're too good to be touched."

Meg's face whitened, and she brushed her hand back over her hair. "I don't like . . ." she began.

"Who was this man?"

Meg looked at Mike, and she frowned. "He was a nurse," she said. "A practical—a Licensed Practical Nurse

176

. . ." She spoke with care. "An LPN. He was big. The elevator was full of women—but he insisted on crowding in."

"I want in on this," the man had said. "With all the girlie girls."

"He wouldn't have done that if the cage had been full of men. . . ."

"Oh, Meg. He was probably anxious to get to his duty." She started to turn back to the bench and her work. But Mike grasped her shoulder. "What happened?" he said again.

"Mike . . ."

"Look, my girl. I not only want you able to continue to work here in this hospital, I want you to be happy doing that work. To do this you will have to contact the personnel in various ways. Now it so happens that the personnel also come under my jurisdiction. If we have male nurses who—"

"Oh, he was just being young and fresh, Mike."

And the women—the girls—need not have encouraged him with their giggles and their own pushing. . . .

"He had no business crowding on that elevator; he had no business pushing his way in and making jokes about not minding being a sardine in such a can."

"We try for a fairly relaxed relationship among the personnel, Meg."

"He was relaxed, all right. Jostling the girls, clutching at them . . ."

Mike nodded. "What did *you* do or say?"

"When I had to get out, and push my way through, I suggested that he would do better not to crowd an elevator to such an extent, and I asked him, please, to step off so that I would not have to push him out of the way."

"And he made remarks?"

"Well, yes."

"Do you care to quote him?"

"No, I don't."

"Did you push past him?"

"I had to, yes. And—"

"Can you conceive that this boy was only trying to have a little fun? A joke at the beginning of his long day?"

"I don't care for that sort of joke."

"It takes all kinds of jokes, Meg. And I suppose it didn't occur to you, either, that he was not primarily interested in jostling *you*. I like you, but after all, you're a pretty skinny girl. Weren't there others on the elevator who were more seductive, who would be more fun to squeeze?"

Meg drew a deep breath, and now she did turn back to her work. "I hate men," she muttered.

Mike still stood behind her; she could feel his warmth. "All men, Meg?" he asked her, his voice deep.

She turned her head to look up into his face. Her eyes were puzzled. But she did not speak again, and Mike left the lab more deeply troubled about her than he had ever been before.

It was later in that same week that Judith Chambers came to the hospital laboratory for the tests which were being required of all the students at the college. Six cases of mononucleosis had turned up in town, three of them college girls, and precautions were being taken. She asked if she might see Miss Goheen, and she was shown the way to Meg's lab.

Meg greeted her and let her talk a little about the "kissing sickness," which Judith thought was exciting—

"Unless you get it," said Meg.

The girl shrugged. "Oh, well, I suppose. I don't know *what* Mother would do or say if I did get it."

Meg smiled. She didn't know either, but her surmises—

"I hope I don't get it," said Judith. "Mother has been letting me have my friends at the house—"

"I'm glad, Judy."

"Yes. Sure." She glanced up at Mike, who had come to the door. "I came to give blood," she told him.

"Do you have any symptoms, Judy?"

"I don't think so. They say you're tired—but I never have liked to get up in the morning."

Mike chuckled. "Do any of your friends have it?" he asked.

"I know some. But they are not *kissing* friends."

"Judith says her mother is letting her friends come to the house," Meg told Mike.

"But she watches us," said Judy.

"And so she should!" said Meg firmly.

Judy looked at her uncertainly. "Well," she said then. "I'll get going. This is a swell hospital, isn't it? 'By . . .'"

" 'By, Judith," said Mike. He watched her go through the big lab.

Then he turned back to Meg. "Will you please tell me," he said idly, "what the hell has happened to your sex life, Meg Goheen?"

He had spoken idly, and her reaction . . .

She drew back from the bench and sat huddled down on her high stool. He saw her shake with a strange little shiver. She did not speak.

Nor did Mike. He turned, his crepe-soled shoes not making a sound, and he went through the lab, fast, lest someone speak to him or even look at him, because he was in a state of shock, and he knew it would show.

He had thought he wanted to know what was wrong with Meg. . . .

But now he did know, and . . . and . . .

He went into his office and through it to the small, marble-walled lavatory. He closed the door behind him. And even his doing that shocked him. But if what he guessed had happened to Meg . . . And it had to have happened! Her eyes, her face—the revulsion in both— Blundering ass that he was, he must ask her, "What has happened to your sex life . . . ?"

Oh, dear God, dear God! That poor girl. And Lucy— Lucy knew, and she too had been deeply hurt. Those nice people, those good people. . . .

He wanted to know where, when, who—

But, good God, he had blundered around clumsily enough as things were, asking fool questions, lecturing Meg—and Lucy—

Of *course* he was shocked!

Why hadn't he guessed sooner? Because things like that just did not happen to people like the Goheens! That's why. Doctor he might be, and was. . . .

He brushed the sleeve of his white coat across his forehead, which was beaded with moisture. He turned the faucet and washed his hands and his wrists, getting one sleeve-edge wet. He dashed cold water into his face, then rubbed his skin vigorously with a towel.

Shock. And if he—

What Meg must have gone through! And Lucy. Had they kept their secret from their parents? Mike hoped so. But Meg should have told him, a doctor—

So, he was a doctor, and now he knew the answer to the problem which had been set for him to solve. Poor Lucy.

She had asked his help, and he had thought he was giving it to her.

Ha! He had given with one hand and taken away with the other, leaving Meg herself to cope with the whole mess, including his bungling words and suggestions.

He went out to his desk and sat there, his head in his hands. His secretary knocked, then came in with some papers for him to sign. He hoped she didn't look at his face or notice that his signature was cramped from his need to hold the pen so tightly to conceal the tremor.

The young woman left, and Mike sat on, now turning his chair to look out through the glass at the darkening sky, at the lights which were springing up.

Shock was not a nice sensation. This was, he thought, his first experience with it himself. And a doctor—

Well, he was a doctor. One with three patients, all criticals. Because he himself, Mike Tryon, at this minute was certainly the most critical.

A doctor should not treat himself. Maybe not, but in this case Dr. Tryon must start right there—with himself. Then he must care for Meg and for Lucy.

He wished he could talk to someone. Even obliquely—as Tony Bowlin had talked to him a time or two. He did at Christmas, faced with having to operate on Leonard Keel's aneurysm. Had Mike helped him? Not much, probably, because, after all, he could not possibly understand. And Tony had had to see the thing through alone.

So would Mike have to work this out alone. He had none of Tony's qualities, he felt pretty sure, but he still was going to do anything he possibly could to get his "family" well and whole again. And now—no more bungling. He must work as delicately as any doctor had ever worked to repair the hurt done, to rehabilitate—Meg, Lucy—and himself. He put his hands over his eyes. Oh, dear God, he groaned, why did this have to happen!

When did it happen?

Well, it must have been the night he came home. Last October.

What if Mike had known then? What if Meg or Lucy had then told him, as they really should have done, since he was both friend and doctor? So—then, what would he have done?

Tried to kill someone, probably.

But—he had not known. Meg had gone through the horror alone, or with only Lucy, the poor, frightened girl. And Meg—

What *must* she have felt? Shock, of course. But along with it—panic and anger. Yes, Meg would have been angry. Had she done anything? Gone to the police, or to a doctor, or . . . ?

No. And Mike could begin to understand why. There was nothing she alone could do, and she did not want others to know. Yes, he remembered how she had crawled into a hole or endured companionship with a cold stoniness which must have concealed such tension, such fear and pain. . . .

Now Mike was pacing the office—across the carpet and back, to the windows, to the door, and back. . . .

Meg had tried drinking, but that had only made her feel worse. She could not hold her liquor without making a fool of herself, which was the very last thing she wanted to do.

And after a time—here lately—she had begun to crawl out of her hole. Puzzled by what life had done to her, wanting to live again—though needing to protect herself —needing that above all else. . . .

So, for all the pain it had caused him, Mike was glad that now he knew, that now he could begin to help Meg.

Six weeks after his delicate surgery, Leonard Keel was pronounced well enough to return to his home and, gradually, to resume the practice of law. The first case he would handle, he promised, would be that fool lawsuit his wife had got herself into.

Since the hospital was involved, Dr. Bowlin and the administrator refused to let him handle the defense. "For pure meanness," said Tony, "he'd sell Bee down the river. Donald O'Hara says the family has no case except against one o.r. personnel, and they haven't sued her. But if we'd tell Keel that—"

"You'll make him mad as hops," Mike warned.

"That's fair enough," said Tony hardily; "he makes me that way often."

Like all patients long in the hospital, recovering from a critical illness, Leonard was full of doubts about getting back into the world of well people.

"Are you taking me home?" he asked Bee a dozen times. "I mean, to our house?"

Each time, she quietly said, "Yes."

Then came the day—only two days before his departure—when he asked her bluntly if she were going home with him.

"I've been there all along, Leonard."

"Alone?"

"Except for Alta. She's there in the daytime, of course."

"But you stay at night—alone?"

She had long ago stopped rising to Leonard's bait. "Yes," she said now.

"I imagine our eminent surgeon-friend was ready to relieve your loneliness."

"Dr. Bowlin has been very kind, Leonard," said Bee staunchly. "To you, especially."

"He saved my life, you mean. A thing of dubious worth to either of us, wouldn't you say?"

"No," said Bee, "I would not say such a thing."

"Before I experienced the great fall, you had told me that you were going to divorce me. I suspected that you then planned to marry Bowlin."

"That was months ago."

"You mean he's no longer interested?"

Bee took a deep breath. "I mean, I have not been seeing him, except here at the hospital. He's on the staff here, he is your doctor—"

Leonard peered at her. His blue eyes were very bright. "And that's all," he concluded.

"Yes."

"Hmmmmn." He waved his hand at her. "Go away now, will you?" he asked. "I want to think."

Late that afternoon, Dr. Bowlin came into Leonard's room, as he was accustomed to do at least twice a day, apart from the rounds which he made with students or members of the staff.

This evening, he found Leonard sitting in the gray half-light, and he snapped on a lamp.

Leonard frowned.

"I'd rather not break my neck," Tony explained. "Besides, I need light to read the chart."

"Always the professional."

Tony said nothing; he was reading the chart. Leonard

sat in the armchair, his fingers tapping the arm of it. He wore a dark blue silk robe, with a lighter blue scarf folded into the throat. He was a very handsome man, though he lacked the ruddy color which touched his cheeks when he was in full health. However, he did look quite well, and Dr. Bowlin told him so.

"I should look so," Leonard replied, "since I am well again. For which, I'm told, I should thank you."

Tony shrugged.

"Perhaps," Leonard continued, biting off the words crisply and spitting them out between his lips, "I should remind you that, being well again, I can fight you for my wife on even terms."

Dr. Bowlin hung the chart again on the bed rail. "Yes," he agreed. "And it's better that way, isn't it?"

"Is that why you saved my life?"

Tony leaned against the wall and studied this man. "I save all my patients, Mr. Keel, if I can."

"But you didn't think you were going to save me, did you?"

"There was a chance I would not."

"But I fooled you."

Tony smiled. "No. I fooled you!"

Leonard's lips twitched. "Yes," he said dryly, "it seems that you did. Would you believe me if I said I was glad you gave me this chance?"

Tony shrugged again. "I only know that I am glad I did."

CHAPTER TEN

By MARCH, Meg Goheen was ordering seeds from the flower catalogues and planning her spring and summer work in the yard. She had attended to this task for several years, and this year the family was relieved that she would continue her interest. Things seemed to be going much better for Meg, and for the family.

"We're having a lot of company again, aren't we?" asked the Dean.

"It's what I expected when Mike came home," said Miss Anna.

"But—"

"He was very busy at first, Doyle."

"I thought that perhaps he had other friends and interests."

"I don't know about the interests. But his friends—he brings them here."

"Yes. Yes, he does." And he introduced the Goheens to them as "my family."

Almost every Sunday afternoon, and on some other evenings, Mike would drop in, sometimes with a friend or two—Tony Bowlin, Miller Hubbard from the cancer hospital, the chemist at the poultry processing plant and his baby-doll wife. It was laughable to see the way Meg regarded this girl, in wonder and disbelief. Kenny was an ardent Episcopalian; he talked earnestly to Lucy about the possibility that he might take orders. And his young wife tinkled baby talk to the Dean.

Sometimes Mike brought a medical student or two, or a resident doctor, a flyer whose arm had been broken in a needless automobile crash and who was most impatient about being grounded. Sometimes he brought a girl, or women. Sometimes old friends of the town, people whom the Goheens knew.

But the new ones were safer. . . . They would not notice any change in Meg and comment on it.

In one way and another, they came, often and regularly.

At first Mike watched Meg. If she walked out . . . She did not. Sometimes a situation could be difficult for her, but she stuck things out, and as time passed, things seemed to get easier. On the evening when she engaged in a lively game of darts and crowed in triumph when she won, Mike breathed a sigh of genuine relief.

The next Sunday was a warm, pre-spring day, and he brought a stack of steaks for a barbecue in the yard. That day Tony Bowlin came, and he and Lucy cooked the steaks, enjoying themselves. Mike and Meg and the Dean sat on the back steps and argued about the younger generation.

"These kids are smarter than we were," said Mike, not really knowing.

"No, they are not," said Meg. "We just notice them more. Analyze them—and, oh, dear Joe! there are so many *more* of them!" But no word at all about the young people being nasty, or—

That was a good day. So was the evening of cutthroat bridge, and the Sunday afternoon when Lucy discovered that Miller Hubbard played the violin.

Meg became interested in the contest that was developing between Tony Bowlin and Dr. Hubbard for Lucy's attention. "One of them is going to cut you out, Mike," she told the third doctor, "if you aren't careful."

"I have hidden powers," he said lazily.

And Meg only chuckled.

She was "better" away from home, too. At the hospital she talked with excited interest to the eminent pathologist who was a visiting lecturer at the medical school; she was interested in him, and she was the one who invited him to come to the Goheens' on Sunday afternoon.

"Hey!" cried Dr. Tryon. "I thought you were my girl!"

Meg touched his arm as she passed him, the first time she . . . "Are you jealous?" she asked, with all of her old pertness.

"Certainly," said Mike.

The pathologist—his name was Reeves—followed her. "Are you his girl?" he asked Meg.

She was still blushing when Mike caught up. She hadn't

answered Dr. Reeves. But she hadn't run away from the idea, either.

On the next Sunday, Reeves showed up at the Goheen house. Everyone—a half dozen guests—had gathered in the kitchen where Lucy had agreed to try making some "old-fashioned pull taffy."

"You doctors will burn your hands," she warned.

"We used to do it as kids," Mike remembered.

"But then a blister didn't matter."

Dr. Reeves was welcomed with shouts which somewhat puzzled him. "She thinks a pathologist *can* burn his hands," Tony Bowlin explained.

That did little to clear up the mystery for the newcomer. "I have a case of cold beer in my car . . ." he announced.

"Let it stay there," Meg told him. "My mother don't 'low no cold beer in here. Wash your hands, doctor, then butter them—"

Someone took pity on him and explained about the taffy.

"But the beer . . . ?" he asked.

That was explained, too.

"Good!" said Dr. Reeves. "I've been looking for just such a family."

It was a family again, and Meg, without being coaxed, was coming back, though gradually, into her full place in it.

The Dean, Miss Anna, and Lucy, of course, had always attracted attention. But now, again, Meg was a lure. And she knew it.

"It's a great bunch," Dr. Reeves told Mike the next day.

"My family?" he asked. "They sure are great."

"But it's not really your family, is it? I mean—"

"We're not related, if that's what you mean."

"If I were in your place, doctor, with those two girls available, I'd see to it that I was related."

Mike nodded. "I have plans along that line," he said. "Did you get blisters?"

Dr. Reeves laughed and looked at the palms of his hands. "Not really. Though I may have to lose a molar from that taffy."

It was fun to make taffy; it was fun to help move books from one set of shelves to another, but mostly the fun of going to the Goheen home was the talk. That talk was always good, especially since Meg was ready to take an animated part in it, no matter what was talked about.

Before the study fire on a rainy evening, they could shock Miss Anna, and vaguely disturb Lucy, by the discussion of a recent death in the town. Possibly they had a crime . . .

Mike again stated his purpose of getting a medical examiner instead of a politically selected coroner.

"That man was burned alive," Meg stated emphatically. "I ran most of the tests. There was soot in the air passages, and carbon monoxide in the fellow's blood. *And* there was no bacteria to cause decomposition."

She caught Lucy's upward, questioning glance. "Well, of course," she said, "if decomposition had been present, the body was dead before it was burned. Oh, you have a crime, all right, Mike."

"I'll call you as a witness."

"You may," said Meg. "I'll testify."

Which was good. Three months ago she would have refused any participation.

Of course she had been missing the talking she so liked to do. Sitting mute in a corner had been part of her pain, her punishment—or whatever she called her period of immolation—and she welcomed relief from it. Now Mike thought up ways to start talk going and to keep it going.

The Dean and his problems always proved a fruitful gambit. "What's up with the girls, sir?" Mike would ask.

The Dean smiled and nodded. "What would you do about an unattractive girl, Mike . . . ?"

"Nothing. I don't like unattractive girls."

"They are not my preference either. But they happen. And we have one—she is particularly that way—"

"Spare us the details, sir."

The Dean smiled. "If you wish. Because my problem really lies with the father, who is filthy rich."

"Oh-oh. And you need a new dormitory?"

"Not really, though endowments are lovely, comforting things. But this man—he's a bully, too."

"A lot of rich people are," Meg chimed in. "They think their money can pay for anything."

"It doesn't make his fat daughter popular," said the Dean. "She doesn't belong to the right clubs—nor any club, for that matter."

"I can solve your problem, Dr. Goheen," said Miller Hubbard.

The family looked at him. He was a very nice chap and had immediately fitted into their group. "Sure," he said. "Get Lucy to tell the girl how to be pretty. She must know everything about *that*."

It was Lucy's confusion at which they laughed, their eyes lovingly upon her for the way *her* eyes shone, and her cheeks got pink, and her hands fluttered. "Oh, eat your spaghetti!" she told them finally.

And everyone laughed at that.

"It's the time of year, too," the Dean resumed, "when we renew our teachers' contracts."

"And that makes problems," Mike prompted him.

"It certainly does. Right now there are three teachers we are afraid will not come back next year, and one we are afraid will."

A ripple of laughter encircled the dinner table.

"What will you do, sir?" asked Mike.

"Fortunately, I am only the Dean of students, and won't have to do anything. Except, next year, perhaps, handle a few problems from student-faculty relationships."

"Medicine sounds easier," Mike decided.

Having been recruited from Mike's available acquaintances, most of the people who came to the house with him were from the hospital, and most of them were doctors. Mrs. Goheen commented on this to Lucy.

"They are interesting men," she said, brushing Mums' hair. "And they interest Meg."

"Yes, they do. And some find you interesting, wouldn't you say?"

Lucy dimpled. "I hope so," she said demurely.

"Do they talk to you about bacteria and interns and stuff?"

"Oh, Mums . . ."

"It depends on whether you're alone or not. Yes, I remember. I wonder, though, with Meg—"

"She doesn't give them a chance to talk to her alone. She won't go on dates, Mums."

"They ask her?"

"I am sure they do. I know they have. Especially that nice Dr. Reeves. He really was taken with Meg."

"But she is more like herself lately."

"I know she is. And personally, I'm grateful."

Mums was, too. She, like Lucy, was willing to sit back and listen to the hospital talk. Mike had succeeded in getting four interns from the spring assignments.

"Not of top quality this first time around," he admitted. "But they are better than none. Bowlin and I shall do a lot of work with them."

"I hadn't guessed that interns would be a major problem in establishing your teaching hospital," Dr. Hubbard told him.

"How long have you been with Engert?"

"Eighteen months now."

"And before that you were in Maryland. I've been here only since October. . . ."

"I know."

"And my chief problem has been to establish the intern service. That's partly because this is one of the twenty-four states which will license a doctor without internship."

"Sometimes that isn't good."

"Of course it isn't good. And a first-rate medical school should not endorse it, even if it is a state-supported institution."

"And you talk to me about my problems?" marveled the Dean.

Everyone laughed. Mike, ruefully. "I'll get interns," he assured the others. "I'll make the hospital a bang-up institution. Bowlin is a tremendous help there."

"How will you get your interns, Mike?" asked Lucy.

"If you establish a reputation, my dear, the med students will apply to work in your hospital."

"Won't you have your own medical school to supply you with interns?"

"It doesn't work that way. They all apply through a central placement service, and hospitals ask for interns through the same channels. Of course we shall get some of our own students, but not as things are now. You see, the board, and the legislature, think we should use fourth-year medical students as interns, and let them go elsewhere for their real internship—if any."

"Will that work?"

"Interns, with four years of medical school behind them, have an awful lot to learn, Miss Anna. Would you care to contemplate the ignorance of a man with only three years . . ."

"Mums isn't to be excited that way," said Meg gravely. And again laughter stirred the mood of the room.

They talked about many things on those Sunday afternoons, on those evenings before the fire. Or, as the weather warmed, out on the terrace with the soft whisper of seeds winging down from the trees, of birds preparing for the night, of music from the street at the foot of the hill.

One evening they spoke of the Keels. During the winter, Dr. Hubbard had become interested in Leonard's case—as a surgeon, and as a friend of Dr. Bowlin and Dr. Keel. Now it was a natural thing for him to ask how the Keels were getting along. "I've heard some gossip . . ." he admitted.

The others laughed at him gently.

"Remember," he defended himself, "I am not *in* on the situation. If my hospital were the one where these people functioned—"

"I thought you were asking about Leonard's medical progress," Mike drawled.

"Which I was, to a certain extent. Though I could have put that question on an evening when Dr. Bowlin was present." Miller Hubbard was a thin, weathered board of a man. His face was craggy, his deep-set eyes were sharp. He had a cleft in his chin, but it was a little to one side. The most fascinating thing about him was his inexorable wit and his ability to stick to a subject until the whole matter became his own.

On first meeting her he had become interested in Lucy Goheen, and immediately he set himself the task of interesting the lovely girl in him. Having surveyed her home and her family, he used every suitable means by which to further his cause. The Goheens and Mike—even Lucy— became intrigued by Dr. Hubbard's campaign. Now Meg, at least, suspected that his inquiry about the Keels had to do with Dr. Hubbard's possible competition from Dr. Bowlin. Tony liked Lucy a lot.

He was told that Leonard had resumed his practice of law, that he was back in his office, and had conducted at least one court case—known to this group.

"And I know that Dr. Keel is still working at the hospital," said Dr. Hubbard. "She sent me a case just last week."

"Oh, dear, yes," murmured Miss Anna. "The Barnes child."

Dr. Hubbard smiled at her. "You get around, don't you, ma'am?" he asked softly.

She nodded to him. "If I lose my interest in the people about me," she said firmly, "I shall have become a sick woman."

"I can tell you," said the surgeon, "that there is hope that we can help the Barnes child."

"Oh, good!" Miss Anna knew that the doctor had made her a gift. "But poor Bee . . ."

"In the triangle I have in mind," said Dr. Hubbard, his mobile mouth twisting, "I would say that the husband was taking undue advantage."

"He is," Mike agreed. "He's a brute. A refined one, but —Bee had decided to divorce him. And now . . ."

"She could be called a sacrificial martyr," said Dr. Hubbard dryly.

"Though she must have loved Leonard once," suggested Miss Anna.

"And if her decision to stand by the man is based on a return of that love . . ." Mike conceded.

"It couldn't be a return of it," said Meg. "And to stake her life on her memory of it seems a stupid thing for an intelligent woman to do."

"Then—what does she plan? This 'stupidity,' I might remind you, could be very rough on the third leg of our triangle."

"Bee knows that. But I think her determination is to wait and see . . ."

"Keel is older than she is?"

"Yes. At least fifteen years."

"Tony," said Lucy softly, "considers her dismissal of him to be final."

"Did he tell you that, Lucy?" the Dean asked.

"Not in so many words." She rose to fetch something from the kitchen; Miller Hubbard followed her.

Dr. Hubbard was "interested" in Lucy, but he did enjoy talking to Meg on professional matters which let the Dean pick up his newspaper and Miss Anna doze in her chair. The matter of food molds had seemed to be implicated in certain cases of cancer of the liver in Africa, and of the stomach in Japan. "I'm going to pursue that," Miller told Meg. "You wouldn't know of a good research-lab worker I might steal from Mike Tryon?"

Meg laughed. "I shouldn't advise stealing anything from Mike," she told him.

Dr. Hubbard nodded. "I forgot, for the minute, how high he rates in this family."

"We like you, too, Miller," Meg told him warmly, her dark eyes twinkling. And then she went on to ask him questions about the use of tiny Geiger counters to survey the progress of radioactive phosphorus used as a tracer material in cancer-fighting drugs.

Dr. Hubbard answered her completely. In fact, he talked to her for fifteen minutes on the subject, all the time watching Lucy, noting the way the lamplight lay richly on her bright hair and threw a shadow of her against the wall, the way she used her hands over some sewing, and the way she placed her feet upon the floor. He watched Lucy . . .

Mike watched both girls. He thought, one evening, that his present occupation was like playing—or watching the play of—a game of chess. The "men" were ranged upon the board, they moved—or someone moved them. . . .

Dr. Hubbard had fallen in love with Lucy, but so had Tony Bowlin. In fact, the man seemed smitten with her. He found ways of getting her off to himself. He would, he said, walk Chorley with her. . . .

"Are you going to enter him in the faculty dog show?" Tony asked.

Lucy hunted for Chorley's leash in the hall closet. "I may take him to see all the other dogs," she said. "But he's not a show dog."

"He looks good to me." Tony took the leash from her and attempted to fasten it to Chorley's collar.

"He has too much lay back," Lucy told him.

Dr. Bowlin stood up. "Come again?"

She laughed, her pretty eyes shining, her lips curved upward. "As a surgeon," she said gravely, "don't you know that there should be a ninety-degree angle between Chorley's shoulder blade and his upper leg bone?"

Tony felt of the joint. "Chorley's isn't that—good," he decided.

"No, it is not. And the old dear couldn't care less. Come on, Chorley, once around the block. . . ."

Tony went with her gladly. Now, thought Mike, what

did his attraction to Lucy mean for Miller Hubbard—and for Bee Keel?

Bee and Leonard were other pawns on his chessboard. Mike Tryon himself was one. And he should critically study the moves of that last one. He did so study them and plan them.

He himself suspected that he was getting so involved with the progress of the game that he was not, really, playing his own part. He was sure of it when Miss Anna spoke to him about his behavior.

"You shouldn't analyze people so much, Mike," she told him. "Will you hold the yarn for me while I wind?"

Willingly Mike straddled the footstool and held up his two hands for the hank of red wool.

"You are at an age," said Miss Anna, "where feelings are very important."

"And dangerous," said Mike.

"Oh, yes. Oh, yes. But who wants to be safe?"

Mike looked at the pretty woman in her wheelchair. Even winding a ball of yarn was a tremendous effort for her. "I wish," he said, "that I had been born thirty years earlier, darling. I am very much in love with you."

She tossed her head. "You would have had no chance at all with a man named Goheen," she assured him.

"Nor with his girl, either, I suspect," said Mike glumly.

Anna smiled at him. "A man in certain circumstances, dear," she said gently, "has a right to think of himself first."

Mike nodded and turned his head a little to watch Lucy, who was playing the piano, with Miller Hubbard sitting on the bench beside her. He seemed to adore the pretty girl—and why not? Lucy's disposition was the best; no girl ever was prettier—or more talented in many ways! He, too, "adored" Lucy.

"I'm getting to be an old man," he told Miss Anna glumly.

She laughed happily. "There's a homely phrase, Mike, dear," she said, "which I might use to you. And that is: you should be stirring your stumps."

Mike's blue eyes flashed. "Before it's too late, eh?"

"Before it is too late. I think I hear Doshie coming up the walk."

She did hear Doshie. One heard Doshie, whatever she might be doing. She accompanied herself at all times with a running fire of comment and explanation. Even when alone, she talked to herself.

"I know you have company," she said as she came in through the front door. "I could see the cars in your drive. But then you almost always do have company. Judith, put the strawberries in the refrigerator. Louis brought me a crate from downstate. I'm dividing with you. I can't face freezing all those berries! I knew you could use some, Lucy."

Lucy made some comment of thanks and went out to the kitchen, Dr. Hubbard following her.

"He's fallen hard for her, hasn't he?" asked Doshie, coming over to kiss Miss Anna's cheek. "How are you, darling? Mike?"

"I'm darling, too," he drawled. He nodded his head at the yarn. "You'll pardon me if I don't stand up. How are you, Mrs. Chambers?"

"Me? Oh, I'm fine, I guess. Doctors really don't want that question answered. Where's Meg?"

"She's in the study with the Dean. He's dictating a list he wants typed."

Lucy brought back a large bowl, two smaller ones, and announced that everyone was going to stem strawberries. "I'll get them in the freezer by bedtime," she said.

"In the living room, dear?" asked Miss Anna.

"Well, you're all in here."

"I'd take them to the kitchen. You and Mike, Judy and Miller—you could go rescue Meg from your father."

"It would be better," said Lucy. "Doshie, you hold the yarn for Mums."

Carefully Mike made the transfer to her hands, and he followed the strawberry pickers to the kitchen. Soon the young voices filled the house.

"Sounds good," said Doshie. "And with your girls, you know they are not cooking up any mischief."

"Oh, Doshie!" cried Anna.

"I'm sorry," said Doshie meekly. "Wouldn't it be easier if you held the yarn and I wound?"

"Easier and quicker. But I'd not be using my hands."

"Oh, I see. Was anyone ever more dumb than I am?"

"I expect so," Anna said, laughing. "Did you want something, Judy?" The girl had come into the hall and stood uncertainly in the doorway.

"Yes," she answered. "Lucy said to ask you if you

wanted all the berries frozen or some made into preserves?"

Anna considered the matter. "Tell her to freeze these. We'll make preserves later. Oh, and, Judy!"

"Yes, ma'am?" The girl stood docilely.

"Tell her to save a quart or so for some shortcake. She may ask the boys to come and help eat it."

"You mean the *doctors?*" asked Judy, her face lighting up. "Oh, isn't Dr. Hubbard dreamy?"

"In a nice way, yes," agreed Miss Anna.

"They are both just wonderful!" declared Judy, scampering off.

Doshie sighed. "I'm glad, Miss Anna," she said earnestly, "that I am not eighteen, or even Lucy's age. How will that girl ever decide among three 'dreamy' men—Tony Bowlin, Mike, and now Dr. Hubbard? Has she given you any hint . . . ?"

"Hold the yarn a bit lower, will you, dear?" asked Mrs. Goheen.

Doshie nodded. "I get the message," she admitted.

With April, spring came in good earnest. The trees leaved out, jonquils bloomed, and tulips. Meg planted her flower seeds, set out new chrysanthemum plants and some snapdragons. "You'll have them for the party," said Doshie lightly, watching her work in the flower bed, "in case Mike comes home again."

Meg's face went white, but she did not falter in the rhythm of troweling out a hole, sprinkling in some peat moss, setting the plant carefully into place, covering the roots with crumbled soil.

"She's lots better, isn't she," Doshie asked Lucy, going into the house, "from whatever ailed her last winter?"

"If you're talking about Meg, she's fine."

"That's what I was talking about," said Doshie, picking up the box of starch which she had come to borrow. "Thanks. I'll return it."

Lucy waved her on. When she was finished with the dishes, she went out to tell Meg that it was getting dark. Lucy was wearing a green dress, and since supper she had run a comb through her bright hair and put on a fresh lipstick. Meg wore a denim jump suit, with old sneakers on her feet.

"Are you expecting company?" she asked Lucy.

Her sister shrugged. "We might get some."

"So we might," drawled Meg, patting earth down around the little green plant. "I often wonder who takes care of the sick people."

"They are taken care of," Lucy assured her.

"But to drive twenty miles . . ." mused Meg. "Several times a week! Do you like him, Lucy?"

"Miller Hubbard? Yes, of course I like him. Don't you?"

"I'm not in love with him." Meg rapped her trowel handle on the bottom of still another little red pot.

"Is that what you were asking me?"

"Of course." Meg carefully set the plant and used her fingers to push dirt around it. Lucy had said nothing.

"What about Mike?" Meg asked her.

"Oh—Mike," said Lucy.

"Yes. Remember him?"

Lucy smiled. "Well, of course, I could never marry him, so—"

Meg sat back on her heels and used her forearm to push the hair back from her face. "Why couldn't you ever marry Mike?" she demanded.

"Well—"

"On my account?" Meg's voice sharpened.

"Well, you know— There's always been the two of us. You liked Mike, and I tagged along. I liked him, too. But now you'd better . . ."

Meg shook her head and began to gather her implements, the empty flower pots, and her gloves—she put them all into the garden cart and wheeled it away.

Lucy watched her go. Meg was better. Often she seemed —well. But there were times—one couldn't push her beyond a certain point. She didn't want anyone to kiss her; she still would not drive her car along the Observatory road, and except for earnest group discussion, or a riotous game, she wanted nothing to do with men. Questioned about this, as she was, she said frankly that she just did not like men.

And then, on a summer-warm evening, when the air was like silk, a big moon coming up over the valley, and the blowing trees playing a game of hide and seek with the stars, Meg quietly told her family—her father stretched out in the long chair, Lucy beside Mike on the glider, and Anna in her wheelchair, a filmy wool scarf over her hair and shoulders—that she had decided to enter the medical school in September and study for a degree.

"Oh, Meg . . ." breathed Lucy.

Mike said nothing, but Lucy heard him gulp in surprise. "Didn't you know?" she whispered to him.

He shook his head.

"Tell us about it," said the Dean.

Meg got up from the low basket chair and walked to the edge of the bricks. "I've thought about it," she said. "Since working at the hospital, I've watched the medical students. And I've thought of myself as wearing a mask and cap and assisting at an operation during *my* twelve-week tour of duty in the surgical departments. I could do that. I've seen myself in one of the seminar groups. You know, Lucy, med students go through school in groups of three."

"No, I didn't know," said Lucy, speaking softly, but her voice quivered a little.

"I can't, of course," Meg continued, "guess who my colleagues would be. They'd probably be men, but I think, toward such a purpose, I would get along with them, be able to work with them, I mean."

"It's not an easy course of study, is it, Mike?" asked Miss Anna.

Meg answered her. She came back and sat on the low table, facing her parents, her back to Lucy and Mike. She wore dark slacks and a white blouse; she gestured with her hands. "It is not an easy course," she said. "The pace is fast, and the pressure terrific. But I think I could take that and would find the life absorbing. I—look forward to it, and to internship and residency as well. I know, as a woman, I shall have some additional difficulties. I'll be mistaken for a nurse, and things like that—but if I remain confident about what I am doing, and can really take time with the patients, they will forget that I am a woman and have confidence in me."

They will forget I am a woman, thought Mike. Oh, poor Meg! Dear Meg!

"I've been watching the students," Meg was saying again —"the seniors who are now in our hospital doing their senior duties. And I have been able to identify. I too could examine a little boy in the neurosurgery department, I could operate the lighting during a pathology lecture, and I *know* I could do the bookwork. My whole life, since I was four, has been with books. If I can look forward to a medical career, I also can look forward to a life of study. And I'd hope to do it well."

"You'd be very brave," said Lucy uncertainly.

"I'd have my nerve," Meg corrected with a slight laugh. "Of course, to swing it, I would have to stay here at home. I'd be able to pay some board . . ."

"I'd just dare you to offer," said Dean Goheen vigorously.

"When did you reach this decision?" Mike asked quietly.

Meg did not turn to face him. "Last winter," she said. "I think the trigger, for me, was Tony Bowlin's attitude toward Leonard Keel. He hated the man and had to despise him. Yet, as a doctor, he was able to see Leonard only as a patient. I've found that he sees all people in the hospital only as patients. And I've found that I can, too, in the hospital. Doing my work—I can see them—they *are* only patients."

"If the personnel would just clear out . . ." drawled Mike.

Meg glanced at him across her shoulder. "I am better about that," she said, a slight question in her tone.

"Yes," he said, "you are."

"I've made my application," said Meg, "and been accepted. Perhaps I can continue working part-time at the lab for a little income. I have some money saved. I figure my car should last the four years, and the clothes I have, barring shoes, and stuff. So I think I can swing the money end of this. Of course if Lucy leaves home, and I am needed here . . ."

"Oh, now, look!" said the Dean, sitting erect. "I will not have you housekeep in my home!"

Meg laughed as freely as anyone. "I know," she agreed. "I am your untalented, dumb daughter."

They all sat for another hour discussing this great turn of events. Meg would have encouragement in her project, that was evident. There was an excitement, a happiness among these people who loved each other. Meg felt it and glowed gently. "It's wonderful to be able to look forward and to plan," she said.

Mike went quickly out to his car and brought back a stethoscope, which he gave to her. "To get ahead of the drug companies," he told her.

Meg was unduly pleased, and Mike laughed at her. "Four years of book swatting," he agreed, "a couple of years of intern scut work, a wear-your-legs-to-stumps residency—that's wonderful, all right! What will be your field, funny face?"

"Pathology," she said softly and firmly.

"Fair enough. You'll be good at it."

When the hour was over, Lucy went into the house to turn on lights, the Dean pushed Miss Anna's chair—and Meg walked around to the drive where Mike had left his car. He should be doing bed-check, he had told the others.

At the corner of the house, with the light from the kitchen fanning out ahead of them, Mike put his arm about Meg's shoulder, drew her to him, and he kissed her.

She gave him an upward look from eyes much dilated, then, catching her breath, she turned away.

He followed her. "Meg!" he said.

But she went on.

Her hands were clenched down at her side, and she was trembling—but not with fear, she told herself in surprise. Not with the hatred and revulsion . . . Mike's cheek had been rough against her soft one, and warm. His lips had been firm upon her mouth. His arm had held her protectively.

And—she had liked being there against him, feeling her own slightness against his male strength. Now, *why* . . . ? She walked to the big oak tree and stood there, knowing that Mike would follow her and say something. . . .

"I thought you loved me," was what he said.

She turned to look at him, her head back, her eyes enormous. Mike's hair gleamed like silver in the moonlight, and his skin . . . She wanted to touch it again, and she held her hand firmly behind her against that desire.

"I do love you, Mike," she said seriously. "I always have." She looked beyond him to the house. "And so has Lucy."

He nodded. "That's true," he agreed, "but not in the same way."

"No," said Meg. "Of course not. We are not the same girls. For one thing, I've two more years of living and learning than she has."

"Oh, Meg." He was laughing.

But Meg was not. She wanted to get away from him now to think— Because she had believed, firmly, that never again could a man touch her, or—or— "I'm going in," she said in a muffled voice.

Mike stepped aside. "Good night, Meg," he said.

He watched her go up the steps, in through the entry, and then into the lights of the house. Nodding, he went to his car.

CHAPTER ELEVEN

ON THE FIRST weekend in May, Karen Chambers came home for a visit. The whole street was drawn up into tension before this event, wondering about the girl, wondering about Doshie—and Judy. It would be, at best, a delicate situation. Should the neighbors go to see her—do anything . . . ?

Doshie said that, physically, Karen was well. Doshie too knew that things would happen—or could. "I think I'll leave home," she told the Goheens a dozen times that week.

Even Mike was jittery and told about the med student he'd once known who had had to spend several months in a mental hospital for readjustment. When he rejoined his classmates, the young men had decided that they would treat the guy "just as we treated each other. We did, too. The second day he was back, and we were having a ward walk, this character came up with an off-base diagnosis. Disagreeing with him, I yelled, 'Morgan, you're crazy as a loon!'" Mike shook his head and laughed sheepishly. *"That* isn't what I'd advise anyone to say to Karen."

Louis was to bring her home when he came on Friday night. The next morning everyone found ways of looking down at the Chambers house.

"I saw Bee Keel go in," Miss Anna reported.

"She'd be the best one to go," said Meg.

After lunch Judy came up to the Goheens'. She was smiling widely. "I came to borrow a racket," she said. "Karen wants to play tennis."

"Karen . . . ?" Meg gasped.

"She used to play. And she says she does at the hospital. You'd have a racket, wouldn't you?"

"Yes. Oh, yes, of course. Just a minute—I'll get it."

As she went upstairs, Meg heard Judy telling Lucy that Karen had cut her hair, too. "Not as short as mine. She flips it at the ends."

Coming down the stairs again, Meg could hear Judy still talking about Karen. "We're all so proud of her!" she said.

"You, too, Judy?" Mums was asking.

"Yes, of course. Oh, thanks, Meg. I'll take care of it." She started for the door. Her young limbs were brown and silky, her shorts and blouse were snowy against them. Judy was a cute girl.

"We're thankful about Karen, too," she told the Goheens. "You know—that she can get better. And then I especially feel—you see, it could have happened to me." She stroked Chorley's head with the racket. "I guess it still could . . ." she mused.

"You won't let it?" asked Lucy.

"Oh, no! Well, anyway, I hope not." She went through the door and out along the walk, beginning to run.

"Well!" said Lucy, turning back. "That seems to be a good thing."

Miss Anna was put down for her nap. "Just like a baby," she said cheerfully.

The Dean said he guessed he had better cut the grass. Meg said she would help him. She went upstairs to change, and there she found Lucy with her wet hair bundled into a towel. "Pin up the back ones, will you?" she asked her sister.

Meg agreed. "Anything special going on?" she asked.

"Oh, yes. I'm going dinnering and dancing tonight with Tony Bowlin."

"Really? You'll have fun."

"I think so. He's a wonderful dancer—and looks so exciting. Of course poor Miller called a half hour ago and I had to turn him down. I didn't really think Tony would want him to go along."

Meg chuckled. "Would Hubbard want to?"

"No," Lucy decided. "I expect not. Anyway, I gave him a date for tomorrow. If it's warm, we'll go to the lake."

"That's the life," said Meg. "Two beaux striving for your attention. Of course I'll be left with the Sunday dishes to wash. . . ."

"I plan things well," Lucy agreed, her eyes sparkling.

"You always did," said Meg.

"I know it. Oh, Meg, it's quite a bit like old times, isn't it? Remember how, in high school, we'd have a lot of dates and get things mixed up—"

"Mhmmmn. Though I didn't have too much trouble."

"Why, you did, too! You had plenty of dates, and you got things mixed up."

"Oh, sure. Because I would forget I'd said I would go to the movies with some boy—and he'd only asked me in the first place so I would help him with his geometry."

In the mirror, Lucy made a face at her. "You had fun."

"Yes," said Meg, "I did. It would be kind of fun to go back, too, if only one *could* go back."

"Oh, well," said Lucy. "There's a lot of time ahead of us."

"The good old future," said Meg, as if she were not really interested.

"Well, sure," said Lucy. "It's spring now—and lovely weather. Summer is ahead of us. But the best part is that winter is behind us. Gone!"

Meg reached for a clip. "But not forgotten."

"No," Lucy agreed. "But it is behind us, Meg. We lived through it."

"Yes," said Meg. "And I know it was hard on you."

"That's right," Lucy agreed brightly, "it was. Just about as hard as the time when you gave me the measles you'd brought home from school. Only I was sicker."

Meg glanced at Lucy. "I had completely forgotten that," she said.

"Well, let's forget this, too. Put it away in a box." Lucy reached her hand for the comb.

"I really hope," said Meg on a deep sigh, "that I can find that box."

The next day, while the family was still eating its Sunday dinner, the telephone rang. Lucy went to answer, and came back. "That's the trouble with dating a doctor," she told the family. "You never can really count on him."

"Miller?" asked Meg.

Lucy nodded. "He says he has an emergency. Or—" She leaned toward her sister. "Did you rig something to get help with the dishes?"

Meg laughed. "I would have, but I didn't think of it. Now I'll offer a substitute. How about some golf at the club?"

Lucy looked up, surprised. Meg had not gone to the club since . . . "Sure," she said. "Of course the men will hate us."

"Oh, now . . ."

"They hate all women who golf on Sunday afternoon. Don't they, Dad?"

"Well, we men did think we had a sport . . ."

"You still have football."

"But not for long, I'm sure."

Lucy jumped to her feet. "Well, come along, Meg. Let's get these dishes washed and our shoes changed. Mums, can you manage to amuse the Dean?"

"I'll try," laughed her mother. "I'll try."

It was good to have the girls gay and nonsensical again.

On the fairway of the third hole, the girls stood aside to let a foursome of men play through. "What'll I say if one of 'em comes up to be Miller Hubbard?" Lucy asked Meg.

"Oh, he wouldn't!" Meg protested.

Lucy shrugged. "I'd hope not."

"You like him, don't you?"

"Of course."

Meg swished her club-head idly through the grass. "I think he'd be fine for you," she said.

"He would be," Lucy agreed readily. Meg glanced at her.

"Then . . . ?"

"Then, nothing," said Lucy. "I think I'll get me a red and white check blouse like yours."

"Borrow mine, and don't change the subject."

"What subject?"

"Lucy! We were talking about your marrying Miller Hubbard."

Under the brim of her small canvas hat, Lucy's blue eyes widened. "Were we? I can't imagine why. I couldn't even consider—"

"You're *not* considering Tony Bowlin!" Meg stepped away. "Or are you?"

"No," said Lucy, "I'm not. He hasn't asked me, of course, but—well, he's a really delightful man. We had a lovely time last night. He doesn't miss a turn in the way of thoughtfulness and attention. But—" She shrugged.

"But what? What's your reason?"

The foursome came past them, stopped to say a few things—the short, pudgy man said the girls should stay right where they were. "We'd have the prettiest golf course in the country!"

"Not with you rambling around on it," one of his companions told him. Lucy and Meg laughed and watched the men go on.

Lucy put her hand on the cart handle.

"Why do you talk that way about Tony and Dr. Hubbard?" Meg demanded. "What reason do you have . . . ?"

"Reasons," said Lucy, walking ahead of Meg. "Not just one."

"I'll settle for just one."

"All right. There's my loyalty to Mike." Lucy placed her ball and took a club.

"What's another reason?" asked Meg.

"What did we come out here to do? Talk or play golf?"

"Make your play, and then tell me," Meg suggested.

Lucy was very careful about setting her feet, about the way she held her club, about her swing—and she lifted the ball a good forty feet. She laughed, and Meg with her. Meg had laughed with those four men, too. She—

"Well," said Lucy, "you know I can't leave Mums and the Dean."

"I'll bet they don't know it."

"And then there's you, Meg."

Meg turned to look at her sister in honest surprise. "Me?" she asked. "Why, Lucy, I don't need you."

"Don't you?" asked Lucy earnestly.

Color flagged into Meg's cheeks. "I won't drive," she said, "until those men get farther ahead." Then—"No," she said, "I don't need you. I won't. I'm going to study medicine, remember?"

"Oh, yes, Meg, I do remember, and I—we all—think it is wonderful."

"It is wonderful. To know that I can plan my life, and a good life, too. For a while there—but now——" She approached her ball and swung at it strongly; she stood watching it arc up into the blue sky, across the little lake, and land, rolling only a little, upon the green.

"Wonderful," breathed Lucy.

"Mhmmmn," said Meg. "Now let's see you catch up. Your forty-foot drives won't get us to the ninth before dark. And that's daylight-saving time, too. I'm going to study medicine," she said, "and then I probably will marry Mike, so you had better——" She knew that she didn't plan any such thing, and she felt her breath quicken.

But Lucy believed her and was all afire. "Oh, *Meg!*" she cried. "Have you told him?"

Meg stared at her. "Told him—that I'll marry him?"

"Well, that, too, of course." Lucy giggled. "He'd want to know that. But I meant, have you told him about—that night?"

Meg turned abruptly and walked away from Lucy, going blindly. Lucy caught up with her, leaving her ball to gleam there in the grass. "Meg, dear," she said earnestly. "Meg, *dear!*"

Meg nodded. Suddenly she looked very tired. "Go back and play your ball," she said gruffly.

Lucy obeyed, being rather indifferent about it, and so got it on the green. "How's that?" she asked triumphantly, coming up to Meg and the cart.

"Look, Lucy," Meg said to her. "I want you to tell Mike. I want you to tell him what happened—that night."

"Oh, Meg, I couldn't—" Lucy began. Then she caught at her sister's arm. She was smiling. "There's no need, you see. I'm sure Mike has guessed. At least, he knows what *sort* of thing happened to you."

Meg stared at Lucy. "But he couldn't!" she protested. "Because, you see— Why, just the other night, he *kissed* me. He wanted to kiss me."

"Well, what does that prove?" asked Lucy. "He's kissed me dozens of times."

"But," said Meg, "this was one time, and he wanted— *Once* can be more important!" she declared.

Lucy thought about that. "Yes," she said finally, "it can be."

They had almost reached the seventh hole when Meg dragged her step a little, not wanting to join the half dozen people ahead of them. She and Lucy could wait under the tree. . . .

"Perhaps your Miller Hubbard will come for supper," she suggested.

"If I thought he would," said Lucy, "I'd go straight home and make ice cream."

Meg laughed. "You must be in love with that man."

"Oh, yes," Lucy agreed calmly, "I am."

"Then—"

"But, of course," said Lucy airily, watching Meg out of

the corner of her eye, "if Mike should crook his little finger—"

"Mhmmmmn," drawled Meg. "Or if Robin Hood should come out of these woods."

Lucy giggled. "Or Greco, the dancer, too. Remember when I was so crazy about him?"

"Of course I remember. Him and a dozen other loves you've had."

"But not you, Meg," said Lucy. "You were always faithful to Mike."

Meg nodded. "Steady. Dependable . . . Do you think I should warn Miller that you are a wanton woman?"

"Oh, he knows it," said Lucy.

"Then I'd marry him right off!"

Lucy grasped the cart handle. "I think I might," she said. "If *you* are going to be all right."

"I am," said Meg.

"*Are* you going to marry Mike?"

"Someday, perhaps," said Meg. "For now, working with him and medical school in the fall will be enough."

"Then let's go home," said Lucy. "And I think I should remind you that if you are going to fool around, you had better watch out for another woman."

"If one shows up," said Meg, "and she seems to be the right one for Mike, I'll push for her."

Lucy stopped to stare at her sister. "I really believe you would," she said.

"Well, sure," said Meg. "I love that man."

Lucy nodded and trudged along beside Meg. "No wonder he loves you," she said softly.

Meg said nothing. But her eyes held a shine such as they had not known for months.

"Extraordinary is the word to be used first, last, and repeatedly about this book . . . . Anyone who meets Karen, even on paper, will postpone resigning from the human race."

—*The Saturday Review*

KAREN 60c
Marie Killilea

As told by her mother, the inspirational story of Karen, who—despite a handicap—learns to talk, to walk, to read, to write. Winner of the Golden Book Award and two Christopher Awards.

WITH LOVE FROM KAREN 60c
Marie Killilea

Written in response to thousands of letters, this sequel to *Karen* tells of her growth from seven years old into womanhood and relates more about the open friendliness and spiritual plenty of her family.